P9-CNF-498

Patrick Lapeyre

Life Is Short and Desire Endless

A novel

Translated from the French by Adriana Hunter

OTHER PRESS   NEW YORK

Copyright © 2010 Editions P.O.L
Originally published in French as *La vie est brève et le desir sans fin* in 2010
by Editions P.O.L, Paris, France.
Translation copyright © 2012 Adriana Hunter

Production Editor: Yvonne E. Cárdenas
Book design: Chris Welch
This book was set in 12 pt Granjon by Alpha Design & Composition of
Pittsfield, NH.

10   9   8   7   6   5   4   3   2   1

All rights reserved. No part of this publication may be reproduced or
transmitted in any form or by any means, electronic or mechanical, including photocopying, recording, or by any information storage and retrieval
system, without written permission from Other Press LLC, except in the
case of brief quotations in reviews for inclusion in a magazine, newspaper,
or broadcast. Printed in the United States of America on acid-free paper.
For information write to Other Press LLC, 2 Park Avenue, 24th Floor,
New York, NY 10016. Or visit our Web site: www.otherpress.com

Library of Congress Cataloging-in-Publication Data
Lapeyre, Patrick.
    [Vie est brève et le désir sans fin. English]
    Life is short and desire endless : a novel / Patrick Lapeyre ; translated
from the French by Adriana Hunter.
        p. cm.
    ISBN 978-1-59051-484-9 (trade pbk. : acid-free paper) — ISBN 978-1-
59051-485-6 (ebook)
    1. Triangles (Interpersonal relations)—Fiction.   I. Hunter, Adriana.
II. Title.
    PQ2672.A5856V5413 2012
    843'.914—dc23
                                                                2012008175

Publisher's Note:
This is a work of fiction. Names, characters, places, and incidents either
are the product of the author's imagination or are used fictitiously, and any
resemblance to actual persons, living or dead, events, or locales is entirely
coincidental.

Life Is Short and Desire Endless

The windless sun is starting to burn. The white car is parked just below the road, at the mouth of a sunken lane edged with shrubs and clumps of bracken.

Inside the car is a spiky-haired man apparently sleeping with his eyes open, resting the side of his head against the window. He has olive-colored skin and dark eyes with long, very fine lashes like a child's.

The man's name is Blériot, he has recently turned forty-one, and today—Ascension Day—he is wearing a narrow black leather tie and red Converses.

While the few passing cars appear to ripple along the road thanks to distortions caused by the heat, he carries on scanning the landscape (pastures, grazing animals trying to find shade), staying quite motionless as if counting each animal in his head. Then, still not interrupting his scrutiny, he eventually climbs out of the car, doing a few half-hearted stretches and rubbing the stiffness in the small of his back before sitting cross-legged on the hood.

At one point, his phone starts to ring on the rear seat of the car, but he doesn't move. It's as if he weren't there.

Blériot adopted this peculiar ability to be both present and absent without training or special effort, simply by happening to listen to a piece of piano music while staring at his neighbors' shutters. He realized later that any sound would do, so long as he focused on some point in the middle distance and shut off his lungs like a free diver.

That's exactly what he's doing now, until his lungs threaten to explode and he's forced to let out his breath. He immediately feels a growing weightlessness, imponderability, as the blood gradually flows back to his extremities.

It is only when he lights a cigarette that he realizes he hasn't eaten anything for two days.

HE DRIVES FOR about twenty miles looking for a restaurant with some sort of appeal and then, weary of the search, ends up parking outside a single-story building surrounded by a wooden terrace and five or six dusty palm trees.

The air inside is clammy, almost static, despite the open windows and the big blue fan on the counter. There are few people left at this time of day, just a trio of Spanish truck drivers and an exhausted couple who seem to have lost the urge to talk to each other. The air swirled by the fan sweeps up and down a waitress's face as she busies herself behind the bar, blowing back her blond hair.

It's a normal early summer's day, and Blériot—who's expecting nothing and no one—is just eating his mixed salad while trying to work out what time he will first see the foothills of the Cévennes, when the ring of his cell, which sounds like the fanfare of destiny, breaks the emptiness of the afternoon once more.

"Louis, it's me," Nora says immediately in that reedy, very husky voice that he would recognize among a thousand, "I'm in Amiens with some English friends. I'm meant to be getting to Paris in a few days."

"To Paris?" he says, jumping to his feet to head for the restroom, away from inquisitive ears.

She's calling from a café opposite the station.

"How about you?" she asks. "Where are you?"

"Where am I?" he repeats, because he's used to thinking slowly—so slowly that he's usually last to grasp what's going on in his own life.

"I'm going to see my parents and, right now, I'm having lunch somewhere near Rodez," he starts before realizing—his lips still moving in a vacuum—that they've been cut off.

He calls back several times but each time gets the same recorded voice: *Please leave a message after the tone.*

Just then the light in the restroom goes out, and Blériot stands there in the dark, his phone in his hand, not fumbling for the switch or even trying to open the door, as if needing to collect himself in the shadows to get the full measure of what's happening to him.

Because he's been two years waiting for this call.

WHEN HE GETS back to the table, he sits for a moment gazing at his plate, his hands limp by his sides, feeling something like a hint of fever, coupled with a shiver between his shoulder blades.

Maybe there are girls who disappear just for the pleasure of returning one day, he muses as he reaches for his table napkin. He orders another glass of wine and sets about finishing his cold meat, neither letting anything show nor relinquishing the breezy expression with which he usually disguises his reactions.

While the Spanish truckers embark on a game of cards and, behind him, the couple in crisis still haven't exchanged a word, he sits very upright on his chair, totally self-possessed; nothing, except for the slight shake in his hands, would lead anyone to believe the baffled and emotional state he's been in since that call.

AS HE LOOKS out the window, Blériot feels two contradictory emotions. When he thinks about it, he wonders whether the second—excitement—isn't a sort of screen or decoy intended to take his mind off the first, which has no name but could be something rather like premonition and a fear of being hurt.

But at the same time, the more he thinks this, the more his excitement grows, as if to distract him from his apprehension and show him how lucky he is to be seeing her in Paris. And, before getting back into his car, he tries her cell one more time, with no success. He hears the same recording in English. Which is almost a relief, given how undecided he feels.

Having wisely made up his mind not to change any of his plans, he now calls his parents to let them know he will be with them in the early evening, and then his wife, not for anything in particular, just to talk to her and, in passing, to check that she's not aware of anything.

"Hello?" his wife says. Blériot momentarily feels his legs give way as if he is about to collapse, and he just has time to hang up.

It's the heat, he thinks, catching sight of the couple in crisis escaping in a red coupe like Jack Palance and Brigitte Bardot.

He stays hunched in his car for several minutes, prey to a slight feeling of nausea. As he watches the succession of trucks on the road between the lines of plane trees, he tries to remember when he last saw Nora, two years ago, and realizes that he can't. However much he tortures his mind, he can't find anything, not one sound, not one image. As if he has consciously erased the scene so he can begin it all over again. So that the last time can be revived another time.

THEN HE DRIVES for a long while without thinking of her, driving for the sake of it, through the empty mountains and the high-altitude clouds suspended over the valley in geostationary flight.

Because of the heat, he has all the windows closed and the air-conditioning seeping silently around the inside of the car, like an anesthetizing gas dimming his sense of reality, clouding his short-term memory. Until everything that's just happened to him—Nora's call, her saying she'd be back, the call being cut off—is now affected by such a coefficient of uncertainty that he could just as easily have imagined it.

Perhaps because some events for which we've waited too long (two years and two months in his case) are beyond our capacity to react, too big for conscious thought, and can be assimilated only as dreams.

Blériot snaps awake when he recognizes the outskirts of Millau, its viaduct, its accumulation of traffic on the freeway, its gloomy houses, and its advertisements for hamburgers sparking longing in children and despair in animals.

He takes the next exit, coming off the freeway and ending up in a sort of suburban outpost, passing a maternity hospital, a social housing project, two or three shops that are not yet open, a cemetery—a whole life flitting by—before starting up a long incline toward some hills covered with scrub.

He is the only person on the road, and this makes him drive as carefully as a spy sent on a mission to an unfamiliar country. In front of him, as far as the eye can see, are stony plateaux with the cliff to one side and, to the other, a sheer drop that occasionally reveals a river below hidden in the trees. He then contemplates the fact that, at this altitude, no one is likely to get hold of him, or he them, because there can't be a signal tower for miles.

If he wanted to he could disappear, unbeknownst to anyone, change his name and start a new life in the depths of a lost valley, marry a shepherdess . . . (Sometimes Blériot just loves scaring himself.)

HE PARKS HIS car in the shade at a deserted rest area, stands there for a moment with his nose to the wind, assailed by the smell of resin and cut grass, and rummages through the glove compartment for some sunscreen, which he spreads generously over his face and arms. Then he improvises a little game of basketball to stretch his muscles before getting back into the driver's seat.

He suddenly feels younger.

For two years, shut away in the confines of his heartache, he applied himself methodically to aging. He lived hanging by an invisible thread, not looking up, not noticing anyone else, coping with his humdrum world and his worries, turning his back on everything as if trying to eclipse himself.

In fact he was almost entirely eclipsed when she called him.

Still under the effects of this intervention, Blériot listens absently to some Massenet and now drives with nonchalant delight along these winding roads through the Cévennes hills in the shadows of sweet chestnut trees. Until, far below in the distance, he spots a small village that doesn't seem to appear on the map, and he promptly decides to have a break and go in search of cigarettes.

The village is built of red stone and can be summarized as two roads running parallel to each other toward a disjointed little square around the *mairie* and a café. Blériot stocks up with a packet of cigarettes and, to celebrate his newfound youth, grants himself a draft beer, which he drinks at the bar, listening—without making it obvious—to locals out on the terrace discussing subsidies and agricultural policies, probably more out of boredom than out of any labor-union conviction. In their flat caps, they look like a ring of gossiping mushrooms waiting for nightfall.

Out on the street, he feels dazed by the heat again and briefly leans against the *mairie*, making the most of the shade in the courtyard and the slight breeze cooling his legs. Then he walks across the square and heads valiantly for his car. Not that he's in any particular hurry to see his parents again—if it were up to him, he'd go straight back and order another beer—but, since Nora called him, a gnawing feeling of impatience or anxiety has been urging him forward.

So Blériot folds his tall, thin, almost tubular body behind the wheel, puts his sunglasses on again, adjusts his earphones—once young, always young—and roars off.

2

Given that the time difference between London and Paris is one hour, it is at about four-thirty on that same May day that Murphy Blomdale opens the door to his apartment, puts down his luggage, and, after a couple of minutes, has the chilling sense that Nora is no longer there.

Everything around him feels strangely calm and lifeless: the windows onto the courtyard have been left open, and, in the space of three days, silence has crept into the apartment, infiltrating every nook and cranny, yet having a different resonance from one room to the next. The place has never felt so vast and abandoned to him.

Time itself seems to be standing still, exactly as if this moment of his life, this slice of afternoon, has seized up altogether and nothing will ever come after it.

Shaking off this morbid spell, Murphy carries on with his exploration, going from the living room to his study, then from his study to their bedroom: the closet is empty, the drawers tipped open as if after a burglary, and, instead of frames with their photos in them, all that is left on the pedestal table is a little film of dust and a set of keys.

Enough said.

Anyone else in his position would already have accepted the evidence. But not him. He can't quite believe it. In fact, he peers at himself in the mirror to see whether he looks as if he believes it, but no, he has the eyes of someone who doesn't.

THERE MUST BE some explanation for this sort of denial. Murphy Blomdale is big on voluntarism, he is one hundred percent American, both austere and hyperactive, held up as an example by his bosses; this is a man who is confronted daily by the anarchic tides of the financial world, by the un-predictability of markets, the speed of exchanges, and the volatility of capitals. In short, nothing that might prepare him for being the male lead in a romantic drama one day.

This role that fate has suddenly foisted on him seems to be casting him so badly against type that he'd rather just pretend he hasn't noticed.

Murphy, who's still holding Nora's keys in his hand, glances out at the street to have something to believe in.

He hopes to see the odd passerby or some children fresh from school; they would soothe him by drawing him out of this bad dream. But, at this time of day, Liverpool Road is like a long, baking interstate highway, about as busy as the Gobi Desert.

Light bounces off the sidewalks with unusual, almost worrying intensity.

It then occurs to him to take his phone from his breast pocket and call Nora's number. About a dozen times. She doesn't reply, so he tries to get hold of her sister, Dorothy, in Greenwich, with no success.

She must have moved from London a while ago, he thinks, washing his fingers as if his phone has melted.

To crush his worries and get a more objective angle on the situation, he decides to resume his search in reverse order, starting with the bedroom and bathroom, then the study. All he finds are a shoe forgotten at the back of a cupboard, a leather belt, a mauve scarf, a paperback of Somerset Maugham's short stories, school editions of Milton and Chekhov, plus a few fashion magazines that he tidies onto a shelf with the other things.

Later, when it is all over and he is left with nothing but regrets, he can always put these relics behind glass, with a little sign. In response to this grim prospect, he is just resolving to go back into the living room when the light coming through the window in the hallway reveals the outline of a hand. A hand so distinctive, so alive, that it seems to wave to him before it vanishes.

His legs undertake a peculiar sort of rotation, and he starts turning circles on the spot, arms spread like a skater, his body's movements apparently completely disconnected from his mind. If he didn't instinctively clutch a chair in passing, he would almost certainly end up out for the count on the wooden floor.

Once safely wedged in his chair, Murphy Blomdale stays put for a long time, legs stretched in front of him, one finger uselessly pressing the button on his cell, eyes staring blankly, as if utterly stripped, like a man confronted by his own nonexistence.

3

Blériot does not yet know Nora at this point, so all this is happening in another life.

Here he is with his wife one September afternoon, at the house of friends—the Bonnet-Smiths, small-time landowners who have a place on the banks of the Eure that boasts extensive wooded grounds through which little groups of guests have started to disperse in search of cooler air.

Blériot, who hasn't been talking to anyone except his wife, stays on the sidelines at the bottom of the steps leading to the front door and wonders, as he often does, what he's doing here. So when Sabine tells him rather brusquely (their marriage is going through a tricky time) that their friends Sophie and Bertrand Laval wondered if he'd like to join them for a little walk around, he makes as if to follow them, then changes his mind, firstly because he's hot and also because he'd rather wander through the house.

He has thirty minutes left till he meets Nora. But he is completely unaware of that. And yet he's ready. He needs something to happen to him. At some stage all men probably need a story like this of their own, to convince them that something wonderful and unforgettable happened to them once in their lives.

This is a conviction Blériot once had, when he set up house with Sabine, but he's lost it since. None of which stops him repeatedly telling himself—and it's getting more and more like autosuggestion—that he married the most intelligent and devoted of women, the one best equipped to make him happy, and if he had to do it all over again, he wouldn't hesitate for a moment.

His conjugal affection has never actually been as vehement as he claims, and their relationship, despite intermittent bonds of complicity and tenderness, has become more or less incomprehensible.

In fact, no one in their circle of friends understands it at all.

But Blériot doesn't mind what people say. It's a relationship with no logical explanation, like in myths and legends.

SO, NOW SABINE has gone with her friends, he withdraws into the house in search of a glass of champagne and ends up in front of the buffet, alongside a certain Jean-Jacques, whom he's now running into for the third time this day in the same place.

Incidentally, despite his good intentions, Blériot hasn't managed to establish whether the man's a semiologist or a sociologist. Perhaps because his white suit and buttoned ankle boots are more inclined to suggest an Italian singer. And anyway he has a maddening habit of constantly turning up the collar of his jacket and running his hand through his hair. Even when he's heading for the restroom.

As they don't have much to talk about, they discreetly look away from each other in perfect unison while knocking back their champagne and hoping to spot someone receptive to talk to. The first of them to be rid of the other will have won.

Blériot is the one who gets ditched.

He has eleven minutes to go.

HEARING IT PUT like that, you would think there's a young woman he's never met already standing at the far side of the door, and that when she comes in Blériot will spin round and feel something as sudden and unpredictable as an avalanche.

But no woman comes into the room. He's still by the buffet, champagne glass in hand, stuck between a couple of academics heatedly criticizing a female colleague, and a bevy of former left-wingers who have rallied to the capitalist cause and are now laying into civil servants. It's almost a competition to see who can stoop the lowest.

While Blériot wonders why he should have to put up with conversations like this, his attention is drawn to the right by a stunning young couple who suddenly revive his faith in his fellow human beings.

THE BOY IS quite tall with a slightly indolent, bored quality, and, just to have something to do, he's leafing through an art magazine on a sideboard, while the girl half hidden behind him looks so slight, so transparent that—by comparison—her partner comes across as a giant.

Blériot, now in a heightened state of susceptibility, notices that every now and then she goes up on tiptoe to say something in his ear, and that he has a funny way of tilting his head and turning his brown eyes—which match her own—on her.

They are standing alone, beside the door to the garden, apparently not interested in anyone else, or wanting anyone to take any interest in them. They look as if they're on the alert, ready to flee at the smallest sign of alarm like a timid pair of deer.

Blériot, who keeps losing sight of them because of other guests' comings and goings, now undertakes a discreet maneuver to get closer to them. As a secondary concern, one day he would love to know why it is that beauty makes him so vulnerable and dependent.

Almost as if it were inevitable, just as he is getting nearer to the couple, he recognizes Valérie Mell, a friend of his wife's, waving to him enthusiastically from the hallway. In the time it takes to go over to her, find out how her son is—he's had a motorcycle crash—and to show a bit of sympathy for him, the other two have disappeared. Despite Blériot's subsequent efforts exploring the surroundings and coming back into the house, they are nowhere to be found.

Neither was his wife. A fact he finds reassuring for now.

AFTER THIS THERE seems to be a sort of temporal collapse between the time when he is still there in the house, champagne glass in hand, thinking about the fear that his wife's prickly, capricious nature has always inspired in him, and the time when he walks around the grounds, guided by his predatory instincts, and comes out onto a small covered terrace, almost next to the girl with the brown eyes. Without her partner.

Thrown by this interpolation of fate, Blériot hangs back a little at first and is of course careful not to stare too much.

While, slightly in profile to him, she tilts back on a chair, resting her feet on a stone bench, he checks once more that there's no one in the vicinity, and then, as she doesn't seem to have noticed him, he just stands there, quaking at the thought of disturbing her, yet suddenly incapable of walking away.

LIFE IS SHORT AND DESIRE ENDLESS   19

Approaching her in due and proper form, asking her permission to sit down, finding the appropriate words to engage in conversation—all this is clearly way beyond his abilities.

He's already decided to turn on his heel and leave as silently as he came when, with no hint of affectation, she asks him whether he's a friend of Paul and Elisa's.

"Paul and Elisa's?" he repeats, lowering his sunglasses.

It is now, as he gets closer to her, that Blériot, who never notices anything, realizes her lips are dry and her cheeks pale and silky with a light dusting of freckles around her eyes.

She looks even more unbelievable than she did earlier.

But, although it pains him more than she could imagine, he's honest enough to admit that he doesn't know Paul or Elisa. On the other hand, he does know a Jean-Jacques Baret or Bari, and Sophie and Bertrand Laval, as well as Robert Bonnet-Smith . . . who, according to her, is none other than a friend of Spencer's mother, Spencer being the boy she lives with.

It's all clear.

"Spencer went for a nap in the car," she tells him, still balancing on her chair, hands crossed behind her head.

"He finds these people boring and anyway he can't stand alcohol," she adds with a slight English accent he hadn't noticed at first.

He dreads the fateful moment when she will probably ask him whether he came alone, and would also rather not pursue the subject of Spencer, telling her instead about his disappointment with the other guests—it's usually a unifying subject—with a special mention for the gang of academics on every floor of the house. They're all over the place. Academics standing up, academics sitting down, lying down. You'd think it was a nursing home for teachers.

That's when Blériot sees her smile.

And she has a very pretty way of smiling, showing the tips of her teeth, but he doesn't make any comment.

"WHAT'S YOUR NAME?" she asks all of a sudden, stopping her chair-tilting.

"Blériot," he says. "Officially it's Louis Blériot-Ringuet. Blériot because I'm a cousin three times removed from the aviator, and Louis because my father—who's an aeronautical engineer—must be the only man in the world who wanted to call his son Louis Blériot. I'll spare you the explanation for Ringuet. I try to take comfort from the thought that Louis Blériot-Ringuet has a ring to it, a bit like Sugar Ray Robinson or Charlie 'Bird' Parker."

"You're clearly modest," she says, laughing out loud.

"I was only giving examples, but if it seems a bit long, you could always settle for calling me Blériot, which most of my friends do."

"I prefer Louis," she says, without any explanation.

"How about you?" he asks after a moment's hesitation, as if she's bound to have a secret name.

"Nora," she replies, "Nora Neville. I'm English on my mother's side and half French on my father's. I think my family were from near Le Havre."

"Miss Neville," Blériot says in affectedly solemn tones, "I don't know your parents, but I'd like to thank them from the bottom of my heart for bringing you into the world. I can assure you of my sincerity."

"Call me Nora, just Nora," she asks, returning his smile.

All the same, he can't help noticing that it's a different smile from the previous one, a slightly thoughtful smile.

She seems to have seen right through his performance and is giving him the indulgent smile of a woman who's met dozens like him and knows exactly where they're coming from.

Of course it doesn't occur to him that he might be better off relinquishing his position to someone else.

Because at that precise moment—they've gone for a stroll at the bottom of the garden, away from prying eyes— he feels that, whether or not he is married, whether or not there is a Spencer, the fact that he may be making some sort of mistake doesn't affect the immediate fierce conviction that this girl is destined to be his.

And this feels both very powerful and quite inevitable. What surprises him most isn't that it should be so powerful, but that it should be inevitable.

She is so close to him Blériot feels that, if he accidentally or inadvertently leaned a little too far forward, he would fall into her arms like a sleepwalker. She seems to be

waiting for his reaction, so—although he makes no conscious decision to do this—he settles for touching her ear
with his hand. Nothing else happens. She doesn't brush his
hand away, but doesn't take it either, so that for a few fractions of a second his arm hangs there in the air.

"It's nearly six o'clock," Nora says suddenly—given that
there is now a Nora. "I'm a bit worried."

"Me too," he says, also feeling strangely different.

Together they walk back, glancing toward the gardens
and the house, as if filled with foreboding.

"What are we going to do?" she asks all of a sudden, her
voice stunned. "Do you have any ideas?"

But Blériot, who's never been this much in love, is as lost
as she is.

4

While Murphy Blomdale is apparently sleeping in his chair, Blériot is driving on and on as if all he wanted was to run out of space while a monotonous curtain of plane trees files past and the boundary offered by the horizon keeps backing away. The heat shimmers over the fields along the road as far as the eye can see, with only occasional clumps of trees, and motionless animals drowned in the afternoon light.

After Lodève, he slows down abruptly, putting his thoughts of Nora aside for later and trying to recall the names of the places he has to drive through after leaving the Montpellier road. If he's remembered this accurately, he has to go through La Feuillade until he reaches a small bridge by a chapel, then carry straight on toward Saint-Cernin.

After about twelve miles, when he still hasn't reached La Feuillade, he decides to stop in the next town he comes across. He reviews his map of France again, with all the windows wound down to make the most of the shade. Obviously, none of these villages is indicated on a map of this scale, so he has absolutely no idea which direction he should take to get to this little bridge he may have only imagined. He resolves to leave the car where it is and set out to ask the first passerby he meets.

He heads up a steep little street and crosses a succession of deserted squares with birdsong echoing inside their walls, before coming to an esplanade above the ramparts that serves as a parking area as well as a scenic walk. But he can't see anyone except for a couple of English tourists and four young girls on bicycles pedaling furiously toward puberty.

With his earphones in place, he teleports himself back thirty years to a time when he too cycled along sheer hillsides in the July sun and when the more he pedaled, the more disproportionate and unbroachable the summer seemed.

BELOW HIM HE can make out a row of little gardens along a stream, with their folding chairs and their wooden sheds covered in wisteria, and he stands there for a while, leaning over the parapet, savoring the languid breeze hovering around his legs.

"A nice day to get your stick out," comments someone behind him, a fat man in pants with suspenders.

"To get your stick out?" a startled Blériot says, taking out his earphones.

"Yes, your stick," the other man insists in a hushed voice, as if this constituted an invitation to follow him into his garden shed.

Blériot steps aside and looks at the man's heavy-jawed face. "I was hoping to find someone who could tell me how to get to Saint-Cernin," he explains in order to dispel any misunderstanding. "Do you know which way I should head?"

"Turn left down the hill, then left again," the man says in the same hushed voice.

Blériot, who still doesn't fully understand what he was talking about, thanks him all the same for his kindness, then unceremoniously makes a run for it, leaping down the steps to get back to his car.

As he is getting into his seat he catches glimpses of the gates to a property on the other side of the road, its abandoned driveway partly invaded by undergrowth, looking as if it leads straight to Sleeping Beauty's castle. Which, by some strange correlation, immediately makes him think of Nora.

He wants to say that, for two years, he's wished with all his might that she would come back . . . and now she's come back. But he is perfectly aware you could also say that, for two years, she wanted him to wait for her . . . and he waited. Who was controlling whom? he wonders, while missing his turning after the little bridge. With no other option available, he calls his parents.

"We were expecting you two hours ago," his mother greets him with that impatient tone he knows so well and that brings him right back to reality.

HE IS THE only child of Jean-Claude and Colette Blériot-Ringuet (previously Colette Lavallée), an engineer and headmistress, respectively. When he was born he apparently gave a piercing cry and shuddered with terror as if he'd come down to earth by parachute. Once the cord was cut and the parachute thrown in the garbage, he immediately locked himself away in a silent, esoteric childhood, becoming a solitary little boy, then a puny teenager, while his parents fought furiously behind his back.

The animosity between them in all probability dated back to their early years together, so far back that Blériot—whose interminable youth gave him plenty of time to think about it—assumed that it was only out of spite that neither of them had left the other.

About thirty years later they retired to the family home in Saint-Cernin, where they now live consumed with boredom, vying to cause each other the most torment as a means of passing the time.

When he arrives late in the afternoon, carrying his small suitcase, his father is digging the vegetable plot in his straw hat, while his mother's on the balcony, carrying on with her perennial phone call to her sister.

AS FAR BACK as he can remember, his father has been a bit of a spare part, and—even though he has a degree, has traveled the world and led teams of engineers in Africa and Asia while remaining a faithful and unbelievably patient husband—the servility and expiatory humiliations constantly inflicted on him (preferably in public) have broken his last scraps of resistance. Scolded and constrained to silence, he's now reduced to smoking in the garage and drinking port on the sly. This behavior has to be witnessed in situ to be believed.

Even their own son has to rub his eyes.

Apart from that, he recognizes everything: the bad paintings on the walls, the highly polished furniture, Billy the dog asleep on the sofa (he's so old that Blériot's father claims he still remembers François Mitterrand), the daybed in his room and the pine shelving with its rows of books by Teilhard de Chardin left to him by his great-uncle Albert, and the hundreds of science fiction novels whose every detail he's pretty much forgotten, as if he stopped believing in the future.

He's perusing their titles when his mother, appearing from nowhere, asks him to what they owe the honor of his visit, given he's been gone for six months without calling or sending so much as a postcard.

"I've had quite a lot on my mind," he apologizes, caught off guard. Still, some part of him registers that since he arrived his mother hasn't said a single word about his wife, whom she cordially loathes and who reciprocates in kind.

His father, redundant as ever, is wandering about like a lost soul in the room downstairs, fiddling with a packet of cigarettes that he dare not smoke. When Blériot suggests going into the garden and getting out the Ping-Pong table, he sees something flit across his gloomy face, something as fleeting and undecided as the Mona Lisa's smile.

THEY START WITH a few rallies, gradually accelerating the pace, then, enthused, decide to keep score. While Blériot's still trying to master his shots, his father—who must be over-revving his engines—wraps up the first two games 21–10 before inevitably giving ground and letting the next few get away.

After a brief restorative pause, they start playing again feverishly despite the fading light, and, with his father suddenly reverting to the bouncing gait and backhand game that once wreaked havoc in local tournaments, they almost tie once more: 18–17. Even though his father is quite quickly out of breath, it's still clear in momentary flashes and from some of his moves that he was once young and virile, that he had style, he had class, and he deserved a life other than the one carved out for him by his wife.

Which reminds Blériot that he still hasn't called his.

She answers from the terrace of a café where she's having a drink with her colleagues Sandra and Marco. The hubbub on the street limits conversation to a bare minimum, and Blériot is glad to have such a good excuse to hang up.

As they sit down to eat, his mother—who has pretentiously set the smaller plates on top of the larger ones—immediately takes over all the talking, as usual. About halfway through the meal, when she's done with the litany of hospitalized cousins and divorced girlfriends, she launches into recriminations about their neighbors Monsieur and Madame Cailleux, whom she suspects are sociopaths.

His father, all his concentration on the bottle of claret, merely smiles and nods, like the blessed, freed of any opinion, while Blériot, who has his own on-off switch, is holding his breath while discreetly focusing on a corner of the garden where a big red sun hangs over the trees as it does over Henri Rousseau's jungles. A technique that allows him, thanks only to the weight of thought, to lower the volume so that he in turn becomes a pure being, released from pain.

HE IS SO lost in contemplation he doesn't realize right away that his mother has changed topics and, with a series of bittersweet comments, is back to the reason for his visit. Because there is some consistency in her train of thought. Blériot now has to swallow hard and admit that, due to various circumstances too complicated to explain, he's come to them to borrow three thousand euros, which he will pay back in installments.

If Billy the dog had started singing on the sofa, his parents wouldn't have looked any more flabbergasted. Even his father is wide-eyed.

Seeing the scope of indignation he's stirred up, Blériot has to concede that three thousand euros would be a luxury and, if there was any problem, he could easily make do with two thousand five hundred.

"It can be my little annual gift," he adds shamelessly.

"You can sort it out with your father, I'm not having anything to do with it," decrees his mother, who still seems shaken and chooses to go and shut herself in her bedroom.

So Blériot follows his father into the study and waits for his check with a contrite heart. What he can't tell him is that he too finds this whole business depressing, and that if he'd known he would be reduced to taking money from his parents at his age, he wouldn't have been in such a hurry to grow up.

"Louis, some days I feel like getting into a rocket and leaving the world behind," his father says out of the blue, interrupting his thank-yous—he's given him three thousand.

To make him happy, Blériot follows his father down to the room in the basement that serves as a workshop and that he has fixed up for himself. A table, two camping chairs, and a mattress are laid directly on the cement floor.

He spends whole afternoons here, communing with the radio while he makes his model airplanes.

Blériot says nothing, but something tells him that one day the old boy will sneak down here with his sleeping bag and never come back up.

OUTSIDE, IT IS nearly dark; the trees in the garden seem suddenly to rustle to the winds of days gone by. The only things that can still be seen are the deck chairs on the terrace and the Ping-Pong balls left in the grass.

"Have you and your wife separated?" his father asks as they both stand drinking in the dark, their feet soaked with dew.

"I think it's more likely she'll leave me, when she tires of bailing out my bank account."

"Mine'll never leave me," his father says regretfully.

Every now and then—as they start to get seriously drunk—snatches of music from a party reach them from the village, with bursts of laughter spilling from the sky, and every time they look up their nostalgia grows heavier.

IT IS NOW eleven o'clock in London. When the telephone starts to ring, it takes a good two seconds for Murphy Blomdale to emerge from his daze and realize it isn't his cell but the landline in the living room.

"Hello, good evening, my name's Sam Gorki," says a quavering voice he doesn't recognize; "could I speak to Nora please?"

"She doesn't live here anymore," he replies tartly. There follows a long silence, a few little coughs, like at a concert, then the voice gives out such a long, deep sigh that Murphy immediately deduces that this person can, like him, be categorized as neo-romantic.

"Welcome aboard, Sam."

But the guy at the other end has hung up.

It's a shame, because they could have set up a partnership, instituted proceedings, and claimed symbolic damages with interest. Which, it turns out, reminds him of the small blue box hidden in the desk, and the five thousand dollars he exchanged on Wednesday. He finds the box in its rightful place, but it strikes him as abnormally light, as if all that was left inside it was a bit of ash or dust. In fact, she magnanimously left him a couple of twenties to drink to her health.

At least the message is clear this time, he thinks, pouring himself a glass of brandy in the kitchen.

A minute later, amid the massacre of his earthly hopes, he pours himself another before calling Nora yet again, just for the hell of it, so as to have no regrets, his heartbeat regulated by the rhythm of the ringtone until he hears the message.

She won't answer.

What compounds his devastation is the thought that the name Nora, and the face and body that go with it, will

anchor itself in a very precise area of his brain cells govern-
ing his memory, and he'll probably forget *himself* before he
can forget her.

Everything we can hope for, he will have hoped for;
everything we can lose, he will have lost.

And, as he looks up at the darkness over London, he too
feels his nostalgia grow heavier.

5

One morning he wakes up next to his wife. She is sleeping with her face turned to the wall, so he can see only her mass of blond hair, which reaches the bottom of her shoulder blades. Her nightshirt has ridden up off her chunky thighs, the white skin of her legs. Nothing more. In the past, even in his most fervent dreams, his wife always appeared to him with clothes on. It must be a pathology with a recognized name.

His face gnawed by the usual morning neuralgia, Blériot fumbles his way to the kitchen to make himself a cup of coffee and take a couple of aspirin while he runs himself a bath. In the mirror above the sink he sees a harassed man with dark rings under his eyes and prominent bones.

The bath is so hot that steam stays hovering over the

surface like a fogbank while he lets his body float, legs out-stretched, and thinks about Nora's incomprehensible be-havior since she returned.

Because he's already left a dozen messages and she still hasn't given any sign of life.

Will she answer? Will she answer?

Right now—as he turns on the cold tap with the tip of his toe—Blériot would be prepared to wager she won't answer and he'll lose everything. But tomorrow, because of his pendulum tendencies, he'll think the exact opposite.

After shaving, he puts on a white shirt with a wing col-lar over his jeans and, despite the forecast of high tempera-tures, ties a small black leather tie with the perfectionism and slightly obsessive elegance peculiar to those who spend their lives waiting for someone.

To take his mind off thoughts of Nora, he's taken to spy-ing on the woman who lives downstairs on the far side of the courtyard, a Russian in her eighties who hasn't left her apart-ment for years—he arbitrarily imagines a smell of dusty upholstery and incontinent cats—because she apparently de-cided to watch television to the death. When he watches her eating her bread and jam, Blériot sometimes catches himself envying her for no longer waiting for anyone.

Then he wanders from room to room, waiting for his wife to wake, hovering like a ghost, opening the shutters and looking at the luminous sky.

· · ·

THEY LIVE AT the top of an old building in the Belleville heights where, on some autumn days, they can watch clouds passing beneath them.

Although their apartment is intrinsically ugly and awkward, it does have the advantage of being large and arranged over two floors connected by a small spiral staircase, which means they can mostly avoid getting in each other's way. They've actually perfected an alternating occupation system so that when one of them is, for example, listening to music, the other can get on with what he or she's doing in peace on the floor below. In fact, it's not unusual—particularly when there's tension in the air—for one of them to choose to stay on his or her floor watching television alone, rather than having to put up with the other's commentary.

· He and his wife are basically in the same space, living in the same time frame, sleeping sometimes together—in Sabine's bedroom—and sometimes each on his or her own floor, and yet they seem to live in two different worlds an infinite distance apart. The staircase, the size of the rooms, and the absence of furniture no doubt contribute to this feeling of emptiness that hangs over both of them, even when they're together. So much so that, in the afternoons, Blériot increasingly finds himself wondering, like a child, whether he's alone in this place.

"ARE YOU UP already?" his wife asks, amazed, appearing in her bathrobe with a towel around her head.

Since an eye infection, she almost always wears dark glasses, and, this morning, it makes her look like a blind woman available to her husband's covetous gaze. Right up until he kisses her and suddenly feels her cold cheeks, her tentative physical presence.

"Did your trip go well?" she asks in a tense voice that he finds slightly worrying. Maybe she knows, he thinks before pulling himself together and improvising some minor development in his father's depression.

"I've still got a few pages to finish," he adds, leaving her there and heading to his study, an upstairs room twenty feet by sixteen where, although he's hardly very involved in his work, he can at least think in peace, with some breathing space.

So, to quash his anxieties and postpone scrutinizing his conscience, he hastily closes the door and turns on his computer.

Blériot, who has always kept any sort of career plan at arm's length, as he has any form of social recognition, set himself up as a freelance translator—of English—three or four years ago, rather than continuing to tolerate the pressure from private agencies who paid him peanuts. But, since he's been working for himself, he has to take on pretty much everything and anything to keep his little business going, and translates just as many scientific articles and pamphlets for pharmaceuticals as operating instructions for household appliances.

On good days, he does a bit of freelance work for medical conferences, but most of the time he stays at home and

makes do with what he's offered. And when he's not offered anything he usually has no other option than to fall
back on the generosity of his friends. This sort of desperate
measure partly explains the poor image his wife and parents clearly have of him.

LOOKING OUT THE window—because he's got his head
hanging out the whole time this morning as if Nora's waiting for him outside—he notices a man wearing a jacket,
looking like a Chinese businessman and carrying his sleeping son on his back while his wife trots alongside in the
pounding heat, regularly spraying the child's face with the
help of a small pink flask. Blériot leans forward for a better
view of the scene and keeps his eyes pinned on them until
they disappear around the end of the rue de Belleville, leaving in their wake a sense of irretrievable happiness.

Was he the son? Was he the father carrying the son in
another life?

Lost in thought, he moves in slow motion to sit back
down at his computer.

His tally of activity over the last six days coming pretty
close to nothing, he struggles for part of the afternoon to
translate an article from a medical review devoted to female circumcision in Africa, before throwing in the towel
and going in search of a bottle of beer in the kitchen.

As he climbs back up the stairs, he hears his wife in the
living room singing a Nancy Sinatra song and stops in his

tracks to listen to her. He didn't know she liked Nancy Sinatra.

Bang bang, he shot me down, Bang bang, I hit the ground, she croons in a voice he didn't know she had, a very young, girlish voice that makes him shiver as if her most beautiful quality had just been revealed to him many years behind schedule.

By the time the song ends, every trace of sadness and bitterness has vanished from his mind. The process of disintegration in their relationship seems to have been halted as if by magic. He mustn't touch a thing now.

So he carries on up the stairs, without a sound, and goes into his bedroom.

Taking little sips of his beer, he pulls down the blinds, because he can see his thoughts more clearly in the dark, then lies on the sofa at the end of the room.

Now he can stay still like a good boy. Everything's fine.

He is lying on his side, eyes half closed, like an animal panting in the warmth of dusk.

Everything's fine, he thinks again. He's brought his knees up to his chest now, and, in the half-light of sundown, the blinds look almost white.

6

Blériot doesn't know when they started growing apart. The day he noticed, it had already happened. From then on all he could do was watch, powerless to stop it, as their whole life became poisoned. He saw their relationship crumbling from one day to the next and did nothing, found no better way of coping with it than feebly accepting the state of affairs.

When he skims back through the early years of their marriage, he thinks they must have had their own small share of happiness like everyone else, but he doesn't remember it. He barely recalls their first meeting, one evening at a friend of a friend's house in the suburbs. His memory is so fallible and has such limited range (they met nine years ago) that he can't actually remember how they fell into conversation, nor what they said to each other. He seems to think he listened to her talk all evening.

At the time he was deep in a black hole, on welfare and living off subsidies from his father when he wasn't lucky enough to be housed and fed by some kindly American or Norwegian girl. Because, although he was never among the sexual avant-garde of his generation, nor was it Blériot's first Communion when they met.

Sabine belonged to a quite different world.

She was older than him, divorced; she knew masses of people; she was elegant, physically attractive, intellectually stimulating. She had written a thesis about the Bauhaus and gone on to look after contemporary art collections for a succession of foundations. She clearly knew what she wanted.

She was the exact opposite of him.

In fact, she was the one who wanted him, who gave him her address and cell phone number at the end of the party, telling him he shouldn't hesitate to call, and he played it cool for a good fortnight before dialing her number.

WHY DID HE see her again? Most likely because she wanted to see him.

Either way, it was less to do with love or desire than with a strange vertiginous feeling of submission.

Plus she impressed him; she'd met John Cage and Merce Cunningham, and she adored German literature, with a particular predilection for Elias Canetti. You could almost say he dated her to find out what made Canetti a genius without going to the trouble of reading his work.

One thing is for sure: once he was over the surprise of finding that this cerebral, slightly uptight young woman had a sensual nature he would never have suspected, everything happened very quickly, probably too quickly.

She married him and he married her—not without unvoiced reservations on his part—and they set off immediately to spend a year in Ireland, where she did valuations for a private foundation as he scrounged for work in local junior high schools. And while they were over there the same thing happened to them that happens to all lovers in too much of a hurry who rush into the first hotel they find and end up stuck in the elevator. Years later, they're still trapped and have exhausted every topic of conversation.

Still, those long, intimate chats, the nights spent together, the walks hand in hand in the early months usually give each party an opportunity to glimpse the share of joys or difficulties the other will bring. And it didn't take Blériot long to anticipate that his share of difficulties would be the weightier of the two.

But he played the part. From a lack of confidence, out of immaturity.

If we look at it all now from an objective point of view, he was definitely the less capable in the couple, and therefore in some way the more guilty.

The things most men spend their whole lives looking for—intelligence, tenderness, being understood and indulged—she gave him on a plate, and it was as if he didn't know what to do with them.

Afterward it was too late.

THE OLD VINYL of time keeps going back over the same sequence. Sabine fell pregnant in April; she was forty-two, refused to believe it was happening, and the whole thing was instantly terribly straightforward: he wanted the child with all his might and, with all of hers, she didn't. Because she'd lost faith in him.

He remembers the way she sometimes watched him, neither blinking nor looking away, as if she suddenly had some clairvoyant gift and knew something about them that she wasn't allowed to reveal to him.

About her, he knows nothing.

She loathes confidences about as much as she does reminiscing. He doesn't even know what her first husband looked like, or exactly what she holds against him. As for her family, her sister and her two rather peculiar brothers, she maintains the same silence about them, the same defensive distance, like an impenetrable security system.

However firmly convinced Blériot may have been that she refused to have a child for reasons connected to her own childhood, he couldn't get an explanation from her. Because it was her business, not his, she told him.

To escape from this claustrophobic relationship, he went out almost every evening and wandered through the neighborhood. Walking as others might pray. Walking while she was asleep in her bed, feeling he was going from one room to another in her sleep until he reached the secret chamber where the child's heart beat.

Once back, he collapsed, exhausted. He already knew he had lost. After days and days of quibbling and pointless debate, he let her get on and do what she wanted.

WHEN SHE CAME home from the clinic she lay down between the sheets and didn't say another word.

From that moment on, life together became suffocating. They avoided each other by day and, by night, they lay on their bed like two slabs of loneliness separated by boundless misunderstanding. They could have separated but carried on living together, probably because they needed some sense of order in their emotional confusion—even though each of them had order of his or her own—and because they could think of nothing more terrifying than to surrender their lives to chaos and disintegration.

The compromise still holds today.

Couples—theirs, at least—look rather like incoherent organizations when, in fact, they're an alliance between clearly understood vested interests . . . by dint of which people can become increasingly indifferent to each other or increasingly inseparable.

Sometimes when he thinks about all this, as he looks back over the molecular chain of his disillusions and sorrows, Blériot doesn't know what scares him more, having to leave his wife one day or growing old with her. Either way, this evening, for the first time in a long time, he feels at ease, with no apprehensions, or illusions.

He sings to himself: *Bang bang, He shot me down,* as he drinks his beer by the window.

His neighbor in the building opposite, a great big black kid, has popped his head out of the skylight like Alice in Wonderland and is inhaling the evening air.

Everything's fine, he tells himself yet again.

7

He tried at least a dozen times to get hold of Dorothy by phone; then, although he couldn't say by what mysterious mechanism, the name Vicky Laumett came to mind while he was sorting through his notebooks.

Murphy felt instantly that he had one of the few useful leads that might get him to Nora.

They had been friends at high school in Coventry, met up again in London, had several mutual acquaintances, and, as far as he knew, were still in touch with each other as recently as March.

What he remembers is a pretty, rather short multi-racial girl, whom he must have met two or three times, always accompanied by very tall men who seemed attracted to her exceptionally low center of gravity.

Nora told him that the previous winter she had married

a David Miler, a journalist for a financial weekly. So their number must be somewhere around.

"I'm Murphy Blomdale, Nora's boyfriend," he introduces himself before, dying of embarrassment, he explains the painful situation that led him to call so late.

After a stunned silence—she seems completely unaware that Nora's gone—she warns him right away that she hasn't seen Nora for months and doesn't know anything about why she may have left. That said, if he feels he needs to talk to her—which she can quite easily understand—she assures him that she's absolutely there for him.

"David won't be back till ten or eleven," she says, "so you can come over whenever you like."

ALMOST BEFORE HE'S showered and put on a clean shirt, he's out in the street looking for a taxi. Seeing the crowds and lights on Upper Street after days of isolation, Murphy feels slightly giddy and panicky, forcing him to pause for a moment.

To put the icing on the cake, a limpid quasi-aphrodisiac dusk is settling over London, café terraces are heaving with people, girls are shrieking with excitement, and couples are kissing while the going's good, and he, skulking behind his blue glasses, can feel something sweet hanging in the air, piercing right through him.

Although he may not look it—and this was back when he still lived in the United States—Murphy Blomdale was once a young male student surrounded by female students, but oddly he has no feelings of nostalgia for those years. All those little Bostonian girls with their blond hair and their sentimentality filing through his bedroom like characters in search of an author, all those warped affections and mediocre affairs, the small change of life, all of that, compared with Nora, now seems incredibly far-off and laughable.

As he steps out of the taxi he notices that the air is getting more stifling by the minute, and he's started to sweat.

The apartment where Vicky and her husband live looks out onto a small deserted square surrounded by hotels, a stone's throw from Earl's Court station. Knowing he can't turn around now, Murphy stands by the ground floor window of the building for a minute, a slightly stooped figure, eyes baggy with insomnia, hair scraped back, looking grim and elegant as a widower. He rings the bell.

"It's on the fourth floor, on the right," a voice answers from the intercom.

THE DOOR IS open. Vicky Laumett, dressed all in white, is walking up and down the hallway, talking on the phone. So he stands in the entrance, trying to establish what surprises him more: her size—she seems to have grown four inches— or the sharp look she gives him as she waves him in.

Two hallways later, he can see beyond her to a dazzlingly cold space, styled like a show home, with metal sculptures, and African masks hanging on the walls. Murphy

Blomdale can't say whether it's in good or bad taste, firstly because he's too distressed or too distracted by the presence of the lady of the house to notice, and secondly because he finds objects in general boring.

"I didn't notice the time," she apologizes, taking his hand to show him to the living room.

When they're sitting across from each other, he suddenly feels depressed, in a sort of emotional nudity which fills him with shame as if he were about to cry. He already regrets coming. Particularly (although he doesn't know why he feels this, but it may be because of the way her apartment looks) as he suspects she's a materialistic young woman and not especially sympathetic.

Which is why, in order to hide his dejected state, he's careful not to talk about Nora immediately but to show an interest in Vicky first, in what she does—she returned to university and is just finishing a master's in law—in her plans, her friends, and her husband. She's fairly outgoing, so it's not too hard a task, and they chat away like this for a while. She's simply happy to be talking to him, and he is comforted to find that this girl he barely knew has kindness and humor as well as calm vitality, which makes a welcome change from the people he usually sees in London.

At times, given his distraught mood, he wonders whether she's being a bit too friendly with him, too charming, to the point of sending out the odd unintentionally ambiguous signal. Like the arm she puts behind her head, in a way that seems intended to show off her young breasts rather than to stretch her back.

So much so that, while he hangs on her every word, Murphy ends up convinced she's probably not as serene and mature as she'd like people to think and that somewhere deep inside her some obscure desire still lies hidden, some pubescent arousal that must persist beneath her adult persona.

"WE STILL HAVEN'T talked about Nora," she points out all of a sudden as she brings a bottle of Italian wine into the room—she must have deduced from his troubled state some transference of feelings not usually directed at her, and thinks it would be a good thing to get the conversation on track.

"No, we haven't," he admits, blushing retrospectively about his inappropriate thoughts.

Murphy now comes to the main reason for his visit and tells her in some detail about the research he's done to try to understand why Nora's left (because she's given him no explanation herself); the calls to various people to piece together where she was and when; the hard drive he got to talk, without finding anything, as if she'd carefully erased her tracks.

"I'm now convinced," he says, "that she organized everything, planned everything a long time ago."

A vestige of scruples makes him avoid mentioning the five thousand dollars she relieved him of before leaving.

"The planning idea—I'm not sure I believe that," she says gently as she fills their glasses. "I don't believe it because I know Nora and I know she's too impulsive to premeditate a breakup."

As for the fact that she's given him no explanation, Vicky goes on, that's what she usually does with men—she's not big on debate. Nora's one of those people who reckons there's nothing to explain, not why people love each other, nor why they split up.

"To be honest, Nora's never been very easy to understand," she reminds him, pausing as if to go into reverse.

IN HIGH SCHOOL she was already seen as a strange phenomenon with her piercings and her bleached hair. She was the sort of surly, mixed-up, slightly tubby teenager who goes through life all guns blazing and whom no one, and Vicky emphasizes the point, absolutely no one wanted as a friend. If he sees what she means.

Vicky must have been alone in realizing just how pretty and how popular she would one day be. And when it happened, after the summer holidays, and everyone started gawking at her, goggle-eyed, her problems only got worse.

She particularly remembers something that happened in gym class one afternoon when Nora was still in transition, not very sure of herself, and some tall older boys made the most of an opportunity to carry her off, taking her to their locker room and each having a feel of her legs and breasts.

"It was revolting," she says; "it was like they all wanted a piece of her."

Vicky Laumett, commenting on these images as if reading a voice-over or giving these images her voice-over-style commentary, concedes that she too was attracted to Nora from that point because she'd stayed true to herself and wild, and both of them hated the kissing couples salivating over each other in every corner of the schoolyard.

While *they* liked American actors or the Romantic poets, especially Shelley.

"Would you like some more wine?" she asks.

Murphy, who's listening to her with a sort of devastated, cataleptic calm, waves for her to carry on. He likes her level, slightly dreamy voice as she tells him about all those years when he didn't exist.

"NORA," SHE SAYS—one thing perhaps explaining another—"was the youngest daughter in a dysfunctional family, with a depressive mother who disappeared into the countryside from time to time, and a gambling father up to his ears in debt who worked for the Coventry town council." She can't remember now exactly what he did but, anyway, one year, on Christmas Eve, he made off with the pensioner's club fund, thrusting the whole family into instant shame and poverty.

A year later, almost to the day, Nora made the most of her family's complete stagnation to break away on her own and join a band who were meant to introduce her to funk and anarchy.

After that she heard no more news. Until Nora's sister, Dorothy, told Vicky that Nora had found the love of her life in Paris in the shape of Spencer Dill, and she'd never been so happy. She really talked about it in terms of redemption, Vicky recalls.

But the first time Vicky and Nora met up in London, the following year, and chatted about all sorts of things, including boys, she felt that actually Nora was quite disillusioned, a bit like a princess who no longer believes in make-believe. Nora kept criticizing herself, saying she was cold, selfish, and destructive, and, to be frank, Vicky felt sorry for her.

She doesn't say: then it was your turn.

Murphy doesn't say anything either.

He wonders whether he can suggest that she speak to Nora on his behalf, or whether it would be better to wait until she offers to do this. Supposing, of course, she feels like it. In this baffled state of mind, he pours himself some more wine and watches the thunderstorm outside. He sees white flashes forking across the sky in the distance, and people running to their cars.

"Do you think you could do something for me if she's in Paris?" he asks, turning toward her.

"I don't know," she says with a doubtful little pout, which he takes as a blunt refusal. He realizes that he'd do better not to insist and to leave with some dignity. Anyway, her husband will be here soon.

Outside, around Earl's Court, it's the calm after the storm: people have gone home, the Pakistani stores have lowered their metal gates, dogs are starting to empty garbage cans. Sheltering in a doorway, Murphy smokes a cigarette while he waits for his taxi, stricken by all the pain in the world, both inside and outside himself.

8

The two girls have been sitting on this bench at the railway station for a while now, waiting for the train to Torquay. Nora's getting her to listen to R.E.M. on her headphones, the sun's rising in the sky, she has her thigh pressed up against Nora's, and it's early summer. They're seventeen and they've become a symbiotic partnership that appears on beaches everywhere. When they're not at the beach, they live with Nora's grandparents.

While her husband sleeps beside her, Vicky Laumett has all the time in the world to picture the station, the posters of the day, the windy platform, the green sea in the distance, travelers walking back and forth in front of them, sluggish in the humid air, and the man writing postcards on the bench opposite.

Then, just as deliberately, she pictures Nora's face next

to hers, her fluffed-up hair, pale, slightly consumptive complexion, brown eyes, freckles, and her lips dried by the sea
air, which Vicky keeps wanting to kiss.

She has more than a crush on Nora that summer.

The train still isn't there. They ran away at seven o'clock
in the morning to meet up with some guy called Aaron
Wilson or Milson, whom she personally has never met, but
Nora can't stop talking about him—he's a windsurfing in-
structor, plays acoustic guitar, and, according to her, must
be at least twenty-two or twenty-three—so Vicky's now
torn between curiosity to see him and fear Nora will abandon her so she'll have to come home alone this evening.

Deep down, she'd rather the train didn't arrive.

If, on a geological scale, all the moments in a lifetime add
up to just one instant that summarizes all the others, Vicky
would like this to be it, the one where they're sitting with
their heads together listening to R.E.M. on a station platform, in summer, when the doors to life are still wide open.

LATER, WHEN THEY get off the train—great swathes of
the morning have disappeared—the pair of them head toward the port, tearing down the streets of Torquay, which
are lined with old-fashioned boarding houses like in *Fawlty
Towers*. A slight smell of the sea hangs in the air; groups of
silvery clouds glide across the sky.

On the way, they stop at a hotel terrace to look at the

view of the beach and wait for the feted Aaron to appear, although they're not exactly holding their breath; he's not the angel Gabriel after all—they're agreed on that.

Just then, someone a long way over to their right calls Nora's name, and they turn their heads in unison. Down below them, they see a tall, dark-haired boy crossing the beach toward them, carrying his board over his head.

"That's Aaron," the real Nora says, shielding her eyes with her hand.

They lean on the balustrade a little longer, watching but not waving to him, their perfectly lined-up faces exposed to the sun. They have plenty of time. It's as if just having Nora beside her is enough to distend it.

At first glance, when they meet Aaron in the street, she thinks he's too tall, too smiley, too sure of himself, perhaps because, conversely, she feels vulnerable and doesn't know how to behave once he starts kissing Nora. To avoid any jealousy, he kisses her too—he seems to be a born kisser—and compliments her on her rhinestone-trimmed jeans and her white sneakers.

Compliments that she accepts with a show of perfect detachment while Nora eyes her mischievously as if she already has her own plans.

Once he has put away his equipment, he takes them for lunch in a fast-food bar above the main road, next to a post office with orange-colored windows.

When he isn't kissing Nora and remembers Vicky is

there—well, she *is* sitting opposite them—Aaron fires masses of questions at her as if for some preliminary examination, asking about her taste in music and her favorite TV shows (he adores a series set in a German submarine) while he steals her fries. However hard she tries to perfect her scowl and her monosyllabic answers, she actually finds him kind of funny, with a childish emotional streak that's rather reassuring.

Afterward they head down toward the sea in a sort of timeless, sun-drenched torpor, waffling between lying on the beach or sitting on a café terrace, as if so encumbered by desire—Nora's walking between the two of them—that they're reduced to a semi-lethargic state.

But the seaside, Vicky discovers, does have this advantage: you can keep walking indefinitely without ever reaching a decision. Which is how they end up miles away, sitting on bar stools in a smoke-filled bowling alley.

THERE'S AN INTERRUPTION.

"You know," her husband says in an exasperated voice, "I'd really like to get to sleep without your light in my eyes. Is that possible?"

She switches it off.

If he only knew, she smiles to herself, going straight back to Torquay.

The afternoon's nearly over now. They've come back to the seafront to have an ice cream and are walking along the beach together, their eyes squinting against the reflected sunlight. Aaron is describing the digs he has in his cousins' house, which, he claims, feels a bit like a Soviet apartment or a hostel, with its communal kitchen and shared toilets.

At seven o'clock sharp you have to hurry to get your place in the queue for the bathroom, he explains, otherwise zilch. The hot water tank takes three hours to heat again.

At the time she doesn't wonder why he's telling them all this. In fact, she's only half listening as she walks, because hovering on the edge of her mind is Nora's shifting shadow, its profile etched on the water.

High up the hillside on the far side of the port she makes out a house for sale, with a series of bay windows, and the name of an agency and their telephone number, which ends in 2013. She couldn't say why but she's suddenly convinced she'll remember this number, 2013, seen there glimmering in the sun. As if it were a date, a sort of warning or conspiracy for the future.

"Vicky, I need to talk to you," Nora says ominously, making the most of a moment when they're alone together. "You know I never keep any secrets from you. You know that, don't you?" she insists. "Okay, and I know you won't tell anyone," she goes on before confiding quietly, as if it were urgently important, that she is in love with Aaron and she desperately wants to make love with him.

"Now?" Vicky asks stupidly, in the confusion of surprise.

• • •

LOOKING BACK, VICKY Laumett can still see the whole scene as if from a helicopter: the fading light, the horizon, the white crests on the waves, children crouching on the sand, and the two of them, so young, shaking as they talked like actresses making their debut.

Her saying she doesn't want to be left on her own and Nora saying there's no way that's going to happen and that she loves her at least as much as Aaron.

"I don't want you to leave," Nora reiterates, stroking the crook of her hand with her finger. "Do you trust me?"

"Of course," she says, leaning so her hair mingles with Nora's, and discreetly seeking the salty taste of her lips as a wave of pleasure runs through her.

Then there's no more time to think, or to worry about what's going to happen to her, because Aaron has already caught up with them, a beer can in hand, and announces that his cousins won't be in this evening—they have to go out at about nine or ten o'clock—so they can both sleep in his room.

"There's just a double bed and two chairs," he warns them, drinking his beer, and he and Nora exchange a look loaded with secrets.

It's then, and only then, that she feels she understands where they're going with this.

"That's perfectly fine with me," Nora replies right away—she's among the thirty-five percent of English girls under eighteen who are sexually active. While Vicky, next to her, has the chest of an eleven-year-old and the experience to match.

But the only thing she can think to say is perhaps they should call Nora's grandparents first to ask permission.

Which makes the granddaughter laugh out loud.

"Sure you don't want to call your parents too?"

For fear of ridicule, she doesn't pursue this further. But she already knows she's been taken hostage, and will probably let them talk her into it. Because she's too scared Nora will dump her there and for that to mean it's all over between them.

"Okay, what are we doing?" Aaron asks. "Are you coming with us or not?"

What can she say? Obviously she follows them, given she has no other options.

FROM UP IN her helicopter, she can see herself walking behind them, all pale and virginal, while they stroll in the shallows, arm in arm, as if they've suddenly forgotten she's there.

There are few others around now; the wind has lifted and people have left the beach. In the distance the sun is sinking into a twinkling sea, and she can see a small motorboat ferrying between nowhere and nowhere in such a serene, lonely way that she has a searing urge to cry.

To avoid making a fool of herself she starts running along the shore, whirling her arms and opening her mouth wide to breathe in the sea air.

Once the sun has disappeared, the beach changes in an instant into a desolate gray place strewn with debris carried in on the waves. And it's getting colder by the minute, so they turn back. They walk side by side toward the port, all three of them silent as if playing some competitive non-speaking game, while a manic dog chases flocks of seagulls.

"When are we going there?" she asks, shivering, as if impatient to get it all over.

It's not quite ten o'clock yet, and they don't know what to do with themselves. With the rising tide, the darkness all along the sea wall has a translucent quality as they look on it from above. They walk randomly along various streets, waiting for the moment when they can take possession of the room and sleep together.

Or rather, the moment is waiting for them.

9

The morning sun is beginning to warm through the living room windows as Léonard Tannenbaum, draped in his purple cotton robe and moving with Olympian grace, passes a small cylindrical Rowenta vacuum over his parquet floor.

Still chatting to his visitor, he gently sucks the dust from cacti in pots before cleaning their branches with a Q-tip dipped in demineralized water. Each time he leans over his plants—like Gulliver leaning over his gardens—his dressing gown reveals long, thin, and sedentary legs; it's a wonder they ever supported an imposing physique, sculpted by years of paragliding and rowing.

The disease has stripped his calves, emaciated his silhouette, hollowed around his blue eyes.

"I don't know which way to turn this morning, and

everything's exhausting," he says, closing the curtains to drown out the heat.

One behind the other, they go through into the large bedroom, with its dozens of Chinese statuettes arranged on shelves, and the master of the house dusts them carefully while he goes back to describing the demonstration of Marxist-Leninist Turks he came across yesterday afternoon on the Place de la République, and the grim feeling that their red flags stamped with the hammer and sickle inspired in him.

His visitor, who's seen it all before, merely nods and gazes out the window at the railings of Buttes-Chaumont, firstly because he can't bear overexcited crowds any more than Léonard can, but also because he can anticipate Léonard's tirade about the distortion of collective emotion and the nightmares it can lead to. In any event, Léonard abhors history (he prefers eternity), and his bag's always packed, just in case things take a turn for the worse.

In the meantime, sporting a pair of long see-through rubber gloves, he's busy cleaning some recalcitrant marks on his sofa with the help of a surface-active product, while he carries on holding forth volubly about crowd behavior. Whether it's a symptom of loneliness or a product of his job (he holds a chair in neurology), over the years Léonard has morphed into an incorrigible monologue-maker who won't tolerate sharing his speaking time with anyone, like in a television debate. And, as his condition is far from improving and he now teaches only very sporadically, his visitors reap the benefits of this. Life has become a permanent lecture hall for him.

In the days when he himself was a pupil on the benches of a private institution, the young Léonard Tannenbaum was already as brilliant as he was unpredictable, always scoffing at his teachers and improvising scandalous speeches in general meetings—when he wasn't trying to have a sneaky stroke of his neighbor's knee, that is.

And the neighbor, more often than not, was Blériot.

THE FACT THAT this one-sided love (Léonard must have sent a good hundred letters) managed to metamorphose into mutual and almost exclusive affection was surely due to some astrological conjunction. Even if the relationship isn't entirely without ulterior motives on both sides.

For example, Blériot, who's always in a fix, regularly relieves his former adorer of several spanking new ten-Euro notes on a variety of grounds—that's actually why he's here today. Not to mention the translating jobs he manages to pick up because Léonard is on the science committee of a dozen or so American reviews. There is a chance Léonard once hoped for a return on his investment, but if he did, he never mentioned the fact and must eventually have drawn a line.

In return, because there's inevitably some return, Blériot has to confess his little private affairs to Léonard, doing his best to avoid any beating about the bush or psychological explanations, which deprive us—this is pure Léonard speaking—of our dignity as sinners.

He may still be impressive in the role of spiritual adviser, but he can also play a dissolute priest with just as much conviction, or even a great lady—Madame de Chevry-Tannenbaum—scorned by her friend, who reprimands him for being so ungrateful and abandoning her in favor of a girl whose reputation is all over Paris.

"You see, what breaks my heart, my sweet, is you're getting more and more like a scrounging drug addict," Léonard says as he hands him three one-hundred-Euro bills, "and I'm worried about you. I'd really like to know what's giving you such a high at your age."

Although he doesn't deny his share of responsibility, Blériot does have to remind Léonard that this is only a very short-term loan and that, anyway, it might be better to avoid talking too much about money because the walls have ears.

THIS IS A reference to Rachid, Léonard's companion, who has just come back from shopping and can be heard busying himself in the kitchen.

Although he also acts as a butler, confidant, lover, and adoptive son, Rachid looks nothing like the image most people entertain of a Prince Charming. He's more a great beanpole with a pimply face and a suspect air about him, and he can't help joining in every conversation and wanting to be the only person in the world who's right. Until his exasperated protector has to take serious measures and shake him like a plum tree to get him to see sense.

After which, by way of punishment, he's relegated to the kitchen and forbidden to talk.

This clearly amounts to a form of abuse, and Blériot is well aware of it. He is also aware that, when this happens, he is the torturer's unbiased accomplice, through both his passivity (which often borders on connivance) and the casual habit he's adopted of putting in his earphones and withdrawing to a bedroom as soon as there's a rumpus in the living room.

All this and then an hour later, like today, he ends up sitting at the table contemplating savory pastries and meatballs with herbs lovingly prepared by Rachid, while—as an aside—Léonard complains about his lover's premature ejaculations, attributing them to Muslim overexcitability and taboo-anxiety.

"You *could* wait till he's gone," Blériot points out quietly, because there are days when he finds Léonard's provocations funny and others when, like the braying of a lonely animal, they totally break his heart.

"Contrary to what my colleagues at university believe," Léonard goes on, "I don't think about my students or my patients very much—well, no more than I think about Aristotle. I think about sex and more sex."

On this occasion, looking intently at his plate, Blériot makes no comment. He's activated his mental projection equipment—MPE—and holds his breath sharply while staring at crumbs dotted about the table, as his vitrified mind reflects the afternoon's play of shadow and light.

It's always at times of inanity and moral collapse like this, when he feels he's reached as low as he can go, that he misses Nora the most and wishes he could call her to come and fetch him.

10

When the phone rings and, for the third or fourth time, he hears Sam Gorki asking in his bleating voice whether Nora's back, Murphy is quick to hang up and turn his mind to something else—he's used to keeping an eye on his seesawing emotions.

For two weeks now, since he spent that strange evening with Vicky Laumett, he's stopped fretting, stopped dissolving into tears, and stopped taking antidepressants. He's hardly drinking anymore either. Knowing how vulnerable he is on this matter, he actually started by getting rid of every bottle of alcohol, and almost banned himself from any social outings, particularly visits with people as intemperate as himself.

All he has left of his painful episode with Nora is a vague posttraumatic discomfort, coupled with a convalescent lethargy and a state of exhaustion that periodically means he has to take stimulants and go for a run in the park, puffing out his own little cloud of morning condensation. This morning he runs for about half an hour, then decides to continue two blocks farther for a swim in the public pool in the hopes of maintaining some muscle mass.

As nine o'clock strikes he is in the shower; he puts on his shirt and his market trader's Armani suit, and, a dozen or so underground stations later—time enough to scan the newspaper and reflect briefly on the state of the world—he is standing outside his office with a clear head, batteries recharged, ready to take on the ups and downs of the financial markets.

THE SPACIOUS GLASS elevator stops on the ninth floor and Murphy Blomdale, badge in hand, falls in step with his colleagues as they head for their workstations, not stopping to think about what he's doing any more than they seem to be, as if they were all driven by some purposeless force and each automatically adopted this smooth expression and energetic gait just in case Miss Anderson's threatening footsteps started snapping behind them.

Following on from the entrance lobby, the main trading room is permanently bathed in a sort of gray half-light, while columns of blue figures scroll across digital screens all day long.

About thirty interchangeable people dedicated to data processing and finance work here, in an atmosphere as sterile as a laboratory, exempt from all political passions and emotional complicity. Each booth is even soundproofed and closed in by a Plexiglas wall, so that its occupant's thoughts interfere as little as possible with his or her neighbor's.

Right now, Murphy's thoughts are focused entirely on his boss, the formidable Miss Anderson—a six-foot redhead— who has a tiny glass office at the far end of the corridor where she constantly has to be careful not to move around too much for fear of knocking over the furniture. Deep down, this Miss Anderson he so dreads isn't a bad person, she just has a fiery temperament, which means that if she instructs someone to undertake a particular operation in a particular market, there's no room for procrastination and even less for argument: her wish is immediately enforceable.

Without knowing why (but it must be Freudian), she has harbored a strange and barely disguised aversion to Murphy from the very start, and never misses an opportunity to exploit his current vulnerability by reprimanding him in front of his coworkers.

Although the others are sometimes shocked by this routine, Murphy knows how this world works and recognizes that his problems with his boss delight some of them, particularly the dealers, Mike and Peter, who do everything as a twosome like Gog and Magog, and ostentatiously step aside every time Murphy runs into them, afraid of touching him as if, on top of being American and a Catholic, he has the misfortune of being a kleptomaniac.

• • •

AFTER FOUR OR five hours of uninterrupted work and a lunch grabbed on the go, Murphy allows himself a moment's relaxation in the cafeteria six floors up. It's a large monochrome space, lit by a wide window overlooking the Thames, and he likes to sit here drinking a soda and watching his coworkers with the curiosity of an anthropologist studying the behavior of some social group. Aware of the side effects an observer can have on the field of observation, he usually makes himself as invisible as possible and, if greeted, settles for a friendly little wave because he wouldn't want to seem like a poser either.

He doesn't actually know what depresses him more about watching his coworkers—the perpetual adolescence of some or the premature aging of others, something no doubt attributable to overwork and the exponential increase in their alcohol consumption.

All of which makes the presence of the agency's director, John Borowitz, more incongruous than ever. Because, in addition to his near-anachronistic temperance, he is distinguished within the firm by an almost taciturn discretion along with moral rigor that demands respect from one and all. If General de Gaulle had been tall and dark with silvery streaks in his hair, people might have said this man had something de Gaullien about him.

"Are you feeling better?" he asks Murphy with his usual courtesy and the slightly protective tone that a Harvard graduate adopts toward his junior (they are both from Boston). "I still have big plans for you, you know?" he adds under his breath before eclipsing himself, espresso in hand.

The cafeteria is almost empty now. Out on the terrace, shaded by a canopy, two girls having a cigarette scream hysterically when a gust of wind undresses them. It is at times like this that Murphy used to like communicating telepathically with Nora. He would find her sitting quietly, book in hand, in some Soho café, or wandering the paths of Green Park.

"You'll never guess what I've bought," she would cry, brandishing a paper bag.

It was always a guessing game to the tune of two or three hundred pounds—cash only.

Today, try as he might to close his eyes and feel his way, communication is not established.

He knows she's a long way off, lost in some foreign city—probably Paris—and that she's forgotten about him, but, sadly, the telescope of his jealousy is powerful enough for him still to see her hundreds of miles away, bouncing on a bed to a stranger's thrusts.

The thought that she might one day be pregnant by another man pierces Murphy with such aching nostalgia— he's hiding in the restroom at the moment—that he's instantly on the verge of tears.

11

When he checks his voice mail (his father's already called him twice), Blériot is at the bottom of the Jardin du Luxembourg, exactly on the corner of the rue d'Assas and the rue Auguste-Comte, leaning against the park railings, dazed by the heat.

He feels about sixty years old.

With no premonition or warning, he suddenly hears Nora's voice in the last message. And everything he was thinking concerning his mother and father is instantly erased.

It is the twenty-first day after Ascension.

Speaking in English and enunciating her words clearly, she tells him that between five and six o'clock she'll walk past the café where they used to meet at the end of avenue Daumesnil. If he can't be there, she'll call him again without fail on Tuesday morning, she reassures him before saying goodbye.

When he walks back across the park, he cuts a taller figure with a brighter face, so that some people sitting on their benches wonder whether it's even the same man. Blériot, who clearly has the gift to change his age at will, overtakes a jogger, then another, as he heads for the nearest Métro station with the sprightly step of an athlete trained in the art of waiting.

All the same—because he knows his own character well—he struggles not to let himself get carried away and get ahead of the music, so that he can think calmly about the decisions that must be made.

It goes without saying he's aware that, whatever happens, he mustn't screw up this second chance and he should in fact be unpacking it, organizing it, and getting it straight, so that he can use it to establish a lasting life plan. Although he doesn't know where they'll be starting.

It all depends on her and on what she's expecting from this reunion.

As far as he's concerned, all he knows at this precise moment is that he's returning to himself after two years in darkness.

WHILE HE QUIBBLES internally like this and tries not to rush ahead, he feels he's being carried by such a strong current, such agitation—which is probably nothing more than a childish impatience to be happy—that he seems to be bouncing off the sidewalk with every step he takes.

At that speed, of course, Blériot arrives an hour ahead of time at the bottom of avenue Daumesnil, and he commences his lookout through the windows of a van parked a few feet from where they're due to meet, so that he has the advantage of seeing her first.

Now he suddenly feels calm, almost detached, as if, by some dissociating effect, he's not so much living in the present moment as in the memory of this moment, and that everything he can see is printed on a contact sheet of photographs. The clouds flying in formation over Paris are printed on it, and the black car parked down at the dead end, the two blond women coming out of a hotel, the Chinese man throwing bread crumbs to the pigeons and the other Chinese man impatiently turning the pages of his racing newspaper, unaware that he too is in the frame.

NORA ARRIVES TWO years late, at exactly five o'clock.

As she spins around looking for him, there isn't a single sound, no breath of air, the earth's rotation stops for a few nanoseconds—to the surprise of the two Chinese men— while Blériot very clearly makes out the vibrations of his own emotion, like a sort of sound wave whose broadcasting time he measures inside his head.

In fact he recognizes her without recognizing her.

He feels—perhaps because of the van's window—that there is a sort of thin, transparent film between who she was the day she left and who she is today, making her both like herself and imperceptibly different.

Yet she's still just as youthful and dazzling, she has the same fair hair framing her ears, the same freckles—they're almost identifying features—and the same elegance in her white T-shirt under a black silk jacket. But there's something else; her face seems to have changed, is more gaunt, more strained, most likely with apprehension.

Perhaps she thinks he won't show.

But Blériot, wrapped up in the illicit excitement of watching her in secret, doesn't move. Keeping his eyes glued to the window, he tries to capture the feeling of joy afforded by beginnings, when the future is still resting and everything is peaceful.

When he finally comes out of hiding, with his arms in the air as if turning himself in, she pulls a funny face as she sees him, like a spasm of astonishment or shyness, before taking a couple of steps toward him and throwing her arms around his neck with a complete disregard for protocol.

"Oh! Louis, I've missed you so much, so much," she reiterates, demonstrating such enthusiasm she could be mistaken for a young girl who's never kissed a boy.

It's enough to take your breath away.

Even so, Blériot tries to stammer some sort of welcome and to say how he's been waiting for this too, but his cracked voice emits a sort of whistling sound and the only audible words are: "Neville, I knew it, I swear I knew it."

She'll never know what he knew because she's already dragged him inside the café, clamping his hand in hers. These hands that haven't touched for two years are clearly in a hurry to be together. Feverish, slightly clammy hands whose chemical communications immediately make them happy.

ONCE THEIR EYES are accustomed to the dim light inside the café, they automatically sit where they always used to, in the corner near the stairs, and order the same drinks, as if nothing has changed and love's timescale is indefinitely reversible.

With this one disparity: in her personal timeline, it may feel as if a mere fortnight has passed since she left him, but in his physical experience, twenty-five months, three weeks, and five days have gone by.

When he eventually asks how she's getting on with her life in Paris, Nora confides with a hesitant little smile that she's hoping she'll find a job as a hostess, but at the moment she's walking a bit of a tightrope with no job and no money. If she weren't lucky enough to be living in the suburbs, in a house loaned to her by her cousin Barbara, she explains, things would be even more complicated.

Although he doesn't openly say so, Blériot would have preferred a slightly less materialistic discussion where, for example, there might have been some talk of him and her, and of what she'd done without him since she'd been in Paris. But all in good time.

Given that he is both inflammable and timorous, he naturally doesn't dare ask her right away to invite him to her house in the suburbs. And given that she herself gives no signs of impatience—she's ordered a second beer—and is behaving exactly as if they had their whole lives ahead of them, he may have to wait awhile.

Even if, judging by various subliminal indicators, he comes pretty close to thinking they do both have the same thing in mind.

Either way, he has to be the one to suggest taking a taxi—it seems to be all she was waiting for—to get her to knock her beer back and finish it, covering her top lip in froth.

SO THEY HEAD off together toward the porte Dorée looking for a taxi stand, still holding hands, their legs oddly weightless, so that at times they seem to be gliding rather than walking, like Fred Astaire out for a stroll with Judy Garland.

Which, once the necessary adjustments have been made, gives some gauge of how quickly the natural rapport between them is reestablished and of the pleasure they derive from walking side by side through the streets and kissing in taxis.

In fact they're still kissing when they get onto the belt-way, and this kiss must be the longest in history—Blériot hasn't taken a breath yet—ending miles farther, on a one-way street high up in the Lilas district.

When they step out of the taxi, the evening sun is warm and the small white-brick house—"this is it," Nora says, pushing open the gate—seems to be reflecting the light of an endless summer.

"Do you know what?" says Nora, suddenly showing him her handbag.

"No," he admits.

"I can't find the house keys."

12

They got in through the garden window, pushing aside the shutters.

Their footsteps are now echoing as if in an uninhabited house. Blériot notices boxes piled in the living room and furniture covered in white sheets. Halfway down the hallway is a room with office equipment in it, lit by a single naked lightbulb.

The kitchen seems to be the only lived-in part of the house. It's a luxury kitchen, all stainless steel with a marble counter and a huge glass-front refrigerator.

"What does your cousin Barbara do?" he asks, discreetly putting his arm around her. (It's as if, now that they're alone in the house, they dare not look each other in the eye or kiss anymore.)

"I think she's an auditor," Nora says. "She's away on business half the time. She's on assignment in Singapore at the moment. She's made in exactly the same mold as my sister. I'm the lame duck of the family," she adds, bringing over a bottle and some glasses.

"You still haven't told me what you were doing in London."

"I was doing an acting class over by Camden Road. It was a pretty mediocre class and I don't think I'll have trouble finding something better here," she says, drinking her wine as she leans against the window with her back to the garden.

It must be just after nine o'clock, maybe nine-thirty, Blériot calculates while noticing that the evening light fits her as if tailor-made. He doesn't say anything, just gazes into his glass. Nerves and emotion, which he recognizes from a characteristic thrumming in his inner ear, have made him forget what he wanted to say about acting.

Taking the time to finish his wine and smoke a ciga-rette, he asks cautiously—because there's always room for misinterpretation—whether she'd like it if they went up to her room, because he's kind of had enough of sitting in the kitchen.

"If you like," she says, her brown eyes turned on him.

THE ROOM IN question is large and unfurnished—just a bed and a TV. It's reminiscent of a hotel room with a toi-let nook and a recess that serves as hanging space. Nora's clothes are scattered all over the floor.

"Barbara's promised she'll get me some furniture in September," she explains, turning on the TV and sitting on the
bed with her legs folded under her.

Blériot pauses briefly, a little surprised by this initiative,
before copying her and dropping down onto the bed himself.

Casually, as if not meaning to touch her, he's pressed
himself right up against her, one arm around her waist,
and is starting to nibble gently along her neck and her
shoulder while she just keeps changing channels.

"I hope you've come back to see me and not to see Spencer," he blurts as if suddenly unsure.

"Louis, do you remember our rule?" she says, stopping
on Natalie Wood's anxious face. "When we're together, the
others don't exist. But if it's any reassurance, Spencer lives
in Edinburgh, he's married, and he runs a company his
father left him."

"And the next one?" he asks.

"The next one still lives in London, but if you don't
mind, I'd rather we talked about something else."

There then follows a tiny moment of uncertainty.

"I PROMISE WE won't talk about them again," Blériot tells
her while—apparently distracted—cupping her breasts in
his large hands, almost astonishing himself because our souls
have such peculiar knowledge of bodies outside our own.

But his hands aren't dreaming. These really are her
breasts he's holding.

As if to give him confirmation of this, Nora breaks away for a moment to switch off the TV and comes coolly to sit beside him, pressing her lips to his and undoing his tie—as if she's been doing it all her life.

Once his shirt is off, there in the middle of the room, they carry on undressing each other, unhurried, not losing their heads at all, with almost synchronized gestures. She tugs hard at his jeans—he's already taken off his shoes—and he removes her skirt, feeling as he does the miraculous coolness of her buttocks.

When she's finally lying across the bed with her hands behind her head, Blériot stays standing for a few seconds, his throat tight, in a sort of tactilo-visual ecstasy that sends a shiver through him as he looks at every part of this familiar body, her breasts, her pussy, her hips, her girlish thighs, her long thin feet and her tiny protruding navel which reminds him of the knot on a balloon.

"Do you realize it's been two years, Neville. Two years," he emphasizes the point, leaning over her so his great shadow darkens her eyes.

"You're right, Louis, I've got a lot to make up for," Nora admits. "Make the most of it."

IT'S THE WEIRDEST and most exciting thing anyone's ever said to Blériot.

So here he is now on top of the penitent's body, his face buried in her neck, and they stay like that for a long time, in the dark, silent and shivering, as if they can feel the dopamine circulating in their brains.

Then he lifts himself up onto his hands so he can continue looking at her, and when he starts to move slowly, attentively, and when the strange action of absorption begins—the one that defies the laws of physics because, theoretically, two bodies can't simultaneously exist in one and the same point—Nora's eyes take on an unreal, almost moonlike limpidity.

They don't even know whether it's day or night outside. Blériot feels as if this embrace could go on for hours and hours, as if they're set to break various records that will never be ratified.

Except that out of nowhere, though he doesn't know how, the name Sabine comes to him—Sabine, who's waiting for him alone at the apartment—and he's suddenly suspended in space.

But he shakes his head to dismiss the idea and, carried away by the procreative current, is back in the flow.

There follows a brief period of abandon and shared contentment—every part of both their bodies being equally affected—until Nora grips him suddenly around the neck as if she has something very important to say and gives a long, soft cry in his ear, rather like the sound of a siren.

The next moment her legs twitch with one last convulsion and she leaps to one side, giving a very different cry: she has a cramp in her calf.

"Cramp?" exclaims Blériot as if he's never had a cramp in his life.

13

The following morning he comes out of the house and finds himself in a village-like street high up in the Lilas neighborhood, his senses so raw with fatigue that the tiniest sound startles him. The very daylight burns his eyes.

To relax himself, he takes his iPod from his pocket and listens to Massenet's *Elegy* very quietly as he heads toward the beltway.

Two or three streets farther, he comes across some water carts working their way around a square before setting off down a hillside. Council workers in boots are cleaning the road with hoses. Where they've been, the sidewalks look like tide-swept beaches. The air is very blue.

Under the influence of a subtle time distortion, Blériot feels as if it is already late in the day when his watch says it's barely six o'clock. He recognizes that Sunday-morning calm, the lack of traffic.

Through a half-open window, he notices a man sleeping in his bed, while a little girl beside him quietly sucks her thumb, staring at the ceiling and listening to the radio.

Having tried to call Nora, he's come into a brasserie and ordered a coffee and two croissants, and is sitting on a banquette by the window, suddenly torn between the contented feeling of being alone in this empty place and the discouraging thought of having to go home soon.

Blériot, who still believes in immanent justice, sometimes wonders what price he will have to pay for this life of lies.

Lung cancer perhaps? A car crash? A violent assault?

Whatever it is, he knows there will be something to pay.

His self-preservation instinct even suggests it's high time he told his wife the truth and reclaimed his freedom, in order to save what little there is left.

Though he knows all too well he won't manage that—at least not today—because he's witnessed his own failure to act before, his endless procrastinations, his puerile attachment to the past, but more particularly because he secretly hopes Sabine will make the decision before he does.

One day he'll buzz on the intercom: *It's over,* the machine will tell him, *you can leave, there's nothing left for you here.*

Just to be sure, he'll press the button again. *I said it's over,* the thing will cry, *now leave me in goddamn peace.*

And he'll go. He'll walk out of her life like stepping out of a room, apologizing for getting the wrong door.

BECAUSE OF THE sun—it's suddenly punishingly hot, with not a breath of air—he decides not to walk any farther and takes a taxi at porte des Lilas. The car is air-conditioned and the Vietnamese driver's wearing white gloves. Blériot has put his music back on, and, for a moment, he feels almost happy, as if he couldn't wish for anything.

When he emerges from the taxi outside his apartment complex, he carefully puts away his earphones and sunglasses—like a burglar who's committed his crime and has nothing more urgent to do than hide his big nose and false beard at the bottom of the garden. Then he walks into the building unnoticed.

On the stairs he realizes his mouth is dry and his temples are throbbing.

He finds his wife sitting in the living room, at her computer. When he leans over to kiss her, she tilts her cheek toward him absentmindedly, still typing away on her keyboard as if nothing were any different.

She just seems paler, more distant, perhaps more irritable than usual.

Ever the coward, Blériot then moves around the living room without a word, careful not to knock the furniture, and sits as inconspicuously as possible on the sofa at the far end, in the hope that his humble behavior and crestfallen expression will predispose her favorably.

"I thought it would occur to you to call me," she comments, without stopping what she's writing, so that, for a few seconds, he gets the feeling she's drafting a statement.

This cranks up his discomfort a little further.

"I did think of it, but I thought I'd be back much sooner," he says, wondering whether this could later be used in his defense.

"I'm guessing you were with friends and you were just taking your time," she says, turning to look at him. "You're all the same, really. Sometimes I think you're just as two-faced as the others."

Blériot doesn't know who she means, but, as he has no wish to take the rap for the others, he's keen to correct her assessment and assure her that she's absolutely and completely wrong because he spent the evening working with Léonard.

"We were flat out, the pair of us," he says, "because there were at least twenty pages to translate."

But something about the way she's looking at him stops him from taking this any further.

She comes toward him, fixing him with a formidable stare, with sad, intelligent eyes the like of which he's never seen before, and he looks away, hugging her to him and reciting some act of contrition inside his head.

Even though he knows it's no one's fault.

Given there are no solutions with love.

AT THREE O'CLOCK the air is still just as hot in the apartment, despite the fans. They have lunch together, sitting in the kitchen. Both playing their roles, he as the guilty son, she as the loving, infinitely indulgent mother, always forgiving his offenses, out of sheer weariness or fatalism.

Blériot would so like to take her hand and say something tender and spontaneous, to give him some relief from feeling this unworthy, but no words come to mind.

After a while, he feels his limbs weighed down by the immobility. The stiffness and silence even start affecting his head and he can anticipate the moment when he'll succumb to one of his migraines. It's as if everything has come to a halt inside them and around them. There isn't a single sound outside now. Apart from a drip from the faucet in the sink, there's nothing to prove that time is still passing.

Sitting with his hands flat on the table and fingers spread, Blériot, who seems to be counting the seconds, notices even the grain of the wood, even the shadows of the stainless steel cutlery, like someone under hypnosis.

In fact, the scene goes on so long, is so persistent, that it could be set in marble.

"Louis, how would you like to come to Milan with me?" she asks all of a sudden, as if to draw him out of his reverie. "It's only for two or three days. You could see the city while

I work, get a bit of fresh air, and take the train to Bergamo or Verona. It would be very easy."

"Yes, I'd really like to see Verona again, but I've taken on too many commitments and I'll never manage it," he replies, compulsive liar that he is.

At least this allows him to get up from the table and, with no solution, to sidle into his office.

His wife says nothing, but he feels he's being followed by a pair of X-ray eyes.

HE SPENDS PART of the day in a state of hovering anxiety, his head buried in a dictionary ("sex" and "secateurs," he discovers, have the same root: "secare"), then types a dozen or so lines of his translation on disorders of the lymphatic system before finally calling back his father.

His mother's still just as difficult and the atmosphere at home just as burdensome, his father summarizes through the telephone's crackling, as if telling him about some tropical country where it never stops raining.

"Could you come down one of these days?"

"I don't know if that's possible now," he says evasively.

And with that, only moments later—experts would probably see this as symptomatic of a split personality— he's already longing to call Nora and go to her little house.

A very powerful longing.

As he convinced himself years ago that chemistry is cheaper than psychology, Blériot ends up taking a valium and lying on his bed, staring blankly in the half-light. Curled in the fetal position, he looks like a man on the brink of nervous exhaustion, lost somewhere between his family problems, his issues as a translator, and his fears as an adulterous husband.

TOWARD THE END of the afternoon, to make Sabine happy, he joins her in the living room and watches an old episode of *Star Trek*, resting his head on her shoulder and hugging a large cushion to his stomach as if afraid of the emetic properties of weightlessness.

"Captain, we've sustained substantial damage, but we still have control of the ship," Spock reports to Captain Kirk.

"Get the men back to their posts," replies Captain Kirk, eyes pinned on the incandescent sky.

"Thanks to Spock, all's well that ends well," says Dr. McCoy.

Blériot, though, says nothing. Even if, as far as their problem is concerned, his and Sabine's, he wishes he could be so positive.

"Now, head straight for Tantalus," barks Captain Kirk.

14

By the edge of the pond Murphy Blomdale catches sight of an obese couple dressed like Martians and taking pictures of everything, most likely with the intention of selling the images back on Mars.

The light is so blinding at this time of day that he himself has opted to take refuge in the shade and buy a soda. Afterward, being careful to leave as inconspicuously as possible, he cuts across to Marble Arch and starts running again, a solitary figure on the park's paths, his heart and mind both empty.

Although he has the occasional bleak moment and his life feels cruelly diminished, Murphy is actually no more unhappy than the next man. He's simply more apathetic, more sluggish, as if suffering from a sort of existential deficiency. This morning, for example, he's hardly returned from the park and settled in front of the television before he falls asleep right in the middle of a Chinese film. He has his newspaper on his knee and his head tipped back, in the exact same position as his father and his father's father.

Sometimes he can even feel himself physically aging on this sofa, probably because his immobility abnormally heightens his perception of the passage of time.

WHEN THE PHONE wakes him with a start, Murphy thinks it's Vicky Laumett. *Happy birthday!* a girl cries in French. So it isn't Vicky.

Afterward, he gets it.

"Do you still think about me?" he asks, amazed.

"I can prove I do: I haven't forgotten your birthday."

"Well, I had," says Murphy.

Then there is a very long, awkward pause, as if she is about to burst into tears.

"So, Nora, are you planning to call me once a year?" Murphy asks sarcastically, almost in spite of himself—because it's not in his nature, nor even in his best interests. But we'll have to accept that when you wait that long for someone to give you a sign of life, your resentment takes a while to lose its edge.

"I'll call as often as I can," she says meekly. "It's just, right now, I'm trying to find work in Paris and I also want to find an acting class, so you'll have to give me a few weeks' respite."

Murphy doesn't react immediately. He leaves a moment's hesitation, then, in a detached tone, as if it were a minor detail, he asks whether she's living alone in Paris.

"Do I have to answer?"

"No," he manages after another moment's hesitation, because he clearly knows what he's dealing with. It's even as if the figure of this man she doesn't want to talk about is silhouetted in the room right now, against a wall of silence.

"ARE YOU THERE?" she asks.

"I'm here, Nora. It's you that's not here. Incidentally, I wish you'd tell me once and for all if I should go on waiting for you or if I'd do better to get on with my suffering and move on, like a big boy."

"I didn't say we won't see each other again," she says gently, "I said that, right now, I'm staying in Paris because I've got loads of things to do here and I'm not free much."

A few minutes later, while she recites the list of everything she's planning to do in Paris (adding endless details and tiresome digressions), Murphy stops listening. Or rather, like changing tracks during a recording, he's erased the words to keep only the sound. The sound of her girlish voice, with her breathing, her hesitations, her rhythms and silences and hurried recapping, as if he were suddenly rediscovering the tune of a song.

He doesn't say a thing. He's lying on the sofa, listening to her, suffused with oceanic melancholy.

"Can you hear me?" she asks suddenly in an anxious voice. "You *could* say something."

"I'm letting you talk. I'm just waiting for you to tell me when you're planning to come back to London," he replies, guessing that she'll just say she has no idea again. Because she's chosen not to choose and to have it all her own way.

"I'll let you know as soon as I can," she promises. "Murphy, you don't hate me, do you?"

"No," he breathes into the phone. We are waiting for your promise, Saint Augustine said, taut with patience.

"Oh, Murphy, you'll never change."

He actually hangs up first. He stays there for a while, heart thumping in the dark, then goes to take a shower.

I'M STILL IN love with that girl, he realizes later as he leaves his apartment, asserting it with the same objectivity as if he were saying: Oh look, it's still daylight.

It's not a change in point of view or inclination, it's a change in the breadth of his soul. Something suddenly stopping him from giving up on happiness.

While he walks aimlessly around Islington, breathing the cool wind as it spreads through the overheated streets, Murphy feels a sort of internal excitement coupled with feverish shakiness, and—instead of spending the evening of his thirty-fourth birthday alone—he has an urge to go someplace where he can meet people. So he goes toward the overflowing café terraces that line Upper Street and, when he reaches the Underground station, heads toward Rosebery.

To be truthful, it's his legs that carry him in that direction of their own volition; he seems so like a robot, weightless, tireless, until he returns to his senses when he recognizes the windows of Mercey's Hotel. The hotel where they had their first date.

Despite his insistence, she hadn't wanted to go to his place, because he was officially living with Elisabeth Carlo and she claimed that just wasn't right.

Now, standing outside the hotel, he can see it all. The blue-tinted corridors, the mysterious elevators, the tall-ceilinged bedroom, their two bodies fitting perfectly into each other, the slight smell of sweat, the muffled sounds from the street, the July sunlight.

And, as the memory is ten times more intense than what actually happened—because of the added value supplied by his imagination—it takes Murphy Blomdale's breath away.

15

Despite the distance separating them, it's as if Murphy and Blériot are moving on either side of a thin partition, as transparent as a paper screen, each aware of the other's existence, inevitably thinking about him, but unable to give him a name or a face, so that they both seem to be groping their way like sleepwalkers along parallel corridors.

While Murphy Blomdale leaves work and, worried by the rumbling storm, takes great strides down Fleet Street, Blériot is walking up the rue Belleville under driving rain, bitterly regretting not taking a taxi in order to save money. The rain is now streaming down the sleeves of his jacket. When he reaches the cemetery, he cuts through the pelting rain and takes refuge in the entrance of a Métro station while he shakes out his clothes and dries his hair. Then he waits under his shelter, stamping his feet, among a group of taciturn Pakistanis.

He's onto his third cigarette when the fleeting sight of a girl hanging on the back of a scooter with her white skirt billowing like a parachute finally manages to reconcile him to the rain, while also reminding him that Nora's waiting for him at her house. And just as abruptly as his financial problems made him miserable, the thought of Nora, the thought of how beautiful she is, of her Noraness, restores his optimism.

Blériot doesn't hang around a second longer; he comes out from his shelter, abandoning the Pakistanis to their fate, and sets off toward porte des Lilas between two curtains of rain, guided by the hubbub and lights from the beltway. In the other direction lies the quiet and semidarkness of suburban neighborhoods.

From this point, a sort of familiar gravitation draws him to the small square where they found a brasserie, a square with its black trees and sloping streets streaming with rainwater.

Obviously, all the shops are closed. The redbrick buildings overlooking the road are reminiscent of a 1950s industrial landscape, and Blériot's quite sure he's the only visitor here at this time of day. Until, that is, he notices a man on the far side of the square, a very tall man, wearing a hat, standing at the foot of a tree as if walking a dog.

AS FAR AS he can tell from this distance, the man seems to be watching him from under his umbrella. Two streets farther, on a sudden premonition, Blériot turns around and sees that the man, who actually doesn't have a dog, is walking a few paces behind him.

Although the situation has certainly never happened before, rather curiously it doesn't raise any fear in him. And even when he starts to hurry and look around on every street corner, it's more out of curiosity, as if it were a sort of game between the two of them.

Because the other man is still behind him, lit up by a perfectly round moon.

This colossal but fleeting figure disappears now and then, intercepted by the shadows of trees, only to reappear in the light and come to a standstill at the same time as him, then set off again, adhering to silent, perfectly controlled movements, then stopping once more. While they each catch their breath.

At one point—perhaps because of his height or the way he walks—it occurs to Blériot that it could be Léonard, and he almost calls out to him. But even though he knows his friend has an eccentric streak, he can't think what might have driven him to improvise this game of hide-and-seek on such a rain-drenched evening.

When he reaches a fenced-off construction site, he turns again and can't see anyone. The sidewalks are deserted, water rushing along the gutter. However convinced Blériot may be that the man in the hat was just a projection of his own fears, he still feels relieved. He stays leaning against the fence for a moment, then, as he can't hear a single sound around him now, he decides to continue on his way, rather than lose himself in speculation.

His cell phone vibrating in his pants pocket reminds him at this juncture that his wife has already tried to get hold of him from Milan, that she must be at her hotel and worried by his silence. Which is actually not very considerate of him. But, although he's reading the warnings from his conscience correctly, Blériot knows he's expected but has no intention of giving up on his plans.

Instead, he decides to switch off his cell and change nothing in his course of action. As if somewhere, on a different level of his psyche, he is free to do as he pleases.

NORA IS STANDING small and slim in the doorway to the garden, wearing a pair of shorts and a man's shirt several sizes too big.

"I'm coming," she cries, stepping out in bare feet to open the gate. Because of the puddles it looks as if she's skipping across the lawn on deer's hooves.

"What were you doing?" she asks, kissing him. "I fell asleep."

Once inside, Blériot quickly strips off his wet clothes and pours himself a glass of white wine before going to the bathroom. He doesn't say anything about what's just happened to him.

"Guess what, Louis, I managed to find a job," she tells him through the door.

"Oh, where?" he says, looking for the hairdryer.

"In a hotel, near Charles de Gaulle Airport. Now I'll be able to pay for my acting classes."

When he is with her in the bedroom, Blériot stops for a moment to brush her hair behind her ears and smell her moist skin while he relieves her of her shirt with the dexterity of a conjurer, then, without further explanation, leads her to the bed.

Now that they're lying in silence, head to head, on top of the covers, he caresses her slowly, methodically, as if needing to work through the whole backlog of tenderness he owes her and for which he feels morally accountable. And anyway, they have plenty of time; they have the whole expanse of a night and day before them.

So, between two rolls on the bed, they can chat, drink wine, listen to music, watch images on TV, in other words do all the things they would do every evening if they were a legitimate couple.

AT NORA'S SUGGESTION, they take the opportunity to lay down the parameters of a life plan, in which they would definitely not be allowed to lie to each other, be jealous of each other, say anything aggressive, harbor negative thoughts, or hide any source of hurt from the other.

"It's a plan that suits me very well," says Blériot, putting his finger on her satiny calf.

By dint of which, Nora feels she needs to let him know that a few days ago she called her ex-boyfriend. The one who lives in London.

"It was his birthday and I have to say I'm not too proud of the fact that he sounded so unhappy," she says as she sits on the bed, all defenseless and half naked.

"Are you planning to get back together with him?" Blériot is suddenly worried, pouring himself another large glass of wine.

Sometimes he can't help wondering, as he remembers all the girls he's known who've been going through crises (starting with his wife), why he always comes after other men, and why he's always the one who picks up the pieces of their relationships. They really could find another job for him.

"Do you regret leaving him already?"

"No, Louis, it's not that at all. I'd just like to see him once more," Nora says with an enigmatic smile.

A take-it-or-leave-it sort of smile.

"It's your decision," Blériot acknowledges, trying—in keeping with the terms of their plan—to adopt as casual an attitude as possible on this particular subject. Although he doesn't always take everything she tells him at face value.

"Do you know what?" she says, lying down on top of him and taking hold of his shoulders.

"No," says Blériot, dreading whatever she's going to tell him.

"You make me happy."

"I make you happy?" he reiterates, astonished—he feels so imperfect, so unavailable, so ill equipped to satisfy a woman, especially one her age.

"Yes, because I find you exciting," she says, looking at him with her gold-flecked tiger's eyes.

As they get up, they notice that the night has cleared, with hardly a single cloud. While he is looking around downstairs for something to eat, Nora appears on the stairs poured into a long periwinkle-blue dress, worthy of a Hitchcock heroine.

"Shall we go out?" she asks in English, leaning over the banister.

In the next frame, we see them from behind as they pass through the moonlit garden.

16

At eight o'clock Nora's already downstairs, her face a mess and her hair tousled. They grab a quick hunk of baguette for breakfast and drink the rest of the white wine. In the morning silence, the door on the large refrigerator makes a rubbery noise as it opens and closes heavily. Then they get undressed and trail into the bathroom, listening to the radio.

Blériot stands under the shower, thinking about this entire free day to spend with Nora—his wife's not meant to be back before this evening—and he can feel his whole soul rippling with little waves of happiness. On top of everything, it's an extraordinarily beautiful day.

From time to time, the light from the garden projects their shadows onto the white tiles, two shadows smiling at each other as if they've been smiling for centuries.

When he has shaved he sits down on a stool with his head obediently tilted while Nora, with not a stitch of clothing on, massages his scalp, tidies his eyebrows—*sit still, Louis*—and files his nails like a real pro.

"Life is short," he says.

When he looks at her really close like this—she's bending over him—Blériot feels as if her peering face dissolves into millions of luminous atoms so that she radiates light.

Because she is radiant, as surely as he is happy.

Of course, when you look at this closely, you can notice a slight pimple here or signs of a cut there, but they're minute flaws and precisely the sort that only a lover can distinguish and memorize for his or her own personal delectation.

"I said sit still," she insists while she tries to squeeze a blackhead at the top of his forehead.

Good-natured boy that he is, Blériot immediately removes his hand from between her legs and sits quietly.

WHEN THEY FINALLY leave the house, the sun is already reigning over the city, and its subjects, in their peaked caps and tinted glasses, slink from tree to tree in search of some semblance of cool.

Nora and her lover, who don't have hats, literally hug the walls of buildings and avoid wide-open streets in favor of small, shadowy ones, even if this means ending up somewhere completely unfamiliar, deserted neighborhoods and lifeless squares that they cut across, occasionally having the titillating feeling—it wouldn't take much for them to get undressed in the middle of the street—that they've arrived nowhere.

"Louis, I'm beginning to feel famished," she complains as if it were his fault.

It must be at least two-thirty when, worn out, they go into the only restaurant that hasn't closed for the afternoon. The empty room looks disproportionately large, and its leather benches feel like something from a postwar film. But they make no comment.

They sit discreetly in a corner, their hands politely resting on the table, waiting for someone to be so good as to serve them.

Ils sont venus, ils sont tous là, Charles Aznavour's voice suddenly sings, just as a disheveled waitress, notebook in hand, gives them the choice between an omelet with fresh herbs and steak with mashed potato.

For a moment they exchange glances incredulously.

La Mamma, cries Aznavour from the kitchen. Which unleashes one of those pandemic outbursts of laughter that are a secret specialty of Nora's.

"Steak and mashed potato," they reply, regaining their composure because the waitress is clearly losing her patience.

Then there is total silence in the room again. From time to time the roar of an engine or a flurry of raised voices on the sidewalk reminds them that life is going on outside, and people are working or getting on with their business in the stifling heat of the afternoon.

• • •

THE MEAL IS as mediocre as anticipated, with ridiculously meager portions and near-humiliating service, but it all goes right over their heads without deflating their good mood. Quite the opposite. Nora's so outrageous that Blériot's afraid she might burst into song herself.

While they eat an ice cream, she tells him about something that happened to her in Torquay, when she was sixteen and was on vacation with her friend Vicky Laumett: *I was a bit into girls then,* she admits as an aside, in her surprisingly good French.

None of which alters the fact that they spent most of this particular day on the beach with a boy—his name was Aaron—who then suggested they spend the night in his room. And because they were curious and already slightly debauched, they didn't stop for a minute but followed him home.

The two of them got undressed in the bathroom, both with the premonition that something very powerful, something really shameless—she emphasizes the point—was going to happen and nothing might be the same again, like after a revolution.

"And was it a revolution?" Blériot can't help asking.

"What's the opposite of a revolution?"

"A nonevent."

That's it. In the end, Aaron chickened out at the last minute and suggested they put their clothes back on like good

girls and leave it at that, on the grounds that they were mi-
nors and he was an adult—they couldn't get over it.

"Couldn't he have thought of that sooner?" says Blériot,
who was rooting for the two revolutionaries.

On the strength of that, Nora goes on, to avenge the insult
the two of them made themselves comfortable in the bed
while he spent the night in an armchair in front of the TV.

"He didn't say a word, but his face the next morning said
it all," says Nora, imitating his face.

"And your girlfriend," Blériot asks as he pays the bill,
"do you still see her? What's happened to her?"

"She married some impossible guy in London and she
lives in a huge apartment," she summarizes, with a hard
edge to her voice that he finds disconcerting.

At least Nora's response could mean—but take this hy-
pothesis with a pinch of salt—that, despite her depraved
youth, she's not without judgment or a moral code on the
subject of love.

BACK OUTSIDE, THEY resume their suburban wander-
ings, until they find themselves close to the beltway
and confronted by rows of buildings in a series of long,
regimentally identical streets and people frozen with
boredom at their windows. They turn around here and
decide to take a taxi, which drops them off at the Odéon
crossroads.

All at once, because of the wind and the shadows, the heat seems less oppressive. They saunter slowly up the boulevard, Nora hanging on his arm as if they were husband and wife, one walking openmouthed to swallow the other's happiness, and the other—which is obviously him—keeping his mouth closed to stop it escaping.

They look at posters on movie theaters but talk about something else, go into a shop, then another, and everything feels easy, fluid, the way life as a twosome should be. They buy pointless things, little gifts, scarves, ties, unusual jewelry, as if extravagance made them feel all the lighter.

Nora even buys him a Hugo Boss linen shirt on the condition he gives her his solemn word that every time he wears it he'll remember just how happy he's been with her.

"I promise," says Blériot, putting his lips to the glowing light of her face and gently nibbling her neck and her little ears without anyone noticing, almost as if a fine bubble stretched around them has made them invisible.

Later they walk along the railings of the Jardin du Luxembourg, eating ice creams again, aware of a Blondie song coming from a car somewhere as the sun begins to fade. They know they're going to part. She has to go to Charles de Gaulle and he has to go home before his wife gets back.

"Right, I have to go," says Blériot, still holding her arm, as if their sympathetic systems were so amalgamated that he will take her with him.

17

Sabine is talking to Blériot, sitting with her back to him as she puts on her makeup at the mirror while he soaks in a bath. He suddenly realizes he's washing his hair for the second time that day, not sure whether this manic attention to personal hygiene is related to some purifying ritual or an obsessive disorder.

He plunges his head underwater, and is aware of Sabine's voice in the background telling him yet again to hurry because François-Maurice is expecting them between nine and ten.

"Am I invited too?" he asks, still splashing and gurgling with his bathwater.

"Of course you are," says his wife, who's almost finished getting ready.

His reflex reaction to the thought of spending the evening with François-Maurice and his clique is to withdraw on the spot, claiming any excuse that comes to mind—how tired he is, how late it is, how much work he's taken on in the last few days—but something tells him that, in some ways, it might be wise to agree to this outing as a couple, as much to please Sabine as to avoid a highly risky evening alone together at home.

So, when he is dry and shaved, he puts on his new shirt and his leather tie before pouring himself a martini as a pick-me-up.

"I'm ready," he announces with a gracious smile. A vestige of tenderness even induces him to run his hand over the naked small of her back to feel her cool skin.

"Louis, we're already an hour late," she reminds him, ensuring he keeps his wandering hand to himself.

THEY DRIVE THROUGH Paris along the banks of the Seine, Sabine at the wheel and Blériot beside her with his arm out the window, while the humid night air, the moving outlines of pedestrians, the buildings along the riverfront, and the radioactive clouds reflected in the water are probably being recorded in some secret part of his cortex.

"There are thunderstorms practically every evening," he tells Sabine, just to have something to say, as he furtively eyes the curve of her breasts under her dress.

His wife doesn't reply, her eyes focused ahead as if the windshield wipers were designed by Marcel Duchamp.

"Don't you like thunderstorms?" he asks.

When she still doesn't answer, he eventually assumes she's thinking of someone else and that this someone else, if his intuition isn't deceiving him, could well be her colleague Marco Duvalier, who was meant to go to Milan with her.

As they head through the rainy streets of Charenton, Blériot pictures himself in the future, coming home one evening like a wandering spirit in his own apartment, and finding Duvalier (who, the last he'd heard, was still married and the father of three boys) sleeping in his bed, next to Sabine.

"Don't let me disturb you, I'm just passing through," he hears himself tell his replacement as he looks for his glasses on the bedside table and is amazed to discover that he feels neither pain nor anger but rather an insidious sort of relief.

"Why are you laughing?" his wife asks as she drives around and around a block trying to find a parking spot.

"I wasn't laughing," he protests, swiftly tidying his hair in the rearview mirror.

THEY REACH FRANÇOIS-MAURICE's house, huddled together under their umbrella. She is classy as ever in her low-cut backless dress, kissing everyone like some movie star, while he follows in her wake and must look like the bodyguard or a production assistant, some sort of incidental accessory.

His face means so little to anyone that he could also be mistaken for an extra who's been granted a one-liner: *Good evening, I'm Sabine van Wouters's husband.* (Because she has wisely kept her maiden name.)

Obviously, the part isn't very rewarding, but, if it's any consolation, there are people here who aren't saying anything at all and have to settle for walk-ons, making variously intelligent faces at the far end of the room but not attracting an iota of attention.

While his wife flits from group to group with the easy conversation and social dynamism that are probably hereditary, Blériot—who knows his own limitations—talks to only a few other guests, preferably isolated ones, because his scant energy flags as soon as he has to show interest in more than three or four people at once. Particularly when these people are of mixed ages and mixed sexual and political leaning, as they are this evening. That's guaranteed neuralgia.

SPOTTING THE BUFFET in the next room, Blériot, who has some experience in this, adopts a casual, almost distracted and dreamy air as he cuts across the room before accelerating in the last few strides and taking possession of a bottle of champagne.

"Can I have some too?" asks the woman next to him, who saw his whole performance.

Being a good sport, Blériot pours her a glass. It would probably have stopped at that if something bright and mischievous in the girl's expression hadn't stirred his curiosity by reminding him of someone.

"Martina Basso," she introduces herself, offering a handshake.

"*Enchanté,*" he says, not feeling required to announce that he's Sabine van Wouters's husband.

His pretty acquaintance happens to be an Italian translator—she's translated some Calvino short stories—who has come to Paris to make the most of a sabbatical year. Blériot, who's growing younger by the minute, pours her a second glass of champagne and takes her to a room at the end so they can talk in peace, but he maintains his reserved and modest behavior.

It has stopped raining and someone has opened the windows; they stand side-by-side for a while chatting in the airy, eleven o'clock warmth, gradually aware of a mutual attraction rising within them and a no-less-mutual desire—of course he's the one extrapolating—to dump the other guests and sneak away.

And yet they don't move. As if it is too late and the opportunity has already passed.

Listening to Marina's voice and seeing the sparkle in her eyes, Blériot can easily see why he's happy to talk to her and grateful to be in her company, but no invitation, no signal.

They stay together a moment longer, leaning out the window, time enough to finish the champagne and exchange a few words in Italian—because he once studied Italian—before eventually going their separate ways, brought back within the bounds of their private lives.

● ● ●

WHILE HIS WIFE holds forth among a dozen or so guests clustered like satellites around her, Blériot, feeling redundant, has made contact with Suzanne and Christophe de Lachaumey, who are reputed to be worth millions but one of the world's least gifted couples in bed.

"What time is it?" Suzanne even asks, sounding anxious.

"Twenty-eight minutes past one," replies her husband in a voice like a speaking clock. You can tell they'd pay a fortune not to have to go home.

Meanwhile—and Blériot's onto his seventh or eighth glass of champagne—François-Maurice's wife has arrived absolutely reeling drunk, and this has cast a chill over the evening. When her official lover, Peter, turns up a few minutes later, the temperature drops even further.

The whole thing could be going on in Lapland.

Sadly, succumbing to a sort of alcoholic haze, Blériot doesn't remember the rest.

HE MUST HAVE passed out again in the car, because when he opens his eyes he recognizes the lights on the place de la République and feels instantly sober. Later he watches himself struggling up the stairs, eyes pinned on his wife's legs, while trying his best to gather his thoughts.

"Who was that girl you were talking to earlier by the window?" Sabine asks as she peels off her clothes like a sleepwalker and Blériot, who has the excuse that he's drunk, stands behind her stroking her cold, cold buttocks.

"An Italian," he says.

"Do you know her?"

"Not at all," he replies while his fingers carry on perusing her body, and she doesn't rebel or try to get away.

This docile acceptance, so unlike his wife's usual behavior, wakes him at once. Now he takes her lovely, heavy, pointed breasts in his hands, as if pretending to be a doctor, and orders her to arch back, pressing her arms against the headboard.

"What the hell are you doing, Louis?" she protests.

"You'll see," he replies, not put off.

"Bend a little bit more," he asks, leaving her in that position while he takes his own clothes off.

18

They are younger by two years, almost three.

They're both sitting by the pool in the fading light of a spring afternoon—it must be around five or six o'clock. While other people swim laps, they're peacefully soaking up the sun in their swimming things, dangling their legs in the water.

They still haven't slept together.

But Nora has already moved into his life as if making herself at home. They see each other nearly every day, at about midday—it's their mythological time—and go for a lovers' stroll through the Jardin des Plantes before having lunch together and then, depending on the weather, deciding to go to the movies or the pool.

They don't try to hide. They feel invisible. His wife doesn't suspect anything; neither, apparently, does Nora's partner, and the chance of bumping into either of them in the street is infinitesimal, so they feel they have nothing to worry about. They're not doing anyone any harm, anyway.

MUCH LATER, WHEN he reviews the images of that spring in his mind's eye, Blériot will be surprised that his wife doesn't appear at all, as if she has been edited out.

Nora has gone back to reading *Tom Jones* on her beach towel, offering her pale calves to the sun, while Blériot swims alone, to a perfectly even rhythm, never losing his stride and never taking his eyes off his lane.

On the fifteenth lap of this monotonous exercise, he allows himself a pause, hanging on to the ladder of the small pool, just long enough to admire his favorite reader and to register yet again his amazement that, after so many relationships, she's managed to keep that virginal expression of someone waiting, all patience and gentleness—the same expression you see on certain figures in paintings, posing with their books and rosaries.

Except that in a swimsuit it's difficult to get an idea of people's inner lives.

HAVING FINALLY CAUGHT his breath, Blériot carves the surface of the water once more with vigorous elegance, flanked by two opulent mermaids and four little boys in matching white swimming caps, making them look like quadruplets. To escape the crush, he swiftly disappears underwater and, despite the fastidious nature of the undertaking, begins counting the tiles in the pool. Until the water starts to cool.

Like a marine monster emerging from the depths, he reaches out a huge arm to grab Nora's foot and watches as she laughs and snatches her leg away—suddenly longing to be alone with her.

Blériot has climbed onto the side; the sky overhead is deep and still with small high-altitude clouds sending shadows scudding over the surface of the pool. Two bulky boys with more tattoos than a yakuza are sitting on the diving board, apparently watching their own reflections in the water, while couples snooze peacefully, their bodies resting alongside each other like cellos on beach towels.

"Maybe there are too many lovers and not enough love," Blériot announces out of the blue, prey to some philosophical inspiration.

"What do you mean?" she asks, looking over the top of her book.

"Just what I said," he replies, lying down beside her with his head parked on her stomach.

All around them the place has started emptying and the terraces are almost silent. The only sounds from the pool are the intermittent cries of a few bathers still diving in.

With his eyes closed like a dog lying in the sun, Blériot listens to them jumping into the water and feels he is drifting far, far away in both time and space.

• • •

HE MUST HAVE drifted off for a few minutes, because Nora's now ready to leave, with her bag over her shoulder.

"I think they're about to close, we need to go," she says, gazing at him with big, thoughtful, slightly pre-occupied eyes. She must be waiting for him to make a decision.

Blériot, who's now fully awake, can guess what this decision is, but it's as if the more inevitable it becomes, the more terrifying he finds it. Firstly, he's never had much resolve on the whole question of women, and secondly, his and Nora's respective situations being what they are, he has every reason to dread the next stage, the subterfuge, the lying, the ploys and degradation: in other words, a reprobate existence. He may have had the odd lapse in the past, but they were only ever internalized lapses, nothing that led to any consequences.

All the same, as he and Nora walk along the street, he's well aware that he can't carry on like this indefinitely, poised between the anxieties of unfaithfulness and the depression of faithfulness—given that, in this sort of situation, there's no happy medium.

"In case you were planning on walking me all the way home, I'd better warn you right away that Spencer's there and you'll have to talk to him," she intervenes at this point in her unpredictable way, changing from one minute to the next.

"Would you rather we went to a hotel?" Blériot asks hoarsely.

"I don't know. What I'd really like is for you not to do this reluctantly," she says, putting her arms around his neck and molding her young body to his to prove that she really is a woman.

"We don't have a choice anyway," he points out.

"If you prefer, you can look at it like that," she says, and then outlines two conditions. The first is that she must be home at ten o'clock, ten-thirty at the latest, and the second condition is that there's no way he can take her just anywhere. Particularly not some crummy hotel where they rent rooms by the hour.

"That wasn't what I had in mind either," he reassures her as he looks for a taxi.

AS IF BY mutual agreement, they don't say another word in the taxi, each politely keeping to his or her corner until they are dropped on a discreet street close to the Montmartre cemetery.

"I hope you know what you're doing and you won't regret anything," she blurts unexpectedly, turning to face him.

"Of course. I won't regret anything and I won't forget anything either," he promises, watching her posing in her sunglasses on the steps to the hotel. At five feet four inches, she exudes a sort of lightness, a sense of unfinished childhood that moves and confuses him in equal measure, as if he is afraid the hotel staff might get funny ideas.

They go into the lobby, without so much as one piece of luggage for the sake of appearances, and head determinedly toward the reception desk. It appears to be a rather exclusive hotel with a lounge the size of a movie theater, deep armchairs, vast mirrors, and walls hung with red velvet. At least she can't say he's doing things halfheartedly. While they wait at reception, two concierges hanging on phones take ages to establish whether room 57 was vacated this morning.

"Every time we try calling, there's no one there," apologizes the older of the two, who talks like someone from *The Bald Soprano.*

"There must be someone," replies her colleague, handing them the key to room 59 at last. "Breakfast is served from seven o'clock."

They don't say anything in reply.

Now the die is cast. They walk back across the lobby and the large red lounge, with the agile step of people perfectly at peace with themselves.

"Do you know what?" says Nora as she calls the elevator. "It's the exact opposite."

"The exact opposite of what?" he asks.

"Of what you were saying earlier at the pool. There's too much love and not enough lovers. So there's always some leftover."

"That may be true, but I suggest we think about this afterward," says Blériot, pushing her into the elevator.

19

It's highly likely that if she'd ever known she would be featured stark naked in a novel, Nora would have refused to take her clothes off. And she would have done everything in her power to make sure that, instead, her taste for Chekhov's theater or Bonnard's paintings was mentioned.

But she didn't know. So here she is, quite naked, with her high buttocks, small breasts, waxed bikini line, and slightly large feet, as if she hasn't finished growing.

By the way, she announces, in Coventry she used to know a photographer who was almost twice her age and was infatuated with her legs.

"I promise you I'm not inventing any of it," she says, stretching her legs out over his. "I hope you believe me, at least."

"Of course I believe you," says Blériot, lifting himself

onto his elbows to admire them more easily.

At the moment they're both lying naked and relaxed on the bed, bathed in the cool air of the room. Molded into position by their pleasure but still with some time before them, they're lounging between the sheets while their furious heart rates gradually slow.

The truth is, they're feeling too lazy to get dressed and leave the hotel. They can only just manage to take turns going to the minibar for shots of vodka that they mix with Pepsi and drink in little sips.

SO, THIS PHOTOGRAPHER of hers, she continues as she comes back to sit on the bed, took her to Switzerland once, with the excuse that he was putting together a portfolio for her, and they spent almost a week in a sort of motel, then in a hotel that was way less glamorous than this one.

At first she thought it would be a perfect life, no parents, no worries, no housework, and she'd be stupid not to make the most of it. Officially, she was going skiing with her friend Vicky and Vicky's grandparents, and she scrupulously called her mother every evening to tell her how her skiing was improving and to describe the spills Vicky had had.

"When you never actually left your hotel room," he interrupts, pinching her thighs.

"It's not what you're thinking," she assures him. "This

guy was completely crazy, he shot up the minute he got out of bed and then drank everything he could get his hands on." When he finished a photo session—she leaves the pictures to Blériot's imagination—he'd vanish without any explanation and she spent the rest of the day waiting for him like a prisoner.

"I felt like I was lost in an empty hotel in the depths of this creepy valley."

"There must have been other guests in the hotel," says Blériot, going to the minibar for another drink.

"I don't know," she says. "If there were, they were so discreet I never saw them. Every now and then you'd hear a door slam or the sound of an imaginary shower. That's about it. One day, I cried so much that someone knocked on the wall a couple of times, but I didn't dare answer."

The most incredible aspect of the whole affair was that she'd been warned, and her seducer was already infamous in every high school in Coventry. But obviously the worse his reputation became, the more girls seemed to beat a path to his door.

"It's the Bluebeard syndrome," Blériot points out. "D'you know, Neville, I think you should write your life story."

"I'd feel like I was cheating. Only cheats write their life story."

"You really are weird," he says after a moment's silence, as he strokes the dark nipples on her little breasts.

"Remember we're not spending the night here," she says

all of a sudden, getting up to pick her clothes off the carpet.

OUTSIDE, THE SUN is taking forever to set. Blériot is on the edge of the bed smoking and is watching her walk around the room and trying, just for now, to adopt a completely detached, exterior point of view, as if he were some vague celestial entity and she a solitary young woman walking naked through the half-light of a large, empty house.

A happy, anonymous young woman.

"Are you happy?" he asks, raising his voice because she's gone into the bathroom.

"Very, but I wish you'd hurry a bit," she cries from the shower. "It's nine o'clock."

Blériot hasn't moved. He's trying to remember everything by closing his eyes, like learning a lesson by heart, the swish of the curtain, the hum in the street, the splash of the shower, the sound of the extractor fan, the resonance of her voice—

"Are you ready, Louis?"

When he opens his eyes again, Nora's in front of him in her panties and T-shirt, with the light from the window behind her. Seeing her like this, as if he were still of an age when the mere suggestion of panties was the stuff of dreams, Blériot feels his nerve endings stir again.

"What would you say if I undressed you a second time?" he asks, standing to grab her.

This can't be happening.

"It's nearly ten o'clock," she protests, trying to break away. Spencer's been expecting her home for at least two hours, she needs to change for a party, and his only suggestion is to go back to bed.

Instead of heading down to reception and calling a taxi.

For a moment, Spencer's name stopped him in his tracks. It's the second time she's said his name since they left the swimming pool. When it's one of their commandments never to mention their partners' names.

But just this once Blériot would rather pretend he hasn't heard.

"And anyway, it's hot and I'm tired," she says, moving as if to put on her pants.

"I feel like a newlywed," he says, his body pressed against hers while his expert ear distinctly picks up her subtly panting breath and the little spasm in her throat.

"Just one more time," he insists.

"Well, very quickly then," she decides at last, letting him undress her with her arms in the air as if this were a heist.

Outside it's already dark. They've taken more cans from the bar and have gone right back to bed.

When Nora was positioned on top of him and he felt the muscles palpitating in her groin, he raised himself slightly on his hands to lick the little streams of sweat on her skin as they ran from her neck and shoulders like spring rain.

Two years later, he's still thirsty.

20

Having gauged the mood of the market, Murphy Blomdale sets to work, occasionally casting a puzzled glance
through the partition window at his right-hand neighbor, a
drab, industrious young woman by the name of Kate Meellow.
She is the most punctilious individual and arrives at her desk
every morning at seven o'clock sharp and leaves only when the
lights go out. She claims she even gets up in the night so as not
to miss the opening of the first Far Eastern markets.

Usually, on these occasions, Murphy can't think what to
say to her.

An irony of fate, which takes pleasure in these duplicat-
ing effects, means they are the same age, both from the
United States, have worked side-by-side for weeks on the
same projects, and are both single and the subjects of scrutiny by their coworkers in the agency.

They've been married off in bets ten times.

Kate Meellow, who describes herself as a tall, straight-forward sort of girl with a good sense of humor, sometimes goes to the cafeteria with him and reads aloud editorials and City gossip from the *Financial Times* before unleashing a sort of prerecorded laugh that he personally finds kind of embarrassing, but it seems to entertain other people.

Those of his coworkers, such as Max Barney, who still have a residue of affection for him and see him every morning, sitting at his desk flanked by his rather unusual and virginal intended, are starting to have serious concerns that one day he'll let himself be lassoed.

"Careful, old boy," Max has already warned him, "in the end that lustful Stakhanovite will reel you in."

"Absolutely out of the question," Murphy protests every time, although of course he can't publish a denial or tack a little poster in the entrance lobby.

"What are you doing this summer?" she asks him in the elevator.

"I haven't made up my mind. I'm waiting to see how things look at work," he replies defensively.

The cafeteria's already full. After ten o'clock, more and more people have informal meetings around the coffee machine as if it exerted a magnetic sexual force on them, and their laughter, raised voices, and cell phone ring tones make such a racket that Murphy almost fails to hear his own phone ring.

"It's me," says a hesitant voice, "are you listening?"

"I'm listening," he says, gesturing to Kate Meellow that she can leave.

AT THAT POINT he moved to a nearby room so he could shut himself in there, and, for a moment, while he cleared a table and put down his mug of coffee, he thought he'd got it wrong. He couldn't hear anything now.

"Nora, Nora, are you there?" he keeps saying, feeling as if he's fumbling in the dark.

"I wanted to tell you that yesterday evening I sent you a check for a thousand dollars. I know I owe you much more, but for now I honestly can't do any better. I've only just found work."

"But you don't owe me anything," he exclaims, noticing the two traders, Mike and Pete, watching him through the glass, their eyes glittering like stuffed foxes'.

"I can't believe you're calling me about this," he goes on, turning his back to them.

"I also wanted to hear your voice," she adds kindly. "Sometimes, as time goes by, I think that when I get back to London you might not be there anymore and I won't even be able to find you because you'll have forgotten me."

He's about to tell her that we can't have everything in life and we can't be both in a place and not in it, both faithful and unfaithful. In all logic, then, she can't give him his freedom, as she did when she left him, and at the same time ask him to be her prisoner.

But he can't do it. He's too afraid that, if she takes him at his word, he'll end up free and miserable.

"Actually, do you know what?" she says. "I get the feeling you're just fine without me and you're desperately trying to prove to yourself it's not true."

"I'm not trying to prove anything to myself at all," says Murphy just as Miss Anderson, chest out and nostrils quivering, barges into the room.

"Meeting in ten minutes," she barks before slamming the door.

"Nora, call back soon," he whispers into his phone. But she must have hung up, because he doesn't hear another word.

WHILE THE OTHERS hurry toward the meeting room, he stays a moment longer, drinking his coffee, and peers through the slats of the blinds to watch swift-footed pedestrians and cars gleaming in the morning sun, suddenly gripped by a feeling of nostalgia—but nostalgia to the power of ten. Rather than wallowing in self-pity (at his age you get the relationships you deserve), Murphy decides to make the most of life and skip the hedge fund meeting, before changing his mind as he spots Miss Anderson hovering, arms crossed over her chest.

So he sits at the very back of the room, as close as possible to the door, then, when the route is clear and everyone's eyes are closed because Borowitz has such a magnetic voice, he surreptitiously slips out on tiptoe toward the elevators.

In the street, he pauses briefly when he reaches Cheapside, buffeted by the wind, eyes turned to the sky, drawn by the shifting clouds as if his feet were about to take off from the sidewalk.

He has no particular plans, so he lets the crowd carry him toward Moorgate and St. Mary Moorfields, where he decides to go in.

IN THE SHADOWS and sepulchral cool of the church, Murphy, who believes in the communion of saints and the effectiveness of their intercession, reels off a long prayer on his pew before examining his conscience and succumbing, in spite of himself, to a depressing contemplation of Nora's indecisive behavior as well as his own indecision.

While sounds from the street waft through the side doors, Murphy remains absorbed in his thoughts and is gradually aware of something like a vast silence descending deep inside him.

That must be what he came here for.

Outside, the retired, the unemployed, and the misfits, all those left behind by the economic boom, sit in rows in the sunshine on chairs in the park, like the last links in a food chain. Seeing them like that, Murphy finds himself dreaming once more of the day when he'll lead an exemplary life, an obscure, anonymous life, entirely devoted to other people—even though, with the best intentions in the world, he wouldn't know where to start.

Later, hearing three o'clock strike, he gives a sudden shudder of loneliness at the thought of Nora walking through the streets of Paris at this exact moment.

HE RETRACES HIS steps to the financial district to go back to the office—he'll claim he had a doctor's appointment—and is just ordering a sandwich from a café close to Temple when, in the far corner of his field of vision, he catches sight of a dog as old as Methuselah. A scrawny one-eyed dog that looks like two dogs spliced into one, with a Dachshund's head and a poodle's bottom. It creeps cautiously toward him as if ashamed of its appearance. Murphy is absolutely not looking for a dog, and there's little chance that this unknown creature should be looking for him.

On a compassionate impulse, he does hand him a piece of his bread, and the dog makes the bread disappear so instantaneously he might have been a conjurer in a former life. In two gulps, he's swallowed the whole sandwich. Then the grateful animal stands there with his head laid gently on Murphy's knee until, touched by such perseverance, Murphy picks his gasping old body up in his arms and, unabashed by curious onlookers, starts talking earnestly into his ear to explain that he now has to return to work, so the dog better think about finding another benefactor.

"Do you understand?" he asks.

The dog, unsure, carries on gazing at him with eyes shrouded by cataracts, while Murphy has the peculiar feeling that, as he hugs the animal to him, he has grown much older than he was moments ago.

The more he hugs him, the older he feels.

As if by some sympathetic phenomenon their two life spans have joined, and they will now grow old together.

21

They're in the kitchen, drinking white wine. It must be late, one o'clock or two. Nora's in her skimpy nightdress, balancing on a chair with her feet resting on the table— every inch of her thighs revealed—while he sits on the windowsill because he likes the sound of the rain in the garden.

For some time now she's been telling him about her new acting classes near Trocadéro, and the parts she dreams of playing someday, like the eponymous *La Jeune Fille Violaine* or Nina in *The Seagull*.

"I've never seen *La Jeune Fille Violaine* or *The Seagull*," he admits.

"You could at least have read them. You must read something."

"I spend my life reading and translating medical texts. So, apart from that, the sum of what I've read this year must be one science-fiction book, two whodunits, Churchill's memoirs, and, on a friend's recommendation, I started Leibniz's *Theodicy*. I think that's about it."

"You read weird stuff. One day I'll give you *The Seagull* if you like."

The actors who play Nina Zarechnaya, she explains, mostly take their inspiration from other Ninas they've seen at the theater or from people they've met, imitating the way they speak or move. As a result, the effect is almost always disappointing. Because everyone already knows Nina.

Now *she*'d like to incarnate someone who doesn't exist yet.

"Do you understand?"

He understands and he doesn't understand. Either way, he's taken with the idea of loving a girl who doesn't exist yet.

Still, he finds something disturbing, something slightly worrying about the way she talks about acting, with that exultant voice visionaries have when they start preaching about the Truth.

But he keeps this to himself.

"I THINK THERE'S someone outside," she snaps, getting up with her glass in her hand.

"Do you think?" he says, looking out at the street.

They've turned out the light like burglars when the police go by on their rounds, and are standing in the dark,

Blériot framed by the window, Nora hidden behind him—
he can feel her nipples through the fabric of his shirt.

"I feel like I've seen him before," he says, recognizing the
figure in the hat by the glow of a hazy moon. He is struck
again by the resemblance to Léonard Tannenbaum.

Just to be absolutely sure, he discreetly calls Léonard on
his cell phone and gets his voice mail.

There's no one outside now. They close the window and
go upstairs, leaving the bottle to chill.

"You can't be serious. I'm completely exhausted," she
complains as she follows him.

"Two years," he reminds her, lifting her nightdress.

WHEN HE LEFT her by the garden gate, Blériot leaned
forward to meet her lips in the dark, and Nora took a step
to the side, laughing.

The second time he missed again.

You might as well try kissing a cloud.

He walks toward porte des Lilas under his umbrella,
turning at regular intervals to check he's not being followed. The streets are utterly deserted. Somewhere the
driving rain makes the trees shiver in an invisible garden.

Once he reaches the rue de Belleville, he carefully calls
Nora. She's already half asleep.

"Do you love me?" she asks.

All at once he feels relieved, and has an urge to jump
into the gutter with both feet.

• • •

AT HOME—HIS WIFE'S away in Marseille—Blériot has hardly finished undressing before he's overwhelmed by dizzying tiredness, followed by an instant annihilation of his faculties, as if he's struck down by some potent hypnosis.

He dreams he's at a variety show with his wife—the red curtains in the room remind him of the Olympia—and during the intermission he's taken to one side by a short, fair-haired man with a bony face and a squeaky voice who suddenly tries to twist his arm.

"That's Marie-Odile's cousin," his wife tells him calmly, as if that explains things.

Cashing in on the element of surprise, the other man pushes Blériot with all his strength into the stairwell, until there's a risk he might fall, so Blériot pushes back and they tumble down a whole flight like this.

At the bottom of the stairs, someone separates them. They both straighten their clothes and shake hands like gentlemen.

What amazes him now—because he's simultaneously at the bottom of those stairs and in the projection room of his dream—is that in the last few seconds Léonard's mournful face has been substituted for his attacker's.

Even though there's no connection whatsoever between them, he thinks from up in his projection room.

A few images later, he's in his theater seat as if nothing happened—he must be in the middle of a paradoxical sleep pattern—and he's sitting next to the little blond guy, who now seems to be in the best of moods. He's well aware that he should theoretically be sitting next to his wife—in his dream he's hopelessly in love with his wife—but he's too exhausted to ask for explanations.

"It'll be Claude François's turn soon," the other guy tells him, touching his knee.

"Oh, isn't he dead?" Blériot cries with a jolt, waking.

THE FOLLOWING MORNING, when he has showered and dressed, he's still wondering what Léonard was doing in the middle of all that.

With no taxis around, he walks to the Buttes-Chaumont park, stopping now and again to breathe the cool air and get into the right frame of mind to confront someone who's not known for being an easy conversationalist.

"It's me, Blériot," he announces after pressing the inter-com button.

Silence.

"Blériot, my sweetie, if it doesn't bother you, I'd rather we saw each other another time," says a weak voice he has trouble recognizing. "I'm really not fit to be seen."

"I absolutely have to see you. It's very important," he insists.

Eventually, he hears the buzzer and pulls open the front door.

Four floors up, Léonard Tannenbaum stands before him in his dressing gown, ashen, damaged, intimidating as a mountain of misery blocking the light of day.

• • •

THE CORNER OF his mouth is torn, his left eye half closed, with a translucent dressing over his eyebrow indicating a heavy cut.

"What happened to you?" asks Blériot, feeling as if he's in a permanent dream.

"What had to happen happened," says Léonard, making an effort to speak clearly; "Rachid left yesterday evening."

When Rachid arrived back from his daughter's house— because it turns out he was married in a former existence— he had a personal crisis, a sort of emotional seizure or psychic meltdown, and started breaking everything in the apartment.

He himself, Léonard says with retrospective fear in his voice, only remembers trying to intervene at one point in the living room, begging him to come to his senses, and Rachid instantly brandished his fists and threw himself at him, screaming.

"After that, everything goes blank."

"He didn't pull his punches," Blériot comments, examining the swollen eye.

"Still," says Léonard, having recovered some of his eloquence, "I most likely got what I deserved and what we all deserve, such as we are, when we can't love the people who love us."

Because Rachid loved him, he says, and—having raised him to the pinnacle of this un-hoped-for happiness—divine retribution threw him down into the very depths. So be it.

• • •

"I HAVEN'T EVEN asked you why you came," Léonard says, sitting in an armchair with the dignity of an aging monarch and turning his face away to hide his impressive shiner.

There's a bit of dried blood on his chin.

Seeing him in this state, Blériot remembers the figure in the hat and is suddenly ashamed of his suspicions.

"It's my money problems again," he apologizes, knowing he'll be readily believed. "I haven't got a cent left, the bank's suspended my account, and my wife's gone off to Marseille."

"Blériot, my dear boy, you're an incorrigible and rather too venal friend," says Léonard, who has nevertheless taken three one-hundred-euro notes from his own pocket.

"Do you want to go and have lunch somewhere together?" he asks, opening a bottle of Vouvray.

"Are you sure you want to go out?" Blériot asks anxiously.

"Do you really think I look that bad?"

A quarter of an hour later, they're walking along the paths of Buttes-Chaumont—one supporting the other—with their big dark glasses and their undertakers' suits, like the Blues Brothers.

"In the end, he stayed just over three years," says the one. "Incredible how quickly it goes."

"Yes, perhaps that's why we never have time to get to know someone," says the other.

22

On this particular day, Louis Blériot-Ringuet is looking out to sea. He's sitting on a lounge chair with his trousers rolled halfway up his calves, while his wife lies on her stomach reading a biography of Picabia. A big late-summer sun pours its still-scorching light over the beach. Beside them, a family of Germans under a large striped parasol is languidly playing Russian Bank, hypnotized by the heat. A Smashing Pumpkins song drifts on the wind. In the distance, people swimming look like no more than clouds of particles deposited on the water.

Blériot, totally consumed with his contemplations, has rolled over slightly on his chair and lowered his sunglasses to cast a quick eye over one of the women nearby, fascinated by the swell of her breasts under her white costume, as if by some stereoscopic apparition.

"Emma's with her brother at their grandparents," she says into her phone. "They just love having them for holidays. After that, their father's looking after them."

He couldn't say why but Blériot feels he's heard this story a hundred times before.

He's turned now to look at the hotel's pergola overlooking the beach, its American and Japanese flags hanging limply from their masts.

Although the afternoon has barely begun, there are five or six white-haired vacationers with oiled bodies drinking cocktails at the swimming pool bar as if to celebrate their immortality.

"You know," the woman next to him goes on, "Sylvain's got his own life now. He shares an apartment with his colleague Fontana. Do you remember him? No, Fontana's the guy whose pants are always too short and he has that tiny little voice like Jiminy Cricket. I can tell you, it's definitely worth seeing them together," she adds, examining her toenails.

Blériot swivels around again. His wife's gone to sleep, her cheek on her book.

"I have to go," he says in her ear. "If you like I'll come for you later."

"Mmmm," goes his wife.

"Let's just say six o'clock, at the end of the coast road," he adds, smacking his moccasins together to get the sand out of them.

When he reaches the boulevard—and stops to get some cigarettes—the noises from the beach evaporate in an instant as if a pair of doors have closed behind him. All he has now is silence and the afternoon's hot breath. He walks through deserted neighborhoods and suffocating streets blasted by a flamethrower, careful to use the strip of shadow against the walls. He can feel his legs dripping already.

At the far end of a black-and-white paved courtyard hemmed in by railings, two old men in undershirts sit motionless at a folding table, like two shadows set against the fabric of summer. A little farther on, gaggles of seagulls call on the empty grandstands of a racecourse.

THE HOTEL HE'S staying at is a large white stucture of seven or eight stories, with galleried balconies along its façade, reminiscent of colonial buildings in photographs. Inside, the lobby and corridors seem peculiarly quiet and lifeless.

Blériot stands in his room for a moment, watching trains passing beyond the blinds, before deciding to take a shower and finally tackle his translation on neurotransmitter activity.

He stays there for part of the afternoon, sitting at his computer in his shorts, then calls Nora.

Her cell phone is switched off again. Unless he's done his calculations wrong, this is the fifth or sixth time he's tried to get hold of her since the day before yesterday. And every time he feels the same small pain, tucked at the very limits of awareness, spiraling back to life.

To take his mind off it, he watches the trains as they run parallel to the horizon while the sun starts to sink over the sea. The pink railway station, slotted between rows of buildings, looks as microscopic and improbable as a Monopoly station with clouds scudding overhead.

Just before six o'clock—he's translated two hundred and fifty words—Blériot leaves the hotel with his jacket flapping in the wind and his earphones in, and goes down the long slope to the beach, swift as a gust of wind.

All along the boulevard yellow light is now spreading between the palm trees in the park while blackbirds hop manically across the lawns. He stops a moment to call Nora—as if she would be interested in blackbird behavior—then hangs up yet again and sets off toward the coast road at a run.

NOW WITH SABINE, he affects a casual expression and a studied normalness intended to reassure her—when, inside, he already feels he has his back to the wall. And, hand in hand like any other tourist couple, they set off at a leisurely pace to find a shady café terrace. They have plenty of time.

They don't have children.

"We haven't been to a hotel together for at least two or three years," he points out as he orders martinis.

"I asked you to come to Milan with me and, once again, you found a way to get out of it," she replies, her eyes masked by tinted lenses.

Sometimes, because of these hidden expressions, Blériot can't help wondering what she really thinks about the state of their relationship. Assuming of course that her multiple activities, both social and professional, leave her enough time for introspection.

"You could have come to Marseille with me too," she adds. "You'd have been very welcome."

While she tells him about her trip to Marseille and the offer one Jean-Claude Damiani made for her to work on the Titus-Carmel exhibition with him, Blériot, still listening, is surprised to find himself momentarily envying the man in front of them for his solitary state as he reads his racing newspaper and chomps cashew nuts.

Because that's the point he's reached.

Walled in by his fears like Tannenbaum.

So as not to ruin their evening and to resist the accumulation of dark thoughts, whose source he understands only too clearly, he suggests they have dinner early in a seafront restaurant and then go either to the movies to watch an Italian film or to the casino.

"You choose," she replies, probably because she is happy just strolling and chatting with him, while the sun takes forever to set on the Promenade des Anglais and they can already feel the chill of the summer's end in the side streets.

The pain we inflict, he remembers all of a sudden, is the big question in life.

But what else can he do?

For now, he hasn't reached any decision.

• • •

OUTSIDE THE MOVIE theater, Sabine is busy checking the show times when Blériot, on a whim, takes a step back, then two, then three, gradually eclipsing himself into the shadows before turning the corner of the building and dis- appearing with his hands in his pockets.

Once he begins moving, everything becomes clear and straightforward. Life is a piece of cake.

He takes a bus, gets off it at random, and walks along the first rising street he finds, then carries on up an inter- minable flight of steps until he reaches a small, lamp-lit square complete with benches, where he catches his breath. He's switched off his cell phone.

Not bothering to stop or think a moment longer, he fol- lows a steep path running between terraced gardens and finds himself in complete darkness, a few dozen yards far- ther, straddling prickly bushes that part and swish back together as he passes.

From time to time he thinks he can hear someone call- ing his name and he hurries up the hill, grasping stones with a sort of animal vitality. He emerges onto a kind of windswept promontory and can see the lights along the coast all the way to the airport in Nice. Overhead, bright filaments ply endlessly across the sky like a shower of me- teorites. Blériot—or rather the entity that has taken the name Blériot—now starts running and waving his arms as if to catch them.

This time, he's stepped through the looking glass.

All around him, the chirring of insects hidden in bushes ebbs and flows to the same rhythm as his excitement.

MUCH LATER, CUTTING across the hillside on his way back, he is brutally sobered by the sight of a young couple sitting on the grass.

He doesn't know how long he's been gone.

He comes out into the light at the top of the steps that lead down to the small square with its benches under the lime trees, and hurriedly switches his phone on again.

"I got a bit lost earlier," he apologizes, struggling to control his breathing and to talk as naturally as possible.

Sabine says nothing. But he knows he had it coming.

At a quarter to midnight, he meets her at the bottom of the stairs.

"We still have time to go to the casino," he jokes, jumping the last few steps as if just returning from a run.

"Louis, you scare me," she says, not looking at him.

23

On the sixth day they fly back to Paris. Out in the streets the wind is damp and the trees shrouded in gray. There's a bitterness in the air as Blériot nips in between cars, aware of an end-of-holiday grumpiness and a sense that everyone's exasperating everyone else. He hurries up the rue de Belleville, earphones in, already missing the days when he went to see Nora without rushing or anxiety because she would be waiting for him on the doorstep, and he could stock up on happiness just by going to her house.

When he reaches Les Lilas—he knows the route by heart—he walks past the gym and the *mairie*, takes a succession of small streets lined with anonymous little houses, and reaches hers at a run, panting with apprehension.

Everything is as he imagined it. The house looks shut down, the gate and shutters are closed, the garden empty.

Mail addressed to her cousin Barbara Neville is still in the mailbox.

Even though Blériot knows perfectly well that Nora can disappear without warning or explanation, and return in exactly the same way, right now he can't help thinking—as he feels sort of extrasensory goose bumps spreading over him—that this time it's all over.

His watch says ten past twelve.

HE'S TAKEN HIS earphones out—Percy Sledge must bring him bad luck—and, just in case, he calls her on his cell. Several times. Like someone trying more than anything to win a bit of time to think.

In fact, it's not so much her absence that frightens him as her silence.

It occurs to him that they've always led such compartmentalized lives that he doesn't know where to look for her or whom to call. He doesn't know the name of her acting school or of the hotel she works at in Roissy, and, what's more, he doesn't have an address for her family or for her ex-boyfriend in London.

Because he was stupid enough to say he didn't have a problem with her seeing the guy again, she must have taken him at his word.

When, to him, it was completely theoretical permission and he would very much like to have negotiated its ramifications.

Utterly despondent, he turns off his phone and then stands waiting in the middle of the street, in a state of calm bordering on catalepsy, while still making an effort to breathe evenly and keep his head held high, so as not to be swallowed by his fear.

Blériot is aware that it's pointless staying here any longer on this sidewalk—unless he wants to make a complete spectacle of himself for the neighborhood—and he would probably do better to move on and walk away. So he sets off down the street, following its gentle incline, not bothering to wonder where he's going, because there are circumstances in which, whatever we do, we never go anywhere.

HE WALKS IN a state of near weightlessness until he reaches a square with a bar. It is dark inside and Blériot is struck by how numb he feels, as if under anesthetic. In fact, his arm's so heavy he can hardly raise his glass.

The last time she disappeared, he remembers, he waited for her for hours in a café, drinking one beer after another, unable to stop sweating. The following morning, there was an e-mail: *Love me do. We won't be seeing each other for a long time.*

It was two years.

When Nora called him on Ascension Day to tell him she was back, his pain had obviously aged. All the same, he can clearly remember that as he climbed into his car to drive to his parents, he already knew, thanks to some baleful foresight, that he'd soon be kicking himself.

And yet the fact that she appeared after two years, the fact that she took him to her house, and that they did what they did, must mean she cares about him. She was under no obligation.

None at all, he repeats to himself. But this flash of understanding almost instantly fizzles out.

HE IMAGINES SHE must have gone to her depressed boyfriend in London, unless there's someone else, some unknown quantity, no cleverer than the rest of them, who'll feel his own pain when the time comes.

She's had so many lovers, so many lives dovetailed into one another, you'd be forgiven for thinking she secretes an active substance when she comes in contact with men, one that singlehandedly makes them fall at her feet.

In any event, one thing's for sure; he won't wait two years for her to call again.

Because there are ways and ways of doing things.

Outside, the sky is still brooding, the wind wet and cold. However much he quickens his step, the rue Belleville still feels endless, like going the wrong way on a conveyor belt. As he walks, though, he can't help staring at every couple he sees, eyeing each female figure and turning around with every burst of laughter as if everything were about to start again.

But there's no remission today.

BLÉRIOT HAS COME home. He's come back to cry into his wife's petticoats and to sign a full confession.

Luckily, she's not there. Which is probably just as well for him.

He goes upstairs to sit at his desk and finish his translation—he's almost six days behind schedule. But while he tries to concentrate, eyes focused on the screen, the recurring thought that he might never see Nora again paralyzes his decision-making faculties.

He hesitates over every word.

In these circumstances, it's usually better to give up the battle. Which is what he does.

From two o'clock until five o'clock, he lies on his bed in the gloomy afternoon light—it must be the longest day of the year—keeping himself busy smoking and automatically checking his cell phone like someone holding his breath and navigating the depths of an unfathomable sorrow.

From time to time he gets up to go to the bathroom and emerges increasingly overwhelmed by the productivity of his digestive system.

A combination of gas and bacteria, there, that's all that'll be left of us, he thinks, flipping his cell phone open again.

Sometimes—this is just a variation—he says: *Hello, hello?* As if in training for answering the phone; then he hangs up.

No one's answering anymore.

He feels like he's on acid.

Now he is undressed and has folded his clothes at the end of the bed, and he sits on the covers, stripped to the waist.

In one hand he holds a glass of beer, and with the other he scratches his chest, like someone wondering what sin, what breach he can have committed to warrant being punished with such loneliness.

He scratches so hard that tiny drops of blood even start beading across his skin.

It could be a scene from "In the Penal Colony," but without the desert or the machine.

Including Kate Meellow and himself, there are already six of them in the elevator: Paganello the careerist, Sullivan the alcoholic, Brown the womanizer—Murphy Blomdale sometimes feels he's surrounded by archetypes—and Barney the depressive. But then Miss Anderson, going to considerable effort to squeeze in, joins them and the machine seems to accelerate suddenly.

Two seconds later it delivers them in the lobby, where groups of people are gathering and calling to one another, abuzz with the excitement of leaving the office and going for a drink near Blackfriars.

On this matter, market traders are no different from firemen or construction workers.

Murphy is flanked by Kate and Max Barney, and he's wondering whether it wouldn't be better to go toward

Fleet Street to avoid the rest of the gang, when someone who seems to have appeared from nowhere cries: "Hello, you!"—if, indeed, he's the you this person means.

The apparition is standing across the doorway, darkly silhouetted against bright daylight that blinds Murphy for a fraction of a second.

"Hello, do you recognize me?" she says, coming closer with a sort of cool assurance.

She has stopped in the doorway while he walks forward, feeling as if he's being drawn across a magnetic field.

And she's the one who holds her arms out first.

"YOU MUST BE horribly angry with me for not warning you," says Nora as if she were saying: You must think I've aged horribly.

"Not at all," he protests, pressing himself to her and feeling once again the living warmth of her body while people around them, who must suspect something's going on, are sidling away like bemused shadows.

He hugs her to him again, then steps back to look at her.

She laughs so prettily, wrinkling her nose and looking so childish, so petulant, that you might almost think this was their first meeting and that time is merely an illusion of perspective.

It's only now that he notices she's wearing a raincoat with a little polka-dot scarf and is carrying a big travel bag.

Murphy, suddenly reminded of more practical consid-
erations, doesn't know whether he can suggest she come to
stay with him—aiming high—or whether he should settle
for asking her, without appearing to press the point, where
she's planning to sleep tonight. With her sister, Dorothy?

"My sister gets on my nerves," she replies. "She spends
her time moralizing, on the grounds that she's three years
older than me and has a master's in economics. I wouldn't
recommend spending an evening with her."

Briefly perplexed, Murphy eventually makes the decision to call a taxi to take them to the center of Islington, as
if this were just a sentimental pilgrimage with no commit-
ment on her part.

"With this bag, I'd rather we went to your place first,"
she says once they're in the taxi.

Seeing as she's the one suggesting it.

Murphy then kisses her neck discreetly and doesn't ask any
more questions or try to understand by what astronomical
combination of circumstances she has been sent back to him.

WHEN THEY ARE at the apartment where they once lived
together, and have dumped their things at last, they both
have a moment of uncertainty and look at each other without knowing what to do, suddenly self-conscious.

The emotion and unusual nature of the situation, coupled with a degree of caution on both sides, makes them
tend toward a waiting game.

Particularly Murphy, who paid a high price for being so trusting and knows only too well that, beneath her gracious exterior, Nora can be aggressive and moody when she carelessly reveals her true feelings.

"Could you pour me a glass of wine?" she says, as if offering to seal their reconciliation and embark on a new era.

"Of course," he exclaims, ashamed of being so remiss and not unhappy to have something to keep him busy in the kitchen.

"You're still reading the Bible," she comments as she studies the piles of books on the table.

"On occasion. To be absolutely honest," he explains while searching for the corkscrew, "reading the Bible isn't so much a crutch as an emotional regulator."

That's probably down to his nerves.

"You're reading Leibniz too," she says, amazed. "Who actually *is* Leibniz?"

"A major Christian philosopher and an important mathematician," he says, amused by the face she makes.

When they're both sitting on the sofa in the living room with their glasses of wine, like back in the good days, they look a little like two actors rehearsing a scene from married life—she's resting her head on his shoulder—but who have unfortunately forgotten their lines.

"I do love this apartment," says Nora, getting up and quickly improvising a brief nostalgic speech about each of the rooms, even the smallest, and the habits she got into in each of them, and what time of day she liked to be where.

"You know, you can move in for as long as you like," he hears himself say, because the unexpected kindness and sensitivity she's been displaying in the last few minutes have touched an area of his brain that's rarely stimulated, and are starting to break down his lines of defense.

"First, I'd like to have a shower, and then supper at Dangello's," she says with a laugh, not indicating that she's heard his offer.

"Whatever you like," says Murphy, though he personally would have preferred something a bit more low-key and cozy than Dangello's. But he won't mention that, because she exerts such dominance over him that it robs him of his free will.

A LITTLE LATER they are striding along St. John Street and Rosebery Avenue, numbed by the wind, huddled together like in the old days, when they were carefree and happy.

Dangello's hasn't changed. They walk into a rococo foyer, greeted by women in starched shirts—they refuse the coat room service—and waiters in equally stiff shirt fronts escort them between the tables to the far end of a large, dusk-dark room.

From the murmurings spreading around the tables, it's quite clear that Nora's entrance, in her leather boots and international adventurer's trench coat, hasn't gone unnoticed.

When calm is restored, the only sounds are the slight clink of cutlery—they order grilled turbot—and the whispering of other diners, occasionally punctuated by unexpected exclamations, from customers of more advanced years who can be identified by their maladjusted hearing aids. In fact, most of the men look exhausted and stooped, while their wives, sitting bolt upright on the edge of their chairs, keep swiveling their heads left and right like platinum periscopes.

Meanwhile Murphy has forgotten what he's supposed to do or say, and is lost in painfully contemplating his guest as she serenely picks at her vegetables.

"Why did you leave, Nora?" he can't help asking quietly, when she's finished.

"For the pleasure of coming back and finding you again. It's the way I am. I need to feel free," she whispers, opening her brown eyes very wide as if to gobble him up.

However heartbreaking this reply may be, under the influence of those eyes, Murphy can't bring himself to hold it against her, and could almost make excuses for her, remembering how very young she was when they met.

He just about manages to ask, with the tiniest hint of irony, whether she now feels free in Paris.

"Very free," she replies firmly, before qualifying this statement by mentioning the invasive presence of her cousin Barbara, who tends to stick her nose in things that aren't her business and wants to chaperone her on every outing.

He couldn't say why, but Murphy has the painful feeling that he doesn't believe her, though he doesn't let anything show.

"Are you planning to stay in London long?" he asks, still quietly, although there's hardly anyone left near them.

"I don't know yet," she says, hiding behind the dessert menu. "Anyway, I'm guessing I can always sleep on the sofa in the study."

"It's up to you," he says, not revealing what he's really thinking.

The customers have left, and the waiters are tired and wanting to get home. Murphy has taken out his wallet—we reap what we sow—and discreetly calls the headwaiter. The bill, please.

Right now, he's paying for her to stay with him, for her to stop lying, for him to stop thinking she's lying, and for their life to have some meaning left. It's all included in the bill.

25

I t's your father," cries his wife, indicating the telephone. Blériot, standing in the bathroom doorway, his face screwed up because of his morning neuralgia, gestures to mean he'll take it upstairs.

"Hello," he says, surprised to find he's breathing hard into the mouthpiece.

"I hope I'm not disturbing you," his father begins; "it's about your mother. I'm calling from a payphone."

He was expecting this.

In the last few weeks, his mother's jitteriness and mood swings have apparently turned into outright hostility, to the point of insulting neighbors and trying on two occasions to strike her husband. The neurological examinations that the hospital carried out, his father explains with the slow delivery of a seventy-year-old on sedatives, found nothing specific and she's back home.

"I'm at my wits' end," he admits.

Blériot, who's not in the best of states either, can tell that, right now, he absolutely has to tackle this and for once prove he can rise to the situation.

"I'll come down by train today," he promises, searching for the reservations site.

"Whatever you do, don't tell her I told you," his father says, as if afraid of being punished.

"Don't worry about it," he says, picturing him all alone at his pay phone.

He finishes washing in the bathroom, gets together a few things, kisses his wife—she's giving him those lovely sad eyes full of understanding—and goes into the street at nine o'clock, freshly shaven and filled with cold despair.

WHEN HE IS sitting comfortably in the train, he first checks that he has no message from Nora, then tilts his seat and listens to Massenet's *Werther* while his happy, insubstantial double through the window flits along country roads with the electric cables and solitary cars.

However he tries to argue it and whichever way he looks at his relationship with Nora, he still finds her just as disquieting, and he really wishes he could think of something else.

So long as it isn't his mother's health.

What then? His childhood, his cycling trips through the

Cévennes, all those years before: before Nora, before Sabine, before being in love for the first time.

Werther doesn't want something else.

All men feel nostalgic for that time when life was still elastic with possibilities.

Blériot rents a car at the station and, after a few miles, finds himself in the desolate expanses of endless scrubland, driving toward the hills with their nebulous bulk and their deserted villages where only the wind and sodden clouds ever go.

By all appearances, the summer has definitively left here too, like those wicked homeowners who board up their houses and escape to the tropics.

After the village of La Feuillade, Blériot remembers he has to turn right and get onto the road that curves toward Saint-Cernin, with its small bridge and the chapel he always uses as a landmark.

BY THE GATES to the house, he notices a sort of ogre rigged in a fisherman's hat, standing in the rain waving to him frantically, and it takes him several seconds to convince himself that this is his father. He's so stooped; his face has gone all gray and his eyes look cloudy and slightly glazed, perhaps because he's filled with emotion or has an infection.

"Louis, I just don't know what to do," he says, not giving him time to get out of the car. "Your mother's killing me. You really have to help me," he insists, repeating word for word what he told him over the phone.

After an altruistic pause, Blériot asks whether his mother knows he's here.

"Of course, she's even got dressed for you. Well, if you can call that being dressed. You'll see in a minute."

At first glance, the house looks unchanged, with its chintzy drapes, its bad paintings, and its framed photographs that remind him of the days when they seemed like a tidy, uncomplicated family.

Billy the dog is still asleep on the sofa.

On the other hand, the upkeep of the house leaves something to be desired. Since the housekeeper was fired, his father has had to do everything, the cooking, dashing to the village, loading the washing machine, the ironing, and washing his wife twice a day, because she'd be inclined to let herself go.

"Do you need me to come with you?" his father asks by the bedroom door.

"No," he replies, looking at him for a moment, because he still can't get used to how much he's changed.

How could the intrepid traveler and dashing Ping-Pong player he once knew have turned into this anxious, dithering old man, who seems afraid of his own shadow most of the time?

WHEN HE WALKS in, his mother is watching television, her legs bare, dressed only in a sort of blue checked smock, half apron, half nightdress. Her face is lit by the screen and looks emaciated; her hair is quite gray.

She looks completely ageless.

"It's September twenty-first, my name's Colette Lavallée and I don't have Alzheimer's," she jokes, as if reading his thoughts . . . before having a go at him for, in no particular order, being selfish, living off other people, and having no feelings for anyone.

"Anyway, you're in cahoots with your father to send me to the hospital."

He shows no reaction.

"But I know you came to pick up your check," she says, jumping to her feet. "Didn't you? That's it, isn't it? Just try denying it. It's the dough you're interested in, my little Louis, I know that, Colette's dough. You're just like your father," she continues, starting to drift about the room.

"You know I came to see you," he corrects her patiently, struggling to hold her in his arms for a moment despite the combination of awkwardness and physical repulsion he always has with her. However hard he tries to remind himself that she *is* his mother, that she cared for him and raised him, no better or worse than any other mother, and she probably loved him in her own way, he doesn't feel anything for her now.

He can't help it. The relevant nerve has been severed.

"Dad's very worried about you," he tries to get her to understand.

"You make a good pair of incompetents," she replies,

adopting her headmistress voice. "And what if I tell you I'm just tired. Do you know what that's like, to be tired?"

Blériot, who's slipped into the mold of his father's fears, thinks she might well slap him at some point.

HIS FATHER'S WAITING in the small room he's set up for himself in the basement. He knows the whole story already.

"What do you expect me to do?" he asks, with the voice of someone wavering between sticking his head in the gas oven and doing it with carbon monoxide in the car. "I've tried everything, put up with everything. As for all that business about the bough bending but not breaking, that's garbage! I'm worn to a shred," he adds.

Because his father can be quite funny when he wants to be.

It's hardly raining now, so, at the end of the afternoon, the two of them go for a stroll along tracks near the house, walking under cover of the trees. The wet leaves look heavy and drip on the backs of their necks as they pass. His father's the only one talking.

In his opinion, there must be some depressive syndrome in the Lavallée family. The grandfather, he recaps, hanged himself after the war; Uncle Charles couldn't do a day's work his entire life; and as for Marie-Noël, Colette's sister who lives in Clermont, she's been on tranquilizers since she retired.

His son, who is therefore the last link in this genetic

chain, isn't too keen to join the debate.

Clusters of cows behind their fences turn their big patient eyes toward the evening because all creatures, Blériot
remembers, all sensible creatures like animals, need time to
gaze in contemplation. He himself actually wishes he could
press his little secret button to grant himself a moment's
contemplation.

But he can't find the button.

Back at the house, they tidy up a bit and set the table for
two, because his mother doesn't want to come down. They
can hear her pacing to and fro overhead, going to the bathroom, coming back toward her bed, knocking things over,
shuffling along the landing. She can't stay still.

"It's like this every evening," his father tells him as they
go into the garden. "I even have to bandage her feet before
I put her to bed. Sometimes there's blood in her shoes."

Blériot's speechless. They can't leave her in this state.

"You've got to call a doctor, whatever the consequences,"
he begs him, "and have her hospitalized again. It's her or
you."

THE FOLLOWING MORNING, as he drives past an estate
on the outskirts of Montpellier, Blériot notices a very dark-
haired young woman waiting by her gate, wearing just a
robe over her pajamas. She must have thrown her things on
in a hurry to intercept the postman or some deliveryman.

With one hand she's holding a simple red striped

umbrella—he's driving at a snail's pace with his eyes pinned on her—while with the other she tries to tuck a lock of hair behind her ear.

She's so perfect, he thinks, so unaware of her perfection, that it would seem quite legitimate to stop his travels right there and politely ask her permission to make babies with her. As he entertains these thoughts, sitting at the wheel of his car, its tires crunch on the gritty surface.

When he draws closer to her, he lowers the window and she leans forward, thinking he needs some information (are you married?), but Blériot settles for smiling and looking her in the eye.

Before driving slowly away, with no descendants.

It was his moment of contemplation.

26

Murphy is with Max Barney and Sullivan—he's the blond one on his right, with the slightly too-big head—walking up New Change under an umbrella, his mind preoccupied with the highs and lows of his domestic life with Nora.

They hear five o'clock strike. As if this were a signal, Sullivan is instantly aware of his thirst and desperately wants the others to have a beer with him. Good friends that they are, Murphy and Max accept the beer, then abandon him to his fate, not unhappy to be rid of him.

While Murphy is still fretting about his unpredictable guest, Barney admits that his future seems pretty uncertain too, and his involvement with the agency has probably run its course—Borowitz has already touched on the subject with him. Weighed down by his failures and the recurring bad luck that's becoming something of a phenomenon (he's onto his fourth job loss in four years), Barney has even started to wonder whether it's all connected to some organized persecution.

"By who?" Murphy asks, emerging from his thoughts. Max can't answer.

What Murphy obviously can't tell him is that his endless muttering during meetings and his disastrous jokes—which are almost always ill-timed—aren't doing much to help his standing with the directors.

As usual, they part outside Moorgate station, and Murphy, succumbing to his worries once more, somehow manages to take the wrong line.

IN THE BUS that eventually takes him to Islington, he has a sudden conviction that when he gets home Nora will have left, the apartment will be silent, everything in its place, as it is every day, but it will all look oddly inert, as if under a spell. He can already hear the sound of his own footsteps along the empty hallway, the full force of the non-being lying in ambush behind the door.

But she's there. She's resting with her legs curled up, on the sofa that she uses as a bed, in the study.

Feeling a sudden, urgent need to unwind, he rushes to pour himself a glass of wine in the kitchen, then comes back silently to sit near her. Somewhere overhead someone's playing a cute ragtime tune on a piano. Murphy draws his chair close to her, and this strange moment, reflected in the mirror of his mind, has the poignant beauty of something that may never be repeated.

"Were you asleep?" he asks eventually, with his hand on her cheek.

"No, I was bored," she says, stretching. "What time is it?"

She was bored, he thinks in private amazement. When she's quite free to go out, go wherever she pleases, and meet whomever she wants.

"How can you be bored after just a few days?" he says, sitting on the edge of the bed to stroke her neck and her warm ears.

She looks at him for a moment as he leans over her, but makes no reciprocal gesture; then she replies in an offhand manner that that's just the way it is, she's bored, and, anyway, she doesn't know anyone in London now.

Murphy is disconcerted by the cohabitation between the old Nora and the new one, and sits there in silence.

"You're missing Paris," he says, looking into her gold-flecked eyes as if he derived pleasure from suffering.

Since she's returned, he could count on the fingers of one hand the number of times she has agreed to broach the subject of her life in Paris. He hasn't insisted. But those four long months have stayed folded away in their wrapping, laid down between them like a gift bomb.

He now feels like pulling the string.

• • •

"I'M GUESSING YOU have someone waiting for you in Paris," he says, and, on the off chance, he mentions Sam Gorki—the guy who's called her about a dozen times.

"Poor Sam, he's been waiting for me for years and years," she says with a laugh to imply that this particular candidate counts for nothing. "I wish all boys were that patient."

At this point, Murphy, who doesn't find it funny in the least, thinks it worthwhile to remind her that he has always been one hundred percent honest with her, and feels he has a right to ask the same of her.

"To ask what?" she blurts, borderline aggressive.

"To ask you to tell me once and for all who you're living with in Paris."

After a moment's thought, Nora sits up on the sofa, lights a cigarette, and points out that we don't *owe* anyone the truth but that, if he really wants, she can tell him his name. Although she can't see what it will get him.

She should tell him anyway.

"His name's Louis Blériot, and I met him long before I met you," she says, watching him and not displeased with the effect she's had.

"Louis Blériot?" he repeats, once, twice, slightly disarmed by this impetuous admission. "What the hell does that mean? Isn't that some aviator's name?"

"If you like. Anyway," she adds, out of sheer provocation, "he's someone I have a whole lot of fun with."

Possibly because he himself is rather too serious, Murphy doesn't want to believe, can't believe, that she could have been attached to someone for so long simply because he's diverting. There must be something else.

"There's everything else," she concedes after a silence, getting up and going to fetch a glass from the kitchen. "He's a very strange guy."

While he sits on a stool and listens to her as steadfastly as he can manage, Murphy gradually realizes that the whole time he lived with her, Nora belonged to someone else—whether or not it was physically—and that he never suspected a thing. Perhaps because he had absolutely no experience of that sort of situation, and had developed no antibodies, no instinctive ability to detect her lies.

Now he knows what he's dealing with.

For a few minutes, he sits there glued to his chair, lost in a sort of emotional fog that stops him from thinking.

"I'M GUESSING," HE says later as he takes her in his arms, "that you're planning to go back to live with him soon."

"I don't live with him," she replies calmly. "And if you were kind, attentive, and had a tiny grasp of psychology, you'd stop asking me this sort of question and, instead, you'd be asking yourself if you still want to live with me."

"Live with you?"

She'll make him drink the cup to the very last drop.

On the spur of the moment, of course, he feels like laughing and saying no, no, and no again, because even if he accepts, in purely hypothetical terms, that she cares about him, he can already feel what this would cost.

So he moves away from her. Surely she can guess from the look on his face that the future of their relationship is being reexamined and that the prognosis isn't very optimistic, because she's now leaning out of the living room window, without a word, her body at right angles to the building, overlooking the street.

Murphy knows at this point that he should tell her it would be better if they split; she's got her life ahead of her and she'll forget him very quickly. But he stays silent.

After a while she sits down next to him on the sofa with her head resting on his shoulder. He has given up the idea of asking any more questions. Anyway, she's not keen on confessions and he doesn't have the power to absolve her. On the other hand, what he'll never understand is this need she feels to betray him and then come back to live with him. But well. Peace and silence on earth and under the heavens. She'll do as she pleases.

"Do you know what, Murphy?" she says, kissing him.

"No," he says.

"I love your innocence."

"My innocence?"

27

That very morning Tannenbaum sent him an e-mail missive of nearly five hundred words. It has a whiff of indictment about it, an exhortation, an electronic epistle to have a go at him for being a forgetful and fairly intermittent friend, and for abandoning him to his fate while he languished in bed. Blériot now remembers that he promised to drop by to see how he was doing and then forgot to, as he's been forgetting everything over the last few days—Nora has something to do with that—to the point where he feels he's lost any sense of his own continuity.

Still, he isn't as thankless a friend as Léonard's pretending to believe, so he immediately drops his translation, gets dressed, and takes a taxi to Buttes-Chaumont, in the hopes of bringing Léonard some comfort. Even if his own heart isn't really in it.

A short man with a swarthy complexion and a drooping mustache who looks vaguely Proustian—Jacques Cusamano, he introduces himself, shaking Blériot's hand rather distastefully—shows him into the apartment and adopts the appropriate expression to inform him that their friend is no better.

"Hang on, it's not serious?" Blériot asks, alarmed, already picturing him at his last gasp.

"He's resting in his room at the moment," the other man reassures him, and kindly offers to let Léonard know he is there.

While he disappears down the hallway, Blériot remembers that Tannenbaum, who is the personification of indiscretion, once confided that he and Cusamano had been at boarding school together, although they hardly knew each other until the day when, by some extraordinary twist of fate, they realized they both had a weakness—what a small world—for very hairy boys with dark complexions.

Only, Léonard put his ideas into practice right away, while Jacques Cusamano, probably being more timorous, is still living with his mother, waiting for Prince Charming.

"You can come through," announces Cusamano from the bedroom door.

LYING ON THE bed like an inert alligator, Tannenbaum has raised one eyelid to watch him enter, and has automatically tugged at his sheets for propriety's sake. His brow is still swollen, his face thinner, his cheeks covered in several days' growth of beard. All around him, piles of books and magazines, bottles like spent corpses, shopping bags, and clothes thrown carelessly onto chairs bear witness to a mood of abandon that has gone on too long.

"As you see, my friend, I'm turning into a bedridden invalid," Léonard says, hugging him.

From his thick voice and sparkling eyes, Blériot deduces he's already had too much to drink.

"Things could be worse; you've got stuff to read, people come to see you, and you've even found yourself a nurse," Blériot points out, helping prop him up with a pillow, while Cusamano has gone to sit on his chair, with a scowl on his face and his hands crossed in his lap.

"Cusa, could you leave us for a moment," Tannenbaum says irritably, and turns to his visitor with an avid smile to get him to describe with complete freedom everything that has happened to him since they last saw each other.

FIRST, BLÉRIOT TAKES the time to swallow hard and adjust himself slightly, as if he's being received for a private audience with his spiritual adviser. Then he embarks on an account of his torments and his addiction to Nora, with the unfortunate consequences that have ensued.

"Are you still living as man and wife with Sabine?" Tannenbaum asks anxiously—he adores issues of conjugal sophistry.

"Of course. Judging by her reactions and the way she speaks to me, I get the feeling she doesn't know," he replies cautiously.

"In that case, it's a minor evil," Tannenbaum concedes. "But, you know, since you became an adulterer and a dissembler, I've been worried about you, my lovely, because you've ruined yourself. I don't know what all this is going to come to. Meanwhile," he adds, patting Blériot's knee enthusiastically, "the pair of us are like two old packages waiting to be delivered."

Blériot doesn't want to say anything, but at the moment he does feel he is the unhappier of the two.

"Still no news from Rachid?"

"That's the whole problem."

Léonard has to recognize that, for now, he's been reduced to supposition, and, in all likelihood, Rachid has gone back to live with his wife. Probably under pressure from his brothers and his daughter. There follow some venomous pronouncements about Rachid's daughter, embellished with a few uncalled-for comments about Muslim families, which Blériot is charitable enough not to hear.

"Metaphysically speaking, I've failed at everything," Léonard announces, turning on the television that sits on the floor. "I have no wife, no family, no friends, and I'm reduced to killing time watching Westerns or porn until two in the morning. It's enough to make you think my interpretation of life wasn't right," he concludes, promptly dropping back into his pillow as if the audience were over.

Blériot doesn't take offense but watches television with him for a moment while the trees in Buttes-Chaumont daub the windows with their orangey hues like in some Technicolor movie from the fifties.

"Perhaps you want to rest?" he says eventually, noticing Léonard's head nodding.

"Television," Tannenbaum says, looking for the remote control, "has an advantage over life's nightmares: you can turn it off when you want to."

Then, reaching toward his shelves for a volume by Péguy, he asks suddenly, "Do you know the most universal secret which has never actually been leaked? The most hermetically secret secret. The secret that's never been written anywhere? The secret," he reads, "that is most universally divulged and yet, from men of forty it has never been handed on beyond thirty-seven, beyond thirty-five. The secret that has never made it down to younger men. Do you know what it is?"

"No. You tell me, Léonard."

"Men aren't happy. Ever since man has existed," he announces in his oracular voice, "no man has ever been happy."

"I suspected as much," says Blériot, just to have something to say, and as Cusamano—whom they'd forgotten in his antechamber—announces visitors.

"Oh, it's Madame de Clermont and Madame de Bernadet!" Léonard exclaims, instantly resuscitated.

Blériot, who's made enough of a contribution, feels happier eclipsing himself as soon as possible. Still, in the hallway he does say hello to Philippe Clermont and little Bernadet, who are discreetly reapplying their face powder in the mirror while Tannenbaum makes a formal gesture inviting them to take seats beside him.

Anyone would have thought it was Yalta. In the last image Blériot has of them as he closes the door, Philippe Clermont is posing mockingly with his large Havana cigar while Léonard, slumped against his pillows, affects Franklin Roosevelt's faraway smile.

28

As a precaution, he's deleted Nora's e-mail—she's finally come back from London—and gone downstairs as if nothing unusual has happened, to make his toast and read yesterday's newspaper, apparently unruffled.

All the same, it's then nearly half an hour before he can open his mouth and ask through the bathroom door what plans his wife has for the day.

She has to go back to Marseille this afternoon.

Having eaten his breakfast, Blériot is careful not to show any impatience, for fear of waking Sabine's suspicions and giving her grounds for barbed comments, and he spends the rest of the morning typing at his computer and pacing his office in a sort of emotional trance.

It is unlikely that an artist wanting to paint an allegory of Tranquillity would have used him as a model.

Every now and then, to calm himself and keep his idle brain busy, he spies on his eighty-year-old neighbor through the window—she's sleeping in front of the TV in her robe as usual.

The less we live, the longer we live, he philosophizes, listening for his wife to leave.

"Can you order me a taxi," she calls on the stairs; "it's two-thirty and I'm already late. Could you also help me take the little blue suitcase down?"

Full steam ahead for the little blue suitcase. Blériot takes his solicitude so far as to carry her big black leather handbag in the bargain. Then he waits until she's in the taxi before getting ready in the bathroom, praying she hasn't forgotten anything.

WHEN HE'S SHOWERED and shaved, he ties his bluesman tie, slips on his old cowboy boots, and immediately feels operational.

In his rush, he slams the door, forgetting his ID and papers inside—as if repressing his identity—and jumps down the stairs four at a time. Then he carefully opens the front door, checks his wife isn't there, and here he is outside, running yet again toward Les Lilas as if time just keeps on rewinding.

The shutters are open, the gate ajar. As he crosses the garden, which is overrun with weeds, he momentarily feels as if he's floating, stripped of all weight. He pushes the door open with a shove.

"It's me," he proclaims, cupping his hands around his mouth.

When he sees her at the top of the stairs in her short dress and pantyhose, Blériot—he'll never change—suddenly feels a sort of chill spreading to his very extremities.

"There you are," Nora says in English, returning his smile. But not moving, as if afraid of his reaction.

"Can I come up?" he asks as gently as he can.

THEY'RE GETTING UNDRESSED in the bedroom, he rather hurriedly, carried away with the thought of going to bed in the middle of the afternoon, she with more circumspection, clearly taking her time—she's still at the stage of undoing the belt on her dress—like someone who's decided to put her enthusiasm on strike. But, right now, he hardly notices. He knows from experience that all these separations and overlong interruptions that are ruining their lives mean they fall out of the habit of each other and they therefore have to be patient.

When the moment he's waited for with such ardent nostalgia finally comes and he's pressed against Nora's body with no dress or pantyhose, he impulsively picks her up in his arms like a naked bride and carries her about the room while she roars with laughter and kicks him.

"Louis, stop it, please!"

Sadly, this moment of happiness, this meager minute of glory, ends as soon as they're together on the bed—he's already between the sheets—where she unceremoniously pushes him away against the wall.

"I don't like you behaving like that," she announces, crossing her legs. "I feel like a whore."

Blériot, rather contrite, stays with his back to the wall and his hands hidden under the sheets for a few seconds while she huddles on the edge of the mattress, ready to get out of bed if he tries again.

"Come on, Neville, what are you playing at?" he asks eventually, leaning over to take hold of her legs, and feeling a combination of arousal and despair.

"Nothing. That's just how it is," she replies, tightening her legs and trapping his hands.

FROM HER JUMPINESS, her stubborn expression, and the tremble in her lip, Blériot can tell she's in no mood to change her mind, and he'd do better not to press his luck. No question about it, all signals are on red.

"I'm guessing," he says, managing to keep control of himself, "that it's your trip to London that's put you in this state."

"It could well be," she says, her arms clamped around her knees.

With his conjecturing turning to anxiety, Blériot asks in his softest, most persuasive voice for her to give him a blow-by-blow account of what happened in London. She, meanwhile, is lighting a cigarette like a renegade when the time comes for his debrief.

She even has the same way of playing for time, getting bogged down in the long-winded background of her relationship with her ex-boyfriend. The whole thing punctuated by a series of digressions about her sister and her cousin, clearly intended to make him a little more confused.

Until he begs her firmly to get to the point and tell him what she did with Murphy. Given that he now has a name.

"Fine," she says, suddenly batting her eyelids incredibly fast, unable to control herself.

And so, talking mechanically, with her eyes fixed on an imaginary teleprompter, she tells him that instead of going to a hotel as she was planning to—she'd booked a room in Camden—she accepted his invitation to move into his apartment, because he really seemed very unhappy and she felt like spending a few days with him.

"I slept on the sofa in the study," she clarifies, as if that makes a difference.

"I hope at least you spoiled this poor Murphy," he takes pleasure in teasing, while avoiding asking overly explicit questions to spare himself pointless suffering.

"Not at all. It's the same rate for everyone," she answers, looking for her clothes on the bed. "Anyway, I knew you wouldn't believe me."

"But I do, Nora, I completely believe you," he insists, inwardly promising himself to piece this information together one day and get the truth out of it. As if calculating a square root.

"I don't ask you about your wife, so leave me in peace, Louis. I'm free to do what I want with who I want."

There's one frank statement at least, Blériot acknowledges. How saintly of her—but then he realizes saintly is only an anagram of nastily.

AT THIS POINT, rather than doing something irreparable, Blériot opts to go over to the window and light a cigarette, because he senses they've reached a decisive moment.

But decisive in what way?

Anyway, he points out, blowing his smoke toward the rain shower, after this relationship with an American trader, there's every chance, statistically speaking, that she'll end her career in the arms of a Russian oligarch or a Saudi emir.

"You've no right to talk to me like that!" she cries sharply, throwing her pantyhose in his face. "How dare you?"

Then she says it again, how dare you, flicking her foot and sending everything flying.

Any hope for rational debate doesn't stand a chance.

Blériot, who rarely measures up to extreme situations, on this occasion has the presence of mind not to add anything more, to know when to stop, like a pilot pulling out of a loop-the-loop at the last minute, just before slicing through the cable of an aerial tramway up ahead.

"It's okay, Neville, I take back everything I've said, let's make peace," he offers suddenly, attempting a soft landing.

At first nothing happens.

Nora's face stays peering so close to his that he can see the texture of her skin and the dark rings under her eyes, while they breathe silently as if listening to the sounds from the street. Then the tension gradually drops, the madness backs away.

"IT WOULD BE really nice if we had a glass of white wine and then went and had supper somewhere," he says once he's calmed down, carefully avoiding a big reconciliation scene.

Because of the driving rain, they go to the local Chinese.

"You'll never guess who I saw a couple of streets away," she says. "The man in the hat. The one who was spying on you, or so you thought."

"Was it him or someone who looked like him?"

"Him, I'm pretty sure. Actually, he was homeless, some poor guy who sleeps in a car parked opposite the stadium."

"Incredible the stuff we can imagine out of fear," he comments after a moment's reflection.

"Fear or guilt, Louis Blériot-Ringuet. I'm convinced there are as many men in hats as there are unfaithful husbands. Don't you think that's funny?"

"No, I think it's depressing," he says as he pays the bill.

They head back early through the empty streets, huddled under their umbrella.

That night, as Nora sleeps peacefully snuggled in her blanket, Blériot thinks of her and Murphy, and can't get to sleep. He suddenly feels as if he's shivering his way along galleries deep underground where the pain of cheated men—all men who've been cheated since the dawn of time—has conglomerated into rock. And the farther he shuffles through the darkness, groping his way along the walls, the more he inevitably forgets his way. Because there are some kinds of pain from which we never return.

29

Nora woke in the middle of the night—he thought he saw a light on the stairs—then she came up again without a word and went back to sleep, leaving one arm forgotten on top of him. When Blériot himself wakes, he's not sure what to do about this arm lying across his chest that's preventing him from moving. Relatively speaking, he feels like a man trapped under a beam, his body beginning to go numb. Because her arm is weighed down with sleep.

He can't lift it without waking her and twisting her shoulder, so he starts to slide it, inch by inch, until it's alongside her body, where it lies awkwardly with the hand turned out. He'll deal with the hand later. For now he's hurriedly picking up his things and getting dressed without a sound before opening the front door and heading into the street in search of an open café.

When he returns an hour later, with his croissants and his English newspapers, Nora still has her eyes closed and everything around her seems to be sleeping as if it's contagious: shadowy corners, the curtains, clothes, the telephone.

Blériot, who can display the patience of a Brahman, sits quietly on the edge of the bed, nibbling on a croissant, with a paper open on his knees.

Every now and then, tiring of trawling through the English soccer results, he leans over her discreetly to stroke her shoulders and the curve of her back in the hope of raising a reaction, a little shudder, but nothing happens.

She's still just as inanimate.

CONCERNED BY SUCH lethargy, he eventually decides to call her name: Nora, Nora, he whispers in her ear as he carefully moves his fingers over her skin, like a burglar trying to find the combination on a safe.

"Nora, darling," he goes on, not discouraged, while with his left hand—he's left-handed—he gently rubs her buttocks.

"Louis, you really are a pain," she says abruptly, turning over and moving his hand away. "I already said I didn't feel like it."

"But that was yesterday," he says in his defense.

"I can promise you that right now I'm not very interested in it," she adds solemnly as if talking about some historical event.

Hearing her talk like that, you'd think she listened to the headlines one morning and discovered that sex was as out of fashion as gingham skirts or huge shoulder pads.

"I promise I won't bother you anymore," Blériot says conciliatorily.

All the same, from her words and her attitude he senses the influence of some new factor, an unknown chemical element that he can't stop worrying about.

"Are you sure this Murphy hasn't got something to do with how little you care about me?" he asks, remembering the scene the night before.

"Absolutely sure," she says with her chin resting on her knees.

"I think it's the opposite; you're a bit depressed and you're already missing the way he loves you."

"You don't understand anything," she says, pushing him away. "I miss his innocence but that's something you couldn't even imagine."

As she stares blankly ahead, Blériot briefly sees a flicker in her eye, a nostalgia for an immaculate sort of love, free of sensory realities. He could almost make a joke of it, but she's looking at him so pointedly at the moment, with such childish earnestness, that he feels stripped of irony, utterly disarmed.

The only thing he can find to say is that if, in some cases, sex can be a kind of burden, then, in his opinion, loneliness is definitely an even heavier one. He decides to stop there, afraid that any additional pressure might provoke another outburst.

"I'VE NEVER TALKED to you about loneliness." She picks up on this unexpectedly, kissing him on the lips, as if to prove to him that joyous events can always spring from painful mysteries.

They stay like that on the bed for a moment, she still kissing him and he clumsily caressing her, but not going any further, in a peculiar suspension of their impulses that still reverberate through them when they're outside in the street.

"I've got an idea," she says, biting into her croissant. "Because the weather's turned nice, I'd like us to get a taxi and blow a load of money somewhere."

Unless he wants to be a killjoy, he obviously can't say no.

"It's my fix, what gives me a buzz," she explains in the taxi. "The minute I have three euros to rub together, I have to spend ten."

Blériot, conscious of her knee against his, points out that that's usually how people end up in financial ruin.

But as he is, in every respect, an adult in a perpetual state of regression who likes nothing better than adolescent women as immature and irresponsible as himself, he can't very easily be too hard on her.

Thrift is not exactly *his* strongest virtue either.

As for the subsequent punishment (confiscated credit cards, frozen bank accounts, and other inconveniences), he knows in advance that instead of bringing him into line, the most it would do would be to force him to find other solutions, given that he always has the option of going through his wife's pockets, or Léonard's.

Except right now, he warns her, he's absolutely broke. But apparently, with what she's earned at the hotel, she can handle it.

All he asks is to believe her.

THANKS TO THEIR compulsive repetitive behavior, they end up near the rue du Bac and the boulevard Saint-Germain again, in luxurious but austere shops where the middle-aged saleswomen have a distinct penchant for extravagant young couples.

Perhaps to compensate for his suffering, Nora buys Blériot a whole batch of ties and a silk scarf, which he obviously dare not refuse because he can tell she'd be hurt.

"I'd love to be really, really rich just so I could give you stuff," she tells him as they walk together in the sunshine and her lovely smile follows them along the shop fronts like a frieze on the Parthenon.

"I'm more selfish. I'd like to be a sort of high-class gigolo who cruises in a huge limousine, drinking Cristal and looking at girls. With not a thought in his head."

"No, you'd be thinking of me," she says, "and you'd be very unhappy."

Later—and this is a sign she doesn't hold anything against him—Nora takes him to a restaurant on the rue de l'Université. The place is empty and their lunch is a peculiar jellied fish garnished with citrus fruit, followed by chocolate cake.

At times like this, when they're sitting alone face-to-face and she settles her big brown eyes on him, he can see that the equation in their relationship is quite simple, almost natural: he loves her and she's cheating on him. That's how it is. He'll deal with it as others have dealt with it.

On the understanding, of course, that his perseverance will be the stronger and, however far she goes in her betrayal, his love will always bring her back.

On that condition, he feels prepared to sign up willingly.

But, in his defense, he is already well under the influence of alcohol.

"NEXT TIME IT'S my turn," Blériot promises as they come out of the restaurant—the weather's turned to rain—because, whatever he may say, he's actually ashamed of benefiting from her generosity . . . or is it her lover's?

"Don't worry about it," she cries through a storm that makes awnings and shutters clatter overhead and threatens to carry off their umbrella.

Caught by a downpour, they take refuge in the first movie theater they come to and spend the best part of the film—it has *Tokyo* in its title—sleeping with their heads resting against each other.

"I really liked the ending," Nora says all the same, when they're back outside.

"It's nearly five o'clock," he notices gloomily. "Do you want to go home?"

While they're waiting for a taxi—she's still the one paying—Blériot claims that when he was a student and already an insomniac, the only place he could fall asleep was at the movies, with a partiality for places that showed Indian films from the '70s.

"Classy," Nora concedes, pressing herself next to him on the taxi seat, just as the driver, with his teary-eyed dog by his side, warns them that the beltway is closed because of a fallen tree and the roads along the river are flooded.

They look up briefly, just long enough to assimilate the information, then start kissing again. But very, very gently, as if to avoid affecting the stability of the planet.

30

Nora, with a swaying gait, is strutting up and down the bed in a sort of flounced, partly transparent dress, and Blériot's sitting on the bedroom floor, checking his messages: his wife calling from her Marseille hotel to say she's already tried to reach him twice at home.

"Do you think it suits me?" she asks, looking at her profile in the mirror. "I'm worried I look fat in it."

Blériot shakes his head to mean she doesn't, still listening to his wife's voice, in which he can't help detecting a slightly strained note.

"But do you prefer this one or the Charleston dress that's tight over the knees?" Nora persists, because she has a photo shoot in the morning.

"Neither, and I don't like photographers much," he says, switching off his phone.

"Stop talking like my father and tell me what you think."

"I'm not talking like your father, I'm just telling you that once again, Neville, and perhaps once too many times, you're heading for serious disillusion."

"The Lord's my shepherd," she sings, revealing her legs to him, "I shall not want."

Feeling despondent, he's come to lie down on the bed without a word.

"Whose do you prefer, your wife's or mine?" she asks, swirling the skirt of her dress like the actress in *Moonfleet*.

But Blériot doesn't feel like talking about his wife.

He looks at her legs for a while in silence, then turns his head away like a child who's had his fill, eyes staring wide at the premature dusk and raindrops on the window.

While she changes her dress and goes to get a drink, he lights a cigarette and settles comfortably on the bed with an ashtray, one arm under his head.

Even if, in mathematical terms, there's no privilege between one moment and the next, that each is equidistant from the other, that doesn't alter the fact that these brief periods of respite are perhaps the only times that make him completely happy.

NORA, WHO'LL NEVER know any of this, comes back in a dress she's borrowed from her cousin; it's in crêpe de Chine silk and has a slit up the side. She asks him gently to make a bit of room for her on the bed.

"I've brought you some potato chips and some English beer," she tells him, putting the tray on the floor. "Do you want me to show you how well it suits me?"

Then, pushing up onto her tiptoes, she warns him, "Of course, without shoes, it won't have the same effect."

She doesn't seem to notice that Blériot, who's splayed out like an insect stuck on its back, has already started exploring the tops of her legs with the help of his tactile antennae.

"To be honest, I really like it, even without shoes," he promises her, skimming his fingers over her lovely smooth thighs and pausing briefly. Because, at this point, his hedonistic system feels so fiercely activated that he has to hold his breath to keep control of himself.

And of course Nora's made the most of this and taken refuge on the far side of the bed.

"You know, you should try things on for me more often, I think it's quite fun, don't you?" he says, sounding like someone doing a qualitative survey in order to establish as soon as possible whether he should reorient his behavior or pursue his intentions.

"I'm not sure we have the same interpretation of me trying things on," she replies just as Blériot catches hold of her ankle to make her tip onto the bed, with the assurance of a man who knows just how far you can go.

Afterward, getting her dress off is inevitably a bullfight.

"Louis, you're such a pain," she complains again, "and I've had enough. You're getting more and more annoying.

Can't you think of anything else?" she screams in his face before launching herself at him and throwing punches so he has to protect himself with pillows.

Luckily, after a few minutes, she gives up the fight, perhaps because she can't be bothered or because she just can't wait for it to be over: she lies down, arms spread wide, and, apart from her panties, quite naked.

There are clinches with worse outcomes.

BLÉRIOT THEN UNDRESSES calmly with his back to her, the way people do on sleeper trains, and checks his messages again before disappearing discreetly into the bathroom.

Only, when he returns, he realizes he's far from tasting his reward.

Nora, who must be a prizewinner at transformations, is now sitting on a cane chair, legs crossed, wearing jeans and a white T-shirt with an image of John Lennon on it.

"And what am I supposed to do in the meantime?" he asks, watching her posing with her fashion magazine on her knee.

"Just the top half," she replies, as if it were some tantric recommendation from her magazine.

"The top half?" he says incredulously.

"The top half," she repeats, revealing her dark nipples, the color of blackberries, and drawing his hands onto her.

Meanwhile, her long bony feet rest on the parquet, the right foot distractedly rubbing the left with one toe, because they must be obeying another thought circuit completely unaffected by what's going on farther up.

"You really are an extraordinary girl," says Blériot, unable to remember where he read that pretty girls almost always have feet that are too big.

RIGHT NOW, SHE has her fingers tightly gripping his neck and her mouth pressed so close to his ear that, thanks to his experience as a sex detective, he immediately distinguishes the change in her breathing.

As if, after a long absence, she has finally picked up the thread of her desire.

Afraid she might lose it again, he avoids talking to her or making any sudden moves.

So they both remain on the alert, taut and panting, while the darkness spreads deep into the room.

There comes a point, although they haven't said a word—the procedure is running perfectly smoothly—when he gently passes his arm under her legs and she lets him pick her up and carry her to the bed.

"Wait, Louis," she says unexpectedly, escaping his arms, "give me a second."

He watches coolly as she nips to the bathroom: a slender ghost, white buttocks, girlish laugh in the half-light.

So young that Blériot suddenly feels old and meditative.

. . .

MUCH LATER AND after considerable insistence, Nora lies down meekly, with her arms by her sides, accepting his desire but not longing for it.

And, in a flash, everything falls silent, the mechanism sets in motion, with her raised on her elbows and him—his lips applied to her skin—moving down her body slowly, like an aquatic ballet, his legs already emerging from the bed, feeling the cold in the room.

Then he comes back up.

While sheets of rain beat onto the window panes, time seems to have been suspended.

The culmination constantly held in check.

Oddly, when it is over she gets out of bed all happy and he rather disappointed. Which would seem to prove that human chemistry doesn't worry about relative compensation in remunerating pleasure.

By way of consolation, she sees fit to explain once again, as she nibbles on her potato chips, that none of *that* really matters to her. Or at least it matters no more than eating an ice cream or bicycling through Paris. There's no hierarchy for her.

"Don't you agree?" she says, handing him a beer she's opened.

But Blériot's heard enough for today. They watch TV for a bit and finish a bottle of wine in the kitchen before going to bed with their shared tiredness and mismatched desires.

"I love you," she says as she turns out the light.

"I know," he says.

"Sometimes, I wish we could be chaste, like children, Louis. Do you remember the letter Mellors wrote to Lady Chatterley?"

"No," he says, waiting to hear.

"'Now is the time to be chaste,'" she recites in the dark, "'it is so good to be chaste, like a river of cool water in my soul.' Don't you think that's beautiful?"

"I do," he says feebly.

He wishes he could say something different about chastity, but the moment has passed and he feels too dispirited. So he takes her hand and they stay there in silence, snuggled in a ball under the covers, knees to knees, and nose to nose like sad Eskimos.

31

M eanwhile, Blériot's been home to rue de Belleville, picked up his mail, changed, and had a frugal lunch of a fried egg and some yogurt before falling asleep on the sofa, listening to the radio. It's now five o'clock in the evening, he's leaning against the window, calling Nora, when, away in the distance, over the top of the zinc roofs of Paris, he notices a great red nineteenth-century sky.

"I often feel really outdated and out of step," he confides. "I think I·don't actually like our era very much."

"You're not the only one, Louis. I'm a young Russian girl from Chekhov's time," she says, letting her bathwater gush into the tub. "Are you free this evening at about ten o'clock?"

"Should be," he says after a slight hesitation. "After Marseille, Sabine's supposed to be going to Barcelona for work."

He and Madame live like that, he explains, clowning. Madame travels, negotiates, circulates with high society, and pays taxes on her fortune, while, back in Paris, he devotes himself to his two-bit translations and lives off Madame's charity.

"And the love of his beautiful English girl," she interjects.

"And the love of his beautiful English girl, if you insist. Anyway, the two of us make quite a pair of misfits."

Then he adds, "Perhaps the only thing we're good at is sex. Which is no bad thing."

"Stop it, don't start all that again," she protests from her bath.

"It's just a statement," he says, turning away and suddenly realizing from a rustle of fabric and the creak of a floorboard that there's someone in the apartment and that that someone is most likely his wife.

A moment later he sees her little blue suitcase in the hall, and the blood rushes to his head so violently he has to support himself on the doorframe.

"Why've you stopped talking?" Nora's saying as he hangs up. Right now, he'd give ten years of his life to be able to erase everything he's just said to her.

Even though he's panic-stricken, he does instinctively put a presentable expression on his face before going to greet Sabine: half smiling, half amazed by this speedy return.

"I'm in the bedroom," she says curtly.

"I didn't hear you," Blériot apologizes, now not sure what to do with his face.

SHE'S PARKED HERSELF by the bedroom door, waiting for him, still wearing her coat.

"Next time, I'll ring the bell," she says, directing a beam of black rays at him, suddenly reminding him of his mother. With no obvious connection to what has gone before, Blériot's weakness makes him flex his knees, lean forward and spread his arms, like a swimmer staring sightlessly from his starting point.

He notices her feet, her short gray socks, her creased pants, while his heartbeat accelerates and his peripheral vision darkens as if he were about to pass out and fall headfirst onto the floor. Before leaving the stage.

But he's still there.

He must have pulled himself back up by leaning on the wall. She's still appraising him with her hypnotic calm, her back wedged against the door, not uttering a word. Any other woman in her shoes would demand instant explanations or throw a chair in his face, but we'll have to assume Sabine is not any other woman. That's their problem.

Because of this never-ending silence, there seems to be something almost palpable, a magnetic dread in the air paralyzing both of them. For several minutes, they stand as still as figures in frescoes from Pompeii, held in suspense, their eyes turned toward the wings, looking at something we can't see but they alone can anticipate.

Perhaps the end of the world.

BLÉRIOT CAN NOW tell she knows everything. She's known everything since the beginning. He's almost expecting her to tell him to pack his things, tidy his desk, and leave the premises forthwith. But no.

"What did you want to say?" he asks, feeling as if he's part of a paranormal performance.

Instead of replying, his wife puts her coat on the bed, removes her shoes, and goes off to make herself a coffee in the kitchen as if he's become transparent. When he joins her there to talk, she takes her cup in her hand, swiveling away toward the window, perhaps to cut off any communication with him.

"Sabine, can you explain exactly what's going on?" he asks, speaking to her back.

As proof of his kindly disposition, he even suggests—in case she can't bear to look at him anymore—that he could go and live at Léonard's place and be forgotten about for a while.

No response. And yet he knows the explosion's imminent. She's had her finger hovering over the red button for years.

"It's your lies I can't take anymore," she starts, rather theatrically, coming toward him. At this point his wife's body seems to increase dramatically in volume, becoming all-powerful and threatening so that Blériot, overwhelmed, can't help recoiling slightly, as if trying to sink into the wall.

"Besides, seeing as lying comes so easily to you, I'm guessing you're lying to her as much as to me," she goes on, making the most of her advantage, "and you're going to ruin her life as much as you've ruined mine."

Blériot wishes he could return the compliment, but as usual he's a little behind the action.

In spite of everything, if lose he must, there is one small correction he'd like to make, he says, emerging from his wall, and that's to remind her that he may have found occasion to lie about various circumstances, but these were lies of omission rooted in his concern for her and the love he bears her. Even if that does make her laugh.

The truth is she isn't laughing at all. She's listening in silence, arms crossed, with a dark, convulsive glint in her eye that he perceives as very worrying.

There then follows an electric pause, during which he feels he can hear himself breathe.

"LET'S TALK ABOUT it then, this 'love' of yours," she retorts eventually, looking him right in the eye and making the inverted comma gesture. "Your love in Nice, for example, when you abandoned me on the sidewalk next to a movie poster, and you disappeared into the countryside."

Scuppered, thinks Blériot as if this were a naval battle.

"And your love in Anvers, when I was ill and had a temperature of 104, and you spent hours and hours on the phone with your English girl in the hotel courtyard."

Scuppered again.

In fact, for a fraction of a second, he has so little recollection of going to Anvers with her, he suspects her of instilling him with false memories to manipulate him.

He never remembers anything now, anyway.

Since she came home so unexpectedly, he feels he's a bit short on thought processes, rather like finding you're short of money. So that when his wife puts him in a position to make a choice—otherwise, she'll draw the obvious conclusion—it takes him a little time to grasp what that choice is and what she's expecting of him.

Her anger, her pallor, and her beautiful, penetrating eyes seem to exert a sort of sexual ascendancy over him that leaves him numb.

"Sabine, just tell me what you want me to do," he asks, demoralized by a feeling of inferiority.

"I've just explained that to you. First, you stop lying to me and cheating on me, and then we'll see. Because we can't go on like this, you know that, Louis," she says insistently but slightly softening her voice. "You're going to have to make a decision once and for all."

"Once and for all," he reiterates, mechanically.

"For all," she confirms.

This produces another pause that Blériot tries to put to good use—staring hopelessly at the windows of the building opposite—to activate his mental protection system. But his wife's presence means he can't concentrate.

"Well, okay then," he concludes strangely, walking out of the room, although he's not sure after the fact whether this was consent or simply an acknowledgment of receipt.

An hour later—he's in the aisles of a supermarket with his earphones in—his wife calls him on his cell to let him know that her former colleagues Marie-Laure and Carlo Simoni have invited them to dinner.

"I'll be back as soon as I've finished," he promises, suddenly realizing that one day she'll stop calling him and they'll never go for dinner with anyone again.

32

N ow is the winter of our discontent," says Max Barney; then, with his hands still pressed to the window, he adds, "and everything leads me to believe it'll also be the winter of my redundancy."

Murphy, sitting behind him, says nothing, too preoccupied with the depressive signals Max has been sending him for some time—he's just found he has glaucoma and two ulcers, all imaginary.

"If it weren't for Borowitz, I don't think I'd stay here either," he says eventually, eyeing the ice-cold sky.

The glum little group that the two of them and Kate Meellow form usually maintains a respectful distance from their colleagues, kept separate by an invisible barrier across the width of the cafeteria, dividing it into two contrasting microclimates. On the other side of this demarcation line, young women from the agency are clustering around the coffee machine under the authority of a new dominant male by the name of Paul Burton who, incidentally, makes quite a point of discouraging some of them by ostentatiously turning his back on them—there's no competition without selection—while encouraging the others with a joke or an attentive remark that comes quite naturally to him. The man clearly has years of experience.

On the subject of Burton, Kate drops her voice to tell them a rather meandering story about one of his mistresses, and although Murphy's not very partial to gossip, he finds himself listening patiently as if his own inner boredom reconciled him to other people's vacuity. After a while, though, he loses the thread of the story and slowly nods off, still listening to Kate's and Max's voices.

The arrival of a gang of analysts puts an end to this peacefulness.

As he rubs his eyes and watches them buzzing about the room with indefatigable ubiquity, Murphy actually wonders why he too was destined to handle financial futures and hedge funds when he would have made a far more convincing academic, or even a preacher.

But we'll just have to take it that he'd already been cast against type.

UNFORTUNATELY, EVERYTHING happened without him having his say.

For several years—radiant, unchanging years—he was in Boston studying Keynes's mathematical ideals and economic theories, until the day when, because his father had lost everything gambling, necessity dictated that he make the decision to leave his empyrean, settle on Earth, and conscientiously earn a living.

Now he has everything. Well, the living but not a life.

He's become slumped and old, and although he may still manage to keep up appearances, he's turned into a pillar of salt inside. Like someone dried to a husk by nostalgia.

Since the evening Nora went back to Paris and disappeared off his radar, Murphy Blomdale's thoughts, whether he likes it or not, have kept coming back to her, as if under some invariable force of physics.

"Do you remember my invitation yesterday?" Kate asks him out of the blue (she'd be good in the thought police).

"No," he admits, turning toward her—always slightly wary when she's in this excited state.

"I said I'd invited some friends over, former colleagues from Barclays, and I was counting on your help."

Murphy is kind enough to make no comment. She must have thought it would be nice for him. He exchanges a last few words with Max Barney and she's still sitting there waiting for his acceptance, looking at him with a reverence, a harmlessly obtuse tenderness that completely disarms him.

"If I do come this evening, Kate, I won't stay long," he warns, instinctively on the defense; then he gets up and goes onto the terrace to smoke.

Murphy sometimes wishes someone could explain to him what sort of moral perversion makes us persuade ourselves that somebody who loves us automatically has inalienable rights over us. As he leans on the balustrade and tries to call Vicky Laumett, he looks out to the bridges in the distance and the mewling seagulls spiraling around them, frantic with hunger.

"Pronto!" says a sleepy man's voice—there are days when life feels like a misunderstanding on a planetary scale. *Pronto?*

KATE LIVES NEAR Euston station—not far from where he lives—in a small, dark apartment with velvet curtains and covered furniture that give the place a confined, funereal feel. The sound of trains can occasionally be heard from outside.

"You can help yourself. I won't be a minute," she says, nipping to her bedroom to make a phone call.

Murphy couldn't say why but he's convinced she's calling her mother in Baltimore. Her mother, who watches over her with avid concern from thousands of miles away, insisting on detailed accounts of how she spends her days. It must be time for their daily call. While he waits for their conversation to end, he draws aside the curtains to watch the first snowflakes swirl above the railway lines, and, as if the snow were beating a rhythm, he gradually feels the tension subsiding in his nerves under a narcotic effect.

Without his even realizing it, his thoughts have returned to Nora. To their first winter together.

To a particular Sunday when they walked down a snowy street high up in Hampstead, treading carefully with their feet apart, in the dusk and in silence. It must be seven or eight o'clock in the evening and all the shops are closed. Whatever happens, they don't want to miss their bus. All the same and in spite of themselves, they carry on walking very, very slowly, holding hands, perhaps because of the patches of black ice they can feel underfoot or simply because we walk more slowly in the past than in the present.

"The others'll be here soon," says Kate, whom he didn't hear coming into the room.

"Do you think?" he says, shivering.

He's stepped away from the window to help her move the chairs and bring the cups and glasses into the living room, while Kate tells him about her quarrels with her sister who lives at her parents' expense in a stunning five-room apartment in Newport and now communicates with her only through lawyers.

Still listening, Murphy becomes increasingly convinced that he'd do well to find an excuse to get away before the others arrive. But at the same time he doesn't dare. Because he has every reason to believe Kate would take it badly.

"Who's coming this evening?" he asks eventually with a semblance of enthusiasm.

"Charles Grocius, who I've told you about; Quentin Bilt," she starts to say but breaks off for a moment until the roar of a train has passed, "Édouard, Franca Lippi, Carol Kussli—who's a pretty incredible person—and a dozen or so others you'll have plenty of time to get to know."

SO, NEVER DROPPING his affability and his rather stereotypical smile, Murphy meets first Quentin Bilt, looking austere as a theology student in his anthracite gray suit (although apparently a technical wizard), but there's something refreshing and frank about him that catches Murphy's attention. Next it's Mike and Édouard, who turn out to be a pair of gossipy, corpulent bachelors, passionate about bickering within the royal family—compared with Quentin Bilt, they're Tweedledum and Tweedledee.

As for Carol Kussli, with her backpack and her snow boots, she's the very picture of the hearty forty-year-old spinster, all calves and kindness, blessed with a pretty, alpine smile, but by the second or third glass of white wine she's offering up her tragic loneliness to all and sundry.

It's apparently not easy finding a volunteer.

Anyway, it won't be Murphy, who's withdrawn to go to the bathroom.

"Is there anyone there?" cries a man's voice. By deduction, it must be Charles Grocius, although Bertrand Russell might have said the same thing.

Murphy has often noticed that life in society is like a badly planned journey, with endless waiting, tedious conversations, inconsiderate people, and toilets that are always occupied.

One thing's for sure, he won't be caught out like this again. Next time, he'll spend the evening at home reading the Epistle to the Romans. All that remains now—his perennial scruples again—is to slip away discreetly without offending anyone. Luckily, Kate's in the living room, monopolized by Franca Lippi, a tall brunette in a fitted jacket who's telling her that, having not opened a book in twenty years, she now reads two novels a day, as if she's had a new lobe transplanted into her brain.

"That's amazing," says Kate just as Murphy gives her a little wave over Franca's shoulder.

There isn't a single sound on the street; the snow has grown deeper on the sidewalks. Snowflakes hang in the air, twirling like moths in the light from streetlamps.

Murphy hesitates a moment; then, buoyed by the pleasure of being free, he starts to run through the snow as if still hoping to catch that bus in Hampstead.

33

For a few fractions of a second—this must be the shortest dream in the history of dreams—a young woman pursued by three lovers (all played by Blériot) takes refuge on the roof of a building, where she balances precariously, her body leaning over the street below and one leg already launched into space.

When he recognizes Nora, Blériot wakes with a start, covered in sweat.

He opens one eye, glimpses his clothes thrown on a chair (he and his wife now have separate bedrooms), his sleeping computer, a jumble of paperwork, and the remains of a meal on a tray. Outside it's trying to snow. It's a day for staying under the covers and reading a book about the retreat from Moscow.

From the sound of doors, he can tell that his wife's already waiting for him downstairs. Since the episode with the phone call he's been constrained to tolerating her mood swings, tears, and silences, her reproach and her control-freakery to the point that life feels more and more like a test of endurance.

Once he's up and has extricated himself from the threads of his dream, like a walker dusting himself as he emerges from undergrowth, he listens to some music, then starts to-ing and fro-ing in the ill-lit bedroom, trying to find a missing sock.

Every time he catches sight of himself in his underpants in the bathroom mirror, he thinks he looks like a yogi.

HE SHAVES NO less meticulously and spreads moisturizer over his cheeks before massaging his temples. All gestures recommended to him by a naturopath to overcome his persistent anxieties. He then goes downstairs, his heart dark and his nerves on edge, dreading his wife's reaction as usual. Because he never knows what mood he'll find her in.

"*Guten Morgen*," he says, hearing his voice boom in the frozen silence of the apartment.

She has her back to him and is busy putting on her boots.

"Could you empty the dishwasher?" she asks while they exchange a neutral kiss in the kitchen doorway. "I'm late."

Feeling his anxiety instantly melting, Blériot promises he'll do the necessary.

"By the way," she adds just as she opens the door, "you wouldn't by any chance like to come to Turin with me? I've been invited to the Pistoletto retrospective next month."

"Pistoletto?" Blériot echoes, his cognitive functions momentarily paralyzed.

Once he's pulled himself together, he has to cite a series of pending translations, as he did for Milan, to be absolutely sure not to make any promises. Because the invitation strikes him as somewhat incongruous, given the circumstances.

But he'd rather keep his opinions to himself and let her get off to work.

NOW THAT HE'S had a chance to think about it properly, he's convinced this is a new strategy of his wife's, intended to keep him under her thumb until his penitence has run its course.

Because of the daily dose of sadness she decants into his brain, Blériot wakes every morning hoping she'll suggest he pack his bags, and every morning she renews his punishment. So that he marinates a little longer in his remorse. And by thinking too much about their relationship, by spending the whole day sifting through all the blunders, tactlessness, and frequent indulgences he's allowed himself, Blériot ends up persuading himself—it must be Stockholm syndrome—that he's only getting what he deserves.

To repair all the damage he's done and completely sur-render his free will, he is now beholden to emptying the dishwasher, being careful not to mix the silver cutlery with the stainless steel cutlery, and scouring the sink and the bathroom—it's ridiculous how servile guilt can make us—before cleaning the floors, shampooing the carpet, and dusting the furniture, until their apartment looks like a model of comfort and family contentment.

By noon, the floor tiles in the kitchen and bathroom are gleaming as brightly in the morning light as if they'd been painted by a Dutchman, because Blériot does everything very thoroughly. He is cast in the same docile mold, the same neurotic submissiveness to his wife, as his father is to his—it must be the karma of men in that family—with the same im-potent resentment and the same element of self-punishment.

While he works, busying from one room to another with his bucket and mop, wearing worn slippers, he actually looks like a prisoner condemned to a long-term sentence—Sisyphus must have looked something like this.

A COUPLE OF hours later, Blériot takes off his uniform, has a scalding-hot shower, and calls Nora to tell her about his strange dream.

She's on another call.

"I'll call you back later," she tells him.

In the meantime, he heats up some leftovers and eats them as slowly as possible because he's got it into his head—this is one of his latest eccentricities—that the best way to counter his agitation would be to slow his chewing process and fragment his every gesture into a succession of tiny equal moments.

Lost in his calculations, he listens distractedly to the sound of traffic and pneumatic drills down in the street, and they almost make him long for the energy of life out there.

Sometimes, as he explores every last inch of his sedentary micro-space, he is gripped by a sort of furious desire to put his feet together and spring out of the circle of his own existence, and for everything to start at the beginning again. Somewhere else, anywhere.

But without Sabine and without Nora—who, by the by, doesn't call him back.

After tidying the kitchen, Blériot has returned to more sensible projects, gone meekly to his office and switched on his computer.

His destitution is so overwhelming and disheartening that, in addition to an article about speech defects, he has resorted to translating the user's manual for a new range of electric shavers. At this rate, he'll soon be translating tourist pamphlets.

OUR ELECTRIC SHAVER, he translates while fat snow-flakes continue to fall outside, *is not for use by individuals who do not have the necessary experience to handle it, nor by individuals with reduced sensory or mental capabilities*—yes, it really says that, word for word—*unless someone responsible for their safety oversees them and ensures they use the device correctly.*

In the event of obvious irregularities in its performance, he continues imperturbably, *the device should be returned to our technical department with the receipt of purchase.*

You have to translate this stuff to believe it.

By way of consolation, at least he can say that his day's been fairly productive, because, as well as his housework, he's almost finished his translation—he has only two or three pages left to go.

When he finally looks up from his work, Blériot sees that it's only half past four, and suddenly feels disoriented by the vastness of the afternoon.

For a while he paces his bedroom, gripped by the same ambulatory mania as his mother, until the alert on his cell phone opportunely interrupts, letting him know he has a message.

It's a text from Nora: *I miss you more and more. Your girl.*

How can someone be devastated and happy at the same time? he muses in amazement, reaching his face out the window to feel the moisture of the snowflakes and wash away his tiredness.

When his wife came home at six o'clock, she found him in exactly the same place, his hair soaked and his head tilted slightly to one side like a horse asleep on its feet.

34

The following morning, all Nora did was return his call at last, ordering him to stop his housework once and for all and come out with her (it was her one day off at the airport), and he promptly decided that his penitence had gone on long enough, and came running. As if she had only to click her fingers.

And everything started again, the turmoil, the lies, the hidden assignations, the hasty reunions, the demented, irrevocable love.

They don't usually see each other for more than an hour or two, preferably on neutral territory, on boulevards away from the heart of the city, or sometimes right in the middle of the suburbs if they want even less risk of being identified. Afterward, like secret agents versed in every subterfuge of a clandestine life, each melts back into the fabric of his or her daily life, she at her hotel reception desk, he in his marital home, where he waits with apparent detachment—nothing in his hands and nothing in his pockets—for his wife's return.

An hour later, though, he quakes at her every question as if his cover's been blown. Something tells him that, where these questions are concerned, he'd do well to consider his words carefully, because he is a multiple offender.

Educated by previous experience, Blériot is well aware he has to be careful about everything, the phone calls, messages, restaurant receipts left in his pockets, withdrawals from the bank—anything, in fact, that might one day be used in evidence against him.

So his life is now run with minute precision.

But a part of him likes this. Because, aside from his fondness for a bit of mystery, he likes the idea of being in a secret organization with Nora, the two of them constituting a unit that can be activated or deactivated depending on the circumstances.

THAT PARTICULAR MORNING, while a great triumphal sun rose over the suburbs, Blériot suddenly felt years younger—that's all part of the double life—as he stepped onto a train, then a bus, to cover his tracks, before heading on foot through the snow-laden streets in a neighborhood of tidy little houses, where he tried, for obvious reasons, to be as discreet as possible.

He comes up to a school, walks along the open fence around a building complex, then, with his collar turned up, sets off down a steeply sloping street edged with brick houses and their still-frozen front gardens, with not a soul in sight. It could easily be a blind spot, a forgotten corner of time.

At the bottom of the street, near the station, he can see the bar that Nora described.

Apart from the manager and a couple of regulars talking quietly and watching a race at Vincennes on the screen above the bar, the place is completely deserted. Blériot orders a glass of Bourgueil wine and sits by the door, with his legs stretched and his arms crossed. All his powers of concentration gathered into this empty moment.

In this tense, obscurely bored state, he watches as people come out of the station one by one and head for the bus stop, but never manages to identify Nora. After a while he calls her, but she doesn't seem to be reachable. It's already eleven and she's almost an hour late. Some days he suspects she does this on purpose.

His exasperation, multiplied by the coefficient of his anxiety, gives him a sudden urge to get up and go back to Paris.

His ringing phone stops him.

"Louis, it's Mom," says a woman's voice with such warmth and enthusiasm that, for the space of a few seconds, he thinks he's dealing with a hoax.

But it isn't. She's been in the hospital just over a week.

Two days before she left, the doctor gave her a chemistry lesson about proteins and amino acids and prescribed her a new antidepressant—Termex, or Temlex—which is working like a dream.

"Right now I'm walking around Nîmes with my friend Jacqueline, Jean-Philippe Lamy's sister, you know, the man who took over from Dr. Bernard. How about you?" she shrieks into the phone.

"Everything's fine. Look, I'll call you this evening." He makes his excuses quickly as, just at the door, he recognizes the girl in a woolen hat smiling at him, baring her little front teeth for him.

The snow itself is smiling.

WITH ITS DARK wooden floor, low table, wilting flowers, and cramped toilet cubicles, the hotel feels like a slightly Germanic inn that's seen better days. The plumbing makes hellish noises and the radiators are cold. But they're happy like this, alone together.

They're leaning out the window, their cheeks touching, looking beyond the railway lines to the jumble of houses and warehouses peculiar to some landscapes on the fringes of cities. The sky is light blue, almost white. Snow is pretty much everywhere and has started melting like the past. Crows perched on their electric cables drop down like dead leaves onto the lawns of nearby houses.

As they find themselves, to their surprise, talking for the

first time of a future when they'll finally live together, occasional trains go past in the distance, so far away that they're reduced to sound waves.

"I'm getting cold," says Nora, closing the window.

At this point, he hasn't yet said anything about his trip to Turin, and—because he knows how unpredictable and explosive she can be—a vague intuition might even persuade him to stick to this safe blackout policy. Unless she herself raises the subject of his future with his wife.

In the meantime, Blériot, who amazes himself with his psychotic ability to lead this double life, has hastily undressed while she's busy in the bathroom.

"Are you coming?" he says, looking at the street through the shutters. She doesn't answer.

HE LIES DOWN between the sheets, closes his eyes, and crosses his hands behind his head, feeling he's being gently carried away as if he were lying in the middle of a river.

At this precise moment, his heart feels pure, his nerves raw, his penis straining like an adolescent's, and he feels as if nothing bad can happen to him.

Nora has, at last, come to sit next to him in her bra and panties, resting her chin on her knees.

"Not now," she says, pushing his hand away. "I've already said I don't like you doing that. It's bloody annoying, Louis."

"If you don't try, you can't get," he points out.

"Is that from Leibniz?"

"No, I came up with it all on my own, can you believe?"

"You are such a pain, Louis! Such a pain!"

"Well, if not now, it can be for later," he concludes, used to dealing with things patiently.

Sometimes he thinks he might just as well be in bed with Queen Guinevere. And that what he might be missing out on in sensory terms can be instantly converted into spiritual gain.

He's resting his head in her lap and hasn't moved for a while, totally preoccupied with inhaling the smell of her skin (white clay and blackberry, he decides, rifling through his memory library).

"It's funny, you talk like a woman with a forty-year sex life behind her," he comments before propping himself up on his hands again and going back to the fragrant nape of her neck and the coiled shell of her ears as if to a focal point of his desire.

"You know," says Nora, moving away slightly, "my contract at the airport ends in March, and I think I'm going to have to go back to London."

"It's becoming a habit," he says, smiling weakly.

SHE'S STROKING HIS cheek and he's closed his eyes again, listening to the shrill vibrations of suburban trains.

"I'll come back to Paris, of course," she tells him, lighting a cigarette, "but I can find as much work as I want there. My sister knows loads of people. Anyway, I'm sure that, even if I took classes for years and years, I'm never going to be Nina Zarechnaya, or young Violaine, or anyone. Except for some English chambermaid."

"You can be my sweetheart, Nora Neville, my one and only sweetheart, my English love."

"Maybe, but I feel like throwing in the towel," she announces despondently. As despondently as if she's seen her whole lifetime in the space of a few months and has learned from it.

Apparently, she doesn't even have enough money to pay for her acting classes now.

"If that's all it is, I've got just what you need," says Blériot, grabbing his jacket from the chair and, as if by magic, producing from the pocket a handsome wad of twenty-euro bills, which he fans out on the bed like a poker hand.

"It's all for you," he insists, pushing it toward her.

Even though he knows that, by definition, we can't buy things that don't have a price, he might be improving his chances of delaying her departure by a couple of months.

"I'll pay you back soon," she promises after a moment's hesitation. "Do you want to go and eat somewhere?"

"THAT WOULD BE silly," says Blériot, who's now lying on his stomach, reaching for his watch on the bedside table. "Sabine's at a private viewing, so we can make the most of having this room a bit longer."

"On your head be it," she warns him as she tries to undo the lock on the minibar, then gives up and lies down on top of him, quite naked.

"Do you know the elevator game?" she asks him, swiftly metamorphosing into such a deft, pliant partner she could be mistaken for a KGB call girl in the arms of an international civil servant.

The comparison clearly pleases her in some ways.

"Actually, *you* could be the kinky spy and I could be the little civil servant who's fallen in love," she says just as a phone rings. "That's your cell."

Blériot, who likes doing one thing at a time, recommends not moving a muscle. So they ignore it while she stays there, raised on her arms, immobilized in a sort of painful stasis that drains her parted lips of all color.

Afterward, they shower and get dressed in no time. It's almost nine o'clock. It's pitch dark outside and the neighborhood is utterly silent. They walk side-by-side through the molten snow, slinking like foxes and coughing in the cold.

When they reach the station platform, Blériot's phone rings again.

"Is it your wife?" she asks, worried.

"My mother," he says fatalistically. "I'll call her tomorrow."

35

With one hour's time delay, the same damp darkness has fallen over London while Murphy and Vicky Laumett sit facing each other in a bar in Blackfriars. She dressed all in white, as she was when they first met; Murphy much more austere in his market trader's suit, his black bag on the bench seat beside him.

Murphy Blomdale may well appear resigned at times, and he may have been living a dull, self-sufficient life for several months, but time hasn't quelled his need to see Vicky, because she remains his only link with Nora. So much so that, to see them whispering together this evening, you'd think they were the last two people on earth to speak a dead language.

"Did you used to come to this bar?" she asks.

"She often waited for me here, when I finished work and we'd decided to eat out somewhere."

Now he only ever comes here on the weekends, almost always alone, he confides. Firstly, because he doesn't have many friends in London, but also because he wants to be here on his own in the very unlikely event that Nora walks through the door.

"I'm still romantic," Murphy muses, looking at her, dazzled by her beautiful, ample figure but not troubled by it, at least not aroused at all.

While they're speaking frankly, Vicky admits that she herself still jumps every time the phone rings, convinced she'll hear Nora's voice at last.

"I don't know if you remember that Bradbury character in *The Martian Chronicles*," she says, "the one who changed sex and identity the minute he met someone."

"I've never read any Bradbury."

"Well, every time, he unintentionally assumes the face of the man or woman that the other person's been waiting years to meet. Like he's becoming a projection of their desire. By the end, everyone's chasing after him and he just becomes this shadowy figure, running away and appallingly unhappy."

Murphy has to agree that it could be a good definition of Nora.

"If you feel like it," she adds mischievously as she gets to her feet, "you could always try your luck in a few months, because according to her sister, Dorothy, she might be coming back to London."

The problem is, he's not sure he'll still be here. The agency, he explains, has already fired a dozen people, and he could easily be in the next round and might have to return to the United States. Which would end up being a double blow, he points out as he helps her with her raincoat. Even though, deep down, he knows very well that as time goes by their relationship would have died a natural death anyway.

VICKY HAS TAKEN a taxi home and, once he comes within sight of Holborn, Murphy continues walking toward Islington, protected by his umbrella, ruminating over his failures and constantly losing his way. At some point, a dog just as lonely as him—a stray with a broken leg and one ear half hanging off—starts following him, making itself as small as it can in the hopes of being ignored.

It must be the other one's brother.

This time Murphy decides to use major tactics immediately and get the animal to understand in firm and definitive terms—from one dog to another—that he has nothing to offer, so it had better try someone else.

A wasted effort. The dog merely steps back a bit, waiting for Murphy to walk on, then falls in at his heels. Followed by a second dog, in no better shape.

At this point, Murphy is reduced to thinking he must look so comic and helpless with his umbrella that dogs, who don't have many opportunities to laugh, all want to walk some of the way with him.

When he comes to Clerkenwell, Murphy has run out of arguments and resigns himself to walking a little farther, cutting diagonally through the crowds, like Saint Roch followed by those two dogs and now relying entirely on a bus to arrive in order to shake them off.

BACK AT HOME, Vicky has undressed and gone to bed without any dinner, feeling slightly nauseous. David still isn't home. She's almost used to it now. She's doing what she often does when her anxieties and her anxieties about her anxieties get the better of her—she's lying on her side with her knees drawn to her body, pressing her hands against her eyes like a child, to find an image of Nora.

Not the Paris Nora, but the first Nora, the one in Coventry, when they were still awkward, shy, and innocently depraved, and, despite all their precautions, their love was clear for all to see. The Nora who used to disappear for days on end and then reappear at any time of day or night, her face ravaged and beaming as she said: *Were you waiting for me?*

Well, what did she think?

The one who used to send her a postcard from a French museum with cherubs and garlands of flowers: *I love you today*, she would write in her small, careful handwriting, underling *today*.

The one she once waited for almost a whole morning at the bottom of a staircase. And this evening she feels she's still waiting for her—the image is there—with her hands deep in her raincoat pockets. Every time the door to the building opens behind her, blown by the draft, she hears the patter of summer rain in the courtyard.

The weirdest part is, she can't remember the rest of the building, or the neighborhood (but they were both still living in Coventry), just that dark stairwell with its wooden banister, as if her memory has become a spiral staircase. A staircase she climbs, feeling her way in the dark, up to the third or fourth floor, the upper floors having vanished, swallowed in oblivion.

When she arrives at the top, Vicky sees herself ringing the doorbell.

"ARE YOU ASLEEP already?" her husband says, amazed, briskly turning on the small lamp that acts as a nightlight.

"No, I'm thinking."

Lost in her mnemonic daydreams, she didn't hear him come in.

"Could you leave me be, David?" she says, because she can't wait to get back to her staircase.

Looking slightly irritated, he takes off his shoes and disappears into the bathroom without another word.

SO SHE RINGS again, goes down, then climbs up, still hearing the sound of the rain from the courtyard.

"Is that you? What's going on?" Nora asks suddenly through the half-open door. (Through the lens of Vicky's memory, Nora looks much smaller than in real life, wearing a shirt that comes to her knees.)

"I was waiting for you downstairs. You said nine o'clock."

"I can't. I'm not alone," she whispers, yanking her thumb as if pointing to someone over her shoulder.

Vicky feels stupid. She didn't realize, she apologizes. Anyway, she won't get in the way any longer.

"Don't be silly," says Nora, pressing Vicky's fingers between her own. "Come whenever you like, I'll explain everything."

After that she can't remember the words. It's as if someone's switched off the soundtrack. She can just see herself running down the steps four at a time, in such a state, such terror of abandonment, that she lets out a sob.

She doesn't even remember the explanations Nora gave her the following day. Just the staircase and Nora's eyes hazy with sleep.

Perhaps that's why memories are beautiful. Because with time, the filter of passing years, they turn into purified products, stripped of the dross of heartache and fear.

"Am I allowed to come to bed now?" asks her husband, looking as if he's waiting his turn as he stands there in his pajamas, his face neither cheerful nor sad.

36

The night sky is high and clear. They've turned off the light and gone out onto the balcony barefoot. They're looking way down below at the deserted streets with their successions of arches and windows glowing orange from the streetlamps—their hotel is at one end of the piazza Vittorio.

Blériot has stopped prevaricating, has leaned toward his wife and is softly nibbling her shoulder as he lifts the hem of her nightshirt, as if this were a ritual gesture of repentance and forgiveness.

He's clearly forgiven.

They stay there a while longer, leaning on the balustrade, not talking, lost in the sheer space and clarity of that sky. Every now and then, barely perceptible cloudy filaments pass far, far overhead, as white as seminal fluid—that's

Blériot's image—and they disperse almost immediately above the surrounding mountains.

"I'm glad you came to Turin," Sabine says, dragging over a chair and putting her feet up.

"Me too, I'm glad I'm here," he says.

Blériot, who's always been secretly bipolar (he's currently in a manic phase), has immediately started kissing her again and pulling against her waist with his left arm—he's sitting to her right—until they tacitly agree to go inside to the bedroom. He then releases her long, tanned breasts from under her nightshirt, and she looks at them as if seeing them for the first time.

Which, incidentally, seems to prove that, despite the exhausting tension they've been living under for weeks, everything is obviously not over between them.

AND ONCE THEY'RE undressed and lying on the bed things do indeed start again just like before, as if nothing had ever happened. They spontaneously use the same words, the same gestures, the same intimate procedures so many years later—perhaps because sex is the reminiscence of sex—before suddenly releasing their embrace and rolling apart, each bathed in sweat.

Now neither of them has the strength to get up. Something that hasn't happened for a very long time, points out his wife.

"Who is this Michelangelo Pistoletto?" Blériot asks to change the subject.

Apparently, it would take a while to explain, but the exhibition was perfect and included works she'd never seen.

Blériot acknowledges that he could have made an effort.

"Will you show me the catalog you brought back?"

"I don't know that the catalog will be much use to you," she says after a while.

As the night draws on, their voices come more and more intermittently, as if borne by a weak electric current.

It must be nearly one o'clock. A draft makes the window smack back and forth.

They both stay there lying on top of the sheets, their legs intertwined, breathing the cool air from the street while the sounds of Turin drift in and out of their gradually dissolving consciousness.

IN THE MORNING they're woken by the telephone.

"Hello?" a voice says.

"Yes?" he says, not recognizing the voice on the other end, or the number on the screen.

"Hello, hello?" the other person says again, like a sort of mechanical bird.

Blériot has hung up, filled with unpleasant premonition.

"Who was it?" asks his wife, still lounging in bed.

"No idea," he replies, hopping over the suitcases to get his clothes.

Following a mysterious transfer of energy in the night, he's woken invigorated, slightly wired, while his wife looks semi-convalescent on her pillow, with drawn features and puffy eyes.

"Are you sure it wasn't anyone you know?" she insists, making the effort to prop herself on her elbows.

"Absolutely totally." He doesn't know what she's trying to insinuate, but he has no desire to be dragged into this conversation.

Sometimes he actually suspects that beneath her appealing exterior—sociable and self-confident—she's kept a depressive core.

The *colazione* arrives just at the right moment.

He's run himself a bath and stays submerged up to his shoulders for a long time with his legs bent and his faun-like thatch of hair floating in the bubbly water as he listens to the pigeons cooing on the roofs. The scurry of their feet on the baking hot tiles.

He climbs out of the tub thin and naked as he'll be on his dying day and hurriedly gulps down another cup of coffee before going to read the paper in the sunshine. His wife will meet him in the piazza.

AT TWO O'CLOCK they have lunch in a restaurant near the banks of the Po, where a dozen or so people sitting with their backs to the sun look as if they're dozing on their chairs. Personally, he rather likes the crushing stillness of Sunday afternoons.

Through the window they watch orange trams, or sometimes orange-and-white ones, going over the bridge toward the hills.

"Are you thinking about someone?" his wife asks, noticing his faraway look. "Your little English girl?" she adds on the off chance.

She's clearly thinking about her more than he is.

"No," he replies, "I'm not thinking about anyone."

Blériot's given up trying to explain that we can never love enough and that he needs both of them—he needs her and Nora—and that if ever he was unlucky enough to have to sacrifice one of them, he would immediately lose the other. Which is what would happen in a legend.

In his double life, he has had to establish a sort of barometric correlation between the pressures they each exert over him, and thanks to this he has found some semblance of balance. When all is said and done, it's as good a theory as any other. Blériot would even be prepared to uphold that any man who hasn't loved two women at once is condemned to remain incomplete.

As he himself isn't.

"It's my treat," he says, taking the bill to prove in passing that he's not as exploitative as she thinks.

AFTERWARD THEY WALK through the hills, following the sun, through cool gardens and the silent wind. In the distance they can see the mountaintops still capped with snow, reminding them of their first trip to Italy, five or six years ago, and the long ski runs in Cortina.

"If we come back to Turin another time, I'd really like to rent a car and go skiing wherever you like," he tells Sabine, who has suddenly recovered her gentleness, her indulgence, and her natural dynamism—her three cardinal virtues. Perhaps because the few moments of stolen pleasure the night before were as beneficial to her as they were to him.

It only remains to hope there will be another time.

They walk through a shady village, then another, without meeting a single person, or worrying about it particularly. They carry on walking at the same pace, shoulder to shoulder, silent and concentrating, like those couples Mikio Naruse films from behind, then they head down toward the banks of the Po with no specific goal.

When they reach the botanical gardens they buy ice creams and sit down on the grass for a while to watch rowers glowing red with sunburn.

"I don't really feel like going back to Paris right away," he admits, lobbing his ice-cream cone in the water. "Couldn't we stay a couple more nights?"

But apparently it's complicated. Their room's booked for just one night.

They could always try to negotiate with the hotel, he suggests.

"I'm very sorry, but you should have woken earlier," is the sour comment from the receptionist, an Italian-Lebanese girl—the shortage of love is everywhere—who stares at them from under her flick of hair.

To top it all, Sabine isn't even sure their plane tickets are interchangeable. All she knows is that they're leaving sometime between ten and eleven. It's as if they suddenly have too much time ahead of them or not enough, which is always what happens when they're together.

THE OBLIQUE RAYS of late-afternoon sun reach under the arches around the square, lighting the quaint old terrace where they're drinking vermouth, Blériot leafing through a paper, Sabine half snoozing on her chair with her legs stretched in the sun.

Making the most of this stillness and under cover of his sunglasses, Blériot photographs her slowly with his eyes—he's taken the precaution of stopping the march of time by holding his breath—while she daydreams and coils her black necklace pensively around her finger, with her head tilted to one side and her beautiful blond hair gathered into a loose bun on the nape of her neck.

Then he lets his breath out in a rush and time starts to flow again, purified and regular, and the hubbub from the streets of Turin fills his ears again.

"Right, what are we going to do now?" his wife asks.

At this precise moment, like a man constantly revolving on himself, Blériot believes with all his strength that he'll never leave her.

"Well, first let's just try to find another hotel," he suggests.

37

He jolts awake, feeling as if Nora is curled up asleep next to him. The room is still dark. Murphy Blomdale reaches his arm across the bed, like an amputee trying to find his phantom limb, and finds nothing but cold sheets. But the impression of her presence persists a few more seconds like a sensory illusion he can't quite shake off.

Nora's visitations started again a few weeks ago, always at the same time in the morning, between five and six, accompanied by the same rush of emotion, the same thundering heart rate—proof that we're electrochemical machines—and always followed by the same brutal and depressing deceleration.

And there he was, thinking he had detoxed from her.

When he gets up, he has trouble putting one foot in front of the other. He manages to open the drapes and fumbles his way to the bathroom to turn on the heat and run the water, taking a certain satisfaction in rediscovering the weightless ease of his daily routine.

Although he's not keen on introspection, Murphy is well aware—perhaps because he hasn't touched a woman for months—that at the moment all it takes is a dream, a small upset, a minor confusion in the morning for him to feel he's instantly crumbling, as if loneliness has made him porous.

If there really is a true self in each of us, he thinks as he gets dressed, a self that is as inexhaustible as a hidden source that never runs dry, even in summer, he has to recognize that his is buried very deep. And he's not sure he'll ever be able to find it. He leans out the window, peering thoughtfully into the future, and suddenly has the strange and almost happy sense that he is a minute detail in an urban landscape, so small he is invisible to the naked eye.

The sun is up now. Blackbirds are singing their end-of-winter trills, and a lemon-yellow light infiltrates Liverpool Road from the side streets, dazzling the first pedestrians.

Before going to the office, he does thirty laps of the pool as usual, punctuating them with a few dives. Being chaste and taciturn, Murphy avoids eyeing the few women thrashing in the water, who, in any case, aren't in the least interested in him. He gets dressed again as quickly as he can, not all that sorry to be reunited with his work bag, his three-piece suit—he's chosen a herringbone fabric—and his Bostonian austerity, all fragments of his identity.

THIS MORNING THE offices and corridors at the agency seem as empty as if there's been a fire alarm.

Feeling slightly disoriented and having checked his watch to see that it is indeed nine o'clock, Murphy goes upstairs in the elevator and sits himself down in the cafeteria in the hope that someone will come to find him, concerned not to have seen him yet. While he waits he buys a muffin from the vending machine, starts leafing through the newspapers, and, being averagely paranoid, wonders whether his colleagues have decided to put him in quarantine.

After a while—he's on his second muffin—Miss Anderson appears, thoroughly embarrassed by her own physical presence, thrusting her torso forward as she tells him that the meeting's started and that, this time, they really are counting on him.

"Are you coming or not?" she asks impatiently.

As if he had a choice.

They're all there: market operators, dealers, brokers, agents, lawyers, analysts—the wan faces of two hundred bank employees—neatly lined up on their molded plastic chairs while the losses figures for the last two months scroll on the screen (nine million, twelve million, twenty-two and a half million) like an avalanche in slow motion.

John Borowitz is perched on the stage, commenting on the results and flicking his silvery locks like an orchestra conductor rehearsing *The Flying Dutchman.*

"It's particularly noticeable that between the eighth and twenty-fifth of this month, ten million pounds in hedge funds went up in smoke," he carries on, talking into his microphone while across the silent room faces imperceptibly fall apart, because everyone's beginning to realize the game is up.

The most distraught have already left the room.

"If you're okay with it, we'll exfiltrate you to Philadelphia in September or October," Borowitz whispers to him afterward in the doorway. "I still have faith in you."

Murphy remains silent.

Professionally, he hasn't lost out. It's just that there are other, more personal factors that he finds quite difficult to assess, given the circumstances.

IT'S LATE MORNING and the cafeteria, usually the nerve center for million-dollar tip-offs and conjuring tricks of variable quality, has swiftly filled with haggard-looking people drifting in aimless circles clutching their cups.

Murphy's used to keeping to himself; he orders two coffees and fills himself a large glass of water from the fountain, curbing his longing for alcohol, before going to console Kate, who's just been let go.

"Well, it was really worth your while working so hard and waking up at four in the morning!" he teases her gently.

But she seems to have accepted the situation. It turns out that recently—in addition to the loathsome atmosphere at the agency—she was so bored by her colleagues' conversation that she even developed an interest in astrology and minor royals in magazines, as if she were going a bit senile.

While he stares distractedly at Kate's charmless features, Murphy can't help thinking about his boss's offer but doesn't know what decision to make about Nora. The very mention of returning to the States seems to have let his anxieties in through a little door in his brain, where they are now weaving their paralyzing web.

He just can't see himself living and working in Philadelphia.

In any event, even if he does have to leave his position in London, at least, like Saint Paul, he can say he hasn't ruined anyone, exploited anyone, or done any wrong.

It's in Saint Paul's Second Epistle to the Corinthians.

People think he's being sanctimonious, but it's just that waiting has probably become his only religion.

"Hope we'll see each other again before you go," says Kate with her feeble antiheroine smile.

"I haven't left yet," he says, inwardly regretting not taking a shot of alcohol.

He gets the feeling it would have made his hands shake with joy.

38

It is now Monday, April 11. Instead of putting himself on hold and trying to monitor his behavior for a few days, just long enough to lay his wife's suspicions to sleep, Blériot is hardly back from Turin before he gets it into his head to go see Nora. As proof that his personality-splitting abilities are intact, he's already forgotten all the resolutions he made there.

So, not wanting to listen to the voice of reason or to think the question over any further, he's dialed her number and invited himself over to Les Lilas on Tuesday and Wednesday, because Sabine is traveling to Strasbourg.

At this stage, we can probably cite maladjusted polygamy.

HE'S JUST CUTTING across the garden, with its water-logged path and tall grass indicating springtime, when she appears on the doorstep, looking incredibly pale in her black mini dress, with her cell phone clamped to her ear.

"I won't be a minute," she calls, waving at him to come into the house.

The red glow of evening lights the succession of rooms inside all the way to the stairs. Blériot sits on the sofa in the living room for a while, looking over toward the window as if at a colorless painting, waiting for Nora to finish. From what he can hear of her conversation, he gets the impression she's talking to her sister in London.

She comes into the room ten minutes later, visibly on edge, with a strange nervous smile that seems to hover in front of her, a couple of inches from her face.

"I'm guessing your trip to Italy went well," she says, pouring him a glass of wine.

Thanks to his special antennae, Blériot immediately knows that she wants a fight, and he's surprised to find himself dreading what lies in store—he actually has a prickling sensation along his spine. He's too familiar with her propensity for tantrums and her tiresome penchant for drama not to want the situation to start degenerating. Particularly as he suspects she's already in a slight state of alcoholic intoxication.

In his haste to break things up, he suggests they put off this conversation until later and go for a walk and find a café terrace to enjoy the sunshine.

But she doesn't want to go for a walk.

"You still haven't told me about your trip," she insists, giving him a homicidal stare that he pretends not to notice.

"There's not much to tell, it was a trip like any other," he replies, his eyes pinned on the label of the bottle of Reisling.

There then follows a long silence, during which they stand facing each other, in profile in front of the window, their glasses of white wine in their hands, in a photographic calm that seems to be preceding the storm.

IN THE MEANTIME, hoping to give an impression of composure, Blériot busies himself adjusting the picture on the television in the living room—he recognizes a young Ricky Nelson on his dappled horse—because there's slightly too much contrast for his liking.

"Switch it off," she orders him, crushing her cigarette in the bottom of the ashtray as if it were a cockroach, then pouring herself more wine and positioning herself in front of him, charged with negative electricity.

No getting away from it, he thinks, having wisely taken a few steps toward the door; it's written somewhere that whatever he does and whatever he concedes to, they'll never manage to settle into a normal existence, a peaceful existence with no dramas or fears or extravagances.

"You were meant to be spending a night or two in Turin," she begins, "and you stayed four days, maybe even five. What was it, my darling? A second honeymoon?"

He feels as if the alcohol has gone straight to his head.

First of all, they stayed three days and he can't see why, even if they did stay an extra day, she should be so upset, he says, because it was mainly a business trip.

"Business," she chokes while her anger rapidly pulls her features into a scowl, and her lips start to tremble and her voice to waver.

"You are such a bastard, such a bastard!"

Even though he was prepared for what was coming, Blériot suddenly looks at her in terror as if there were toads spewing from her mouth.

He's happy to take responsibility and try to listen to her, he replies calmly, but he'd like her to lower her voice by two octaves first, because right now the whole neighborhood's listening in.

What he would actually like to explain to her, he continues, on the condition that she pays a teensy bit of attention, is that he's already unhappy enough with his wife and tired enough of all the lies he has to tell her, not to need Nora getting involved in their marriage. When it's none of her business.

"None of my business"—she picks up on this—"what am I doing with you, then? What are we doing together? Why do you think I came back to Paris? To find some low-paying job? To visit museums?"

And she carries on like this, firing off questions at machine-gun speed and telling him for the third or fourth time—which doesn't fail to disturb him—that, whatever happens, there's a connection between them for life.

"There's no need to be pointlessly melodramatic," Blériot interjects, having waited some time for an opportunity to get a word in. "I'm just telling you about my relationship with Sabine and the trip I went on with her because I couldn't not tell you."

"Yes you could," she says stubbornly.

All right, he could, he concedes. But he can also say nothing, if she likes, and change the subject, aware that she can't bear not having the last word anyway.

HE'S GONE INTO the kitchen to get another bottle of wine and to take two aspirins with a black coffee, because migraine-type shooting pains are beginning to obscure his view of things. In the refrigerator he happens across moldy tomatoes and zucchinis, some frankfurters past their sell-by date, and a pork chop as cold as death itself.

His headache hammering hard between his eyes, Blériot goes to stand by the window for a while to tip his head back and watch swathes of luminous clouds trundling over the roofs. He's also hoping to absent himself from his own life. But try as he might to hold his breath and make his mind go blank by concentrating on the limits of his visual field, his powers don't kick in this time—it's not the first time. With his head out the window, he can still hear Nora's voice behind him, hurling insults from the next room. While he waits for her to calm down, he lingers a bit longer in the kitchen, sitting on a stool like a boxer recovering between rounds.

It's incredible, he realizes, just how much damage this girl can do to him. You would think she was one of those hallucinogenic substances that dilate our perceptions while simultaneously destroying our nerve cells.

And yet he knows he's incapable of walking out on her, slamming the door behind him. So he knows he'll have to go on tolerating this screaming, these recriminations, and these repeated fits of jealousy, and that it will all probably go on for months or years, until neither of them has a single breath of love left.

He knows and he no longer knows.

In fact, he no longer knows what on earth he should do.

WHILE HE IS turned away, looking for his telephone— he must have left it in his jacket pocket—she's practically emptied half the bottle by herself.

"I suppose that was your mother," she says.

"No, my wife," he replies, taking her glass away.

Even though he's in no position to be moralizing, he does allow himself to point out that she drinks far too much and that it's certainly not helping the conversation.

"You stop sleeping with your wife and I'll stop drinking. Fair's fair," she says, taking another glass with a sly little smile.

The problem is that, until there's proof to the contrary, he and Sabine are still officially husband and wife and therefore, he reminds her, they're meant to live as such.

"Well then, make her not be your wife anymore and come and live with me. It's not as if there isn't room for you."

"Funny," he says, amused, "I would never have thought of that. Anyway, Neville, that sounds very much like an ultimatum."

"It is one," she confirms.

With his deferred emotions, Blériot takes a little while to react and to tell her what he thinks of how she's behaving. Because he is well within his rights to be surprised that a girl as emancipated as she is, who has one lover in London and another in Paris, and who's apparently given herself to lots of boys (mostly twice rather than just once), can now resent him for living as husband and wife with his own wife.

"You make me sick, Louis, you make me so sick you can't imagine," she says slowly, almost dreamily, while he gradually gauges the extent of the disaster.

It's not what he meant to say, he replies.

"You make me puke, Louis, you make me sick," she goes on, still just as slowly, before suddenly exploding under the effects of an emotional pressure cooker and screaming as she launches herself at him.

HE STEPPED BACK too late.

He realizes in a flash that his nose is bleeding and he doesn't even have a handkerchief on him.

Overrun by a surge of hatred, a desire to kill or disfigure him, she's moving about the room at frightening speed, one arm extended like a saber.

She's completely out of control, he thinks, struggling to protect himself a little.

"Louis, you make me sick," she says again when it's over and she's leaning on the table trying to catch her breath while he dabs his nose with a towel. "You don't understand anything."

Driven by a sort of clinical curiosity, Blériot has come over to her to study her deformed, slightly contorted face, which for a second likens her to some insidious, unbalanced infantile entity.

"What the hell's happening to you?" he asks, increasingly worried, and at that exact moment she snatches up the telephone to smack him full in the face.

Now his mouth's bleeding.

Before things get completely out of hand, Blériot takes hold of her arms and puts her in an armlock, pinning her against the wall. She then slides down to the ground, and, when he sees her lying dislocated on the floor, he has the heartbreaking feeling of having shot a deer.

He picks her up, and she eventually slumps onto the sofa, probably floored by the alcohol, and huddles against him, pressing her face to his and letting so many tears flow over him that anyone would think they were both crying.

"You're completely crazy," he tells her gently as he strokes her hair, and she cries with her jaw hanging slackly as if in agreement.

• • •

IN A SPIRIT of reconciliation, he gets up to go to the bathroom for a large glass of water and a sedative—she swallows it without batting an eyelid. Then they stand by the window. So a moment of respite, one poor fragile moment of respite has introduced itself into the continuum of their suffering, one during which they both hold their breath.

Now they're sitting side-by-side again on the living room sofa, in complete silence, gripped by a nameless, telepathic dread that it's already too late because this time they've gone too far.

"It's my fault," Nora says eventually, pressing her fists into her cheeks in mortification. "I have no right to treat you like that, it's no way to behave." She starts to cry again, and, hiccupping like a child, she accuses herself of being a liar, selfish, possessive, destructive—especially destructive—and perversive.

"I don't think the word 'perversive' even exists," he reassures her, going back to get another glass of water and a towel to wipe her tear-stained face, and to rub his own forehead and temples with analgesic cream.

"You calm down now and try to get some sleep," he advises, but he can't help himself—he's as sick as she is—watching her gasping little breasts rising and falling beneath the fabric of her dress.

"Do you still want me?" she asks all of a sudden, turning to him with such an infinite clarity in her pale hazel eyes that it frightens him.

"I don't know why you're asking me that," he says defensively, backed up to the wall with his dead man's erection.

"Because I was wondering."

He takes her into the bedroom and lies her down on the bed, removing her little dress—she struggles limply with her legs—and aware that this isn't what he should be doing at all; it's not the appropriate response and she's likely to feel even more lost than before.

But he's so lost himself that he can't see what else he could do right now.

Later, in the middle of the night, Blériot turns to her and whispers in her ear: "I'm leaving you!" like a bullet fired at point-blank range—*bang!*—carving through her sleeping brain.

39

Murphy didn't say anything. He settled for watching her lean her head forward and pinch cherries from a white stoneware dish on the garden table. The others, he seems to think, were talking around them about Tony Blair's recent conversion to Roman Catholicism.

"Would you like one?" she offered, indicating the plate. "They're perfect."

So he reached out his hand to take a handful of black cherries, and his right arm inadvertently brushed past hers.

It was absolutely meaningless, but to this day—that's his hyperactive memory at work—Murphy remembers that moment with great precision. Particularly the golden hairs on her arm and the slight prickling feeling he got from the contact, like a small shock.

As she was trying to listen to the conversation about Tony Blair—and he loathed Tony Blair, even as a neo-Catholic—he pointed out that her blue dress changed color as subtly as Peau d'Âne's "color of time" dress in Jacques Demy's film, and she immediately withdrew into her shell.

He didn't let this put him off—he hardly recognizes himself there—and went on to say he had always loved Demy's films, although, as it happens, he wasn't sure how the French pronounced his name.

"Demi," she said, spitting a cherry pip into her hand.

With her long neck and brown eyes, she clearly had the sort of beauty—but he didn't tell her this—that instills in men's hearts regret for the lives they'll never lead.

So he knew what he was dealing with.

Which doesn't alter the fact that, when the others stood to go for a walk to the pond and she looked as if she would follow them, he immediately fell in step behind her, thirsty for her freshness. As if he himself were a torrid, melancholy summer.

THEY WALKED IN groups of two or three—Tyron and his children in the lead—in the lyrical quiet of an English afternoon, surrounded by birdsong and the buzz of insects. In his highly subjective memory, he seems to think the air was peculiarly light that day, the trees luminous and the currents swift-flowing.

He eventually discovered—she was not exactly the talk-ative type—that her name was Nora Neville and that her sister was Tyron's best friend, Dorothy.

"I think she works for the same company as him," she added, pointing ahead to a small dark-haired girl wearing a flowery dress and a sort of pink straw boater.

"How about you, have you just arrived in London?" she asked, merely out of courtesy.

He can't remember what he said. At the time he had been living in London with Elisabeth Carlo for nearly a year, and he imagines he must have said something fairly evasive.

On the other hand, he remembers very clearly that, with no premeditation, they ended up some way behind the leading group while the people bringing up the rear with Max Barney must have turned back or cut across the fields.

At one point they stopped in front of an electric fence, struck by the silence in that particular spot. A herd of deer lying farther up the meadow watched them point-edly over the top of the grass, and around them were five or six gray hares and a black horse with feathered feet, as if every creature of field and forest were holding its breath as this girl passed, perhaps mistaking her for Julie Andrews.

"I'm worried the others will be waiting for us," she said quietly, as if to avoid frightening the animals.

He thought it was only about another mile to the pond.

. . .

THEY WERE NOW walking across a green meadow with curves as soft as a golf course, and along the way she did tell him that quite recently she'd gone off to live in France, the way some people go off in search of themselves—she had French ancestors—but after eight months in Paris she hadn't achieved anything. She still didn't know who she was, or what she really wanted.

"And what did you do all on your own in Paris?" he asked innocently, before realizing that—out of shyness or an evasive strategy—she had a curious habit of never answering his questions directly and not finishing her sentences. All the same, with each new question Murphy began to see an image of her emerging, like playing connect-the-dots to complete a picture. The image was of a strange, fairly unstable girl who was both sassy and oddly taciturn—apparently she'd just broken up with someone—and who operated under a very high coefficient of narcissism.

So why didn't he backtrack? Which part of his detection system wasn't working?

Why did no alarm bells start ringing to warn him he was going to suffer so much?

Now that they had rejoined Tyron and his group on the edge of the pond, the contrast between the banalities they had to exchange with the others and their silent intimacy may have been too new and too exciting for him to want to project himself any further.

The only thing he was sure of was that he was most likely coming to the end of his time with Elisabeth Carlo.

"I KNEW I'D find you here," says Borowitz, walking onto the terrace. "It's always easier to think in fresh air."

"I don't know," says Murphy, still lost in his trance of memories.

"Well, I hope you'll make the right decision and I can count on you in September."

"I expect so," he replies, glancing around the rooftops—the sky is an oceanic blue—and the glass façades along the embankment.

To the east, over by Canary Wharf, share values are still scrolling across the Reuters tower as if nothing has changed.

"So I can leave you feeling reassured. I'm convinced we'll meet up again in Philadelphia," says Borowitz, crushing Murphy's hand in a surge of emotion.

Downstairs, his colleagues are finishing any last business and starting to put their things in boxes like resigning civil servants. The cafeteria's deserted.

Since Miss Anderson was hospitalized—there's talk of an embolism—her little office looks like a museum where everything has been carefully preserved as it was; her computer, her pencils, her diary, her pack of Lucky Strikes, and the picture of her cat, Bloomsbury.

Emptiness seems to be piling on emptiness.

• • •

MURPHY SPENDS THE rest of the afternoon feeling strained and alone as he sorts through files on his computer, until Kate Meellow appears out of the blue.

"Officially, for the next eighteen days I'm still part of this company," she tells him, perching on a corner of his desk and insisting he tells her in great detail about the latest events affecting him.

"I think I'm going to go to Philadelphia," he says gloomily as he puts his things in his bag.

"Of course, it's your choice, but I've read that in New York former traders have been reduced to selling shirts at Bergdorf Goodman."

"Well, I'll sell shirts, then," he says as they leave the building and he notices he has a text from Nora (*Murphy, I need you urgently*).

So she *is* in London, as Vicky predicted.

Back at his apartment, Murphy falls prey to his analytical prognostications again and wonders whether Nora's trying to say that she needs him for himself, or whether it's just a malicious way of appealing to his charity and getting two or three thousand dollars out of him. If that's the case—and, sadly, he thinks it is—he'll add another thousand dollars as a bonus, so she understands that charity is always greater than malice or venality.

After that it's up to her if she wants to keep thinking otherwise.

He will have given her everything he has to give.

40

H e called her all day, then resigned himself to leaving
a message on her voice mail. The next morning he
started again from nine o'clock, without much hope, calling the landline this time.

"Raymond speaking," a tired-sounding man's voice re-
plied unexpectedly before hanging up, probably thinking
it was a wrong number.

Blériot stood for a moment with his arm held out, his
telephone transformed into a block of ice; then he got ready
quickly and sprinted over to les Lilas, feeling as if he was
living a continuous recapitulation.

A large black car with its doors gaping open is parked
by the entrance to the house, and a man in velvet pants
is buried from the waist up in the trunk. On the far
side of the car, laden with bags of clothes, is a tall blond

woman in glasses who watches suspiciously as Blériot comes closer.

"Is Nora here?" he asks, introducing himself.

"I think she must have made a run for it the day before yesterday, but at the crack of dawn. When we got here the house was empty and the kitchen was in a horrendous state," she tells him with a sardonic little laugh that feels spiteful.

"I'm her cousin Barbara," she explains. Exactly as he thought.

Beyond the hedge and the roses that are past their best, he can see empty bottles poking out of a wooden case, next to piles of books and magazines heaped straight onto the ground. In the background a garden chair he's never noticed before has been left standing in the middle of the garden.

"Raymond Hemling," the man says, emerging from the trunk.

"Do you have any idea where she may have gone?" asks Blériot, still studying the empty chair.

(He's imagining her saying: *What are you complaining about, Louis? You've got what you wanted.*)

THE MAN AND woman consult each other with a brief glance before shrugging their shoulders as if to say, to be honest, right now, that's the least of their concerns.

"In all likelihood, she must have gone back to London to squat in her sister's apartment or with one of her boyfriends," cousin Barbara speculates, looking at him inquisitively.

But he hasn't turned a hair.

Quite the opposite, he's actually rather detached, almost cocky, leaning on the hood of the car with his small cigar in the corner of his mouth while Raymond sheds fat beads of sweat as he hauls cardboard boxes.

And yet he knows perfectly well—somewhere else, in another circuit of his mind—that it's highly likely he'll never see Nora at Les Lilas again and that, as the laws of probability are no more negotiable than those of gravity, soon all he'll have left are his eyes for crying.

While he watches them empty the house (what are they planning to do with it?), Blériot suddenly feels his pain spring as if from a severed artery.

Then it flows in a constant stream.

He just has time to move a few steps and bend over to catch his breath.

"Okay, good luck, my friend." Barbara calls out her delayed revenge as she gets into the car.

THAT EVENING BLÉRIOT'S sitting in a hotel room facing the television, with his legs splayed across the bed and the remote control in his hand, as devoid of responses as if he were brain-dead.

He walked all the way to Buttes-Chaumont in a state of shock, but Léonard was out or asleep so he just kept going and went into the first hotel he found.

Now he's drinking beer straight from the bottle and

watching images from outer space. When the two astronauts are about to climb back into their separate rockets, they turn around weightlessly and look at each other for a long time— a crimson light flares over their visors for a moment—before giving the tiniest wave and returning to their space vessels, knowing they'll never see each other again.

Blériot has turned off the television, thrown his shoes on the floor, and lain down in the dark with his head tipped back, to dream of his unhappiness.

He's lying there, still awake with his eyes pinned to the white window, his arms by his sides, plagued by this haunting thought, as insistent as water dripping into a bucket: Nora's gone and he's going to live without her.

He has a feeling he won't be able to. It'll be too cold.

It will get dark at noon and an arctic wind will blow through deserted streets. Pipes will burst and weeds will grow through cracks in the cement, people will block every opening with mattresses, and in the end, numbed animals will lie down to die, having never known Nora.

That's what the world will be like without her.

IN THIS QUASI-HALLUCINATORY state he finds the strength to get up and go over to the window for some fresh air (the heartache has made him nauseous) while, on the far side of the boulevard, the elevated railway cuts through a sleeping world, lighting the treetops all the way to Stalingrad station.

Filtering the darkness with his eyes, Blériot now notices a taxi parked in the street below, its inside light on, its front door partially open, and its engine still running.

Perhaps she's waiting for him.

I must go down, he thinks belatedly as the car sets off—and the night closes in behind it.

Because despair has its own peculiar acceleration, Blériot then falls into a sort of stupor, lying there with his teeth chattering as if he were laughing.

The digital screen now reads 01:07.

The worst of it must be over. People are going to their rooms. From time to time he hears the sound of the elevator traveling in its glazed shaft like a hypnotic pendulum.

Without realizing it, he's turned onto his stomach, his arms stretched in front of him on either side of his pillow, like a swimmer with a breathing tube discreetly flicking his feet to carve through silent black waters before dropping through layer after layer of undersea trenches.

He wakes at daybreak, his muscles stiff from his underwater endeavors, and immediately calls his wife (because he *is* still married), afraid she may have gone looking for him. She must have turned off her phone.

While he waits before trying her again, Blériot looks at the empty bed with the shape of his body outlined in the sheets, as if taking an imprint of his own disappearance, then he falls asleep on the chair.

41

When he goes home and finds himself face-to-face with his wife in the living room, he has a strange, chillingly precise feeling that he's arrived too late.

They exchange a rather stilted greeting, and Blériot reads in her face a sad and solemn expression that frightens him. She's sitting on the edge of the sofa, her hands flat on her knees and her eyes hidden behind dark glasses, and she's obviously waiting for him to provide some explanations. From her silence, Blériot can tell it won't be easy and this time there won't be any way out.

"Yesterday evening," he begins, clearing his throat, "I felt terrible and I thought I'd better not come home. I took a room in a hotel near Stalingrad. To be honest, I was completely lost."

"You know, it's in that film by Eric Rohmer: *Qui a deux*

maisons perd la raison," she reminds him almost chirpily. "I'm guessing your lovely English girl was with you."

He shakes his head while something cold and dark seeps through him like a soul-destroying memory.

"That's just it." He jumps to his defense; he may well have told her too much about Nora, or not enough.

Actually, they've split for good and that's why—at least just this once he's not lying to her—he didn't have the strength to come home last night.

"Am I supposed to comfort you?" she asks, getting up for her cigarettes.

Blériot shakes his head again, knowing there won't be any more comfort for anyone. In fact, since he arrived home, he's felt as if a general climate of distress has been hanging over them.

"You know, Louis, while I was waiting for you last night I reached a decision," she tells him, speaking so seriously that his throat constricts. "A difficult and completely uni-lateral decision for which I take full responsibility," she ac-knowledges, "but I've dealt with too much and I just want to have a quiet life now."

She sketches out a summary account of their life together and its resulting collapse, and Blériot listens quite motion-less, leaning against the wall, his muscles paralyzed, feeling the blood flowing through his veins one drop at a time.

"To be absolutely frank," she tells him, "there was a time when I regretted not having children with you, but I don't re-gret it now; I think you would have made a hopeless father."

"Sabine, you don't know what you're saying."

"You're right, I don't know what I'm saying anymore. Still," she concludes, "I've decided that when I get back from my parents' house—I have to go there for a couple of days—you will have packed your bags and left the apartment. I honestly think it's the most sensible solution for both of us," she adds, enunciating each syllable separately.

"A couple of days," he echoes, stuck to the wall by his pain like a burned moth.

Then what?

THEY WILL HAVE been together ten years, minus a couple of days.

"If you want some coffee, it's on the table," she says.

This ominous event has obviously been casting its shadow over them for a long time, but Blériot kept pretending not to see it. Despite his pessimism and his cynicism, he couldn't truly believe that they would separate someday, and that they too would not be spared the pitiful banality of ending like that.

"When all's said and done, we're no smarter than anyone else," he points out to distract her briefly from her plans and embark on a dispassionate debate about the uncertainties of married life.

"I never claimed we were any smarter than anyone else," she replies as she tidies her hair in the bathroom mirror. "We were just unhappier than them. And that's why we never did any entertaining. Remember?"

He remembers.

What he finds ridiculous and unfair, he says, and now he too is speaking deliberately slowly, is that they're leaving each other exactly when he's cured and repentant, and when they could start over together, here or somewhere else, abroad.

"But we've spent our whole lives starting over," she interrupts him, "and you know that's just talk. Am I right, or am I wrong?"

Blériot is behind her, sitting on the edge of the bathtub, and they're watching each other in the mirror. Each staring at the other's reflection as if talking to his or her double, to the person they love and have lost and whose eye they're trying to catch in the depths of that mirror.

"Do you have anything else to say?" she asks in a neutral voice.

"No," he acknowledges, feeling he can hear the little click indicating that the present has just become the past.

"Just one thing," he adds at the last minute.

He wants to apologize, before she leaves, for loving her so badly, and to promise he'll wait for her as long as he can, for years if need be.

"But you've already promised me that dozens of times, and, anyway, I really don't want anyone waiting for me anymore," she admits, moving aside.

"It *is* tough for the self-same man," he points out with a forced smile, "to be both made redundant and evicted at the same time."

"That's the way it is," she says, suddenly looking at him with no anger or resentment, but not wanting him to add another word.

So he doesn't.

"Right, I need to hurry," she announces, as if the case is closed and she has other things to do.

Outside, rain and the leaden sky above the rue de Belleville add to the end-of-the-world feeling that hangs over the whole apartment.

Blériot is standing by the window, not knowing what to do with himself. He's still tempted to try to stop her, to grab her bodily and kiss her, but what with his slow reactions and the speed with which she's closing her travel bag, it's clear that time is now moving at two different rates and he has little chance of catching up with her.

"Sabine, come back!" he cries inanely down the stairs. From the astonished expression on her face when she turns to look at him, he abruptly grasps the fact that he no longer exists for anyone.

When it's over—after her taxi has left in the rain—he slumps over, bent double on the toilet, with his trousers down and his tongue lolling right out like a dog's.

BY THE END of the afternoon it's stopped raining. His huge African neighbor and one of his friends have popped their heads through the skylight like two astrologers.

Happy astrologers, that is.

Meanwhile, Blériot's gazing at his wife's things scattered around him—her bags, her shoes, her stacks of files, her boxes of photos, her Pistoletto catalog—with an appalling sense of waste.

Soon he will tiptoe out of the apartment, leaving a good-bye note on her desk and handing the keys to the doorman, and then he will have nothing left of their life together, absolutely nothing, as if their two trajectories' meeting has merely been an optical illusion.

Only their unhappiness might live on after them, like a body suspended in the air in that apartment.

Blériot doesn't want to stay here a moment longer, and while he tries to reach a decision about where to go, he piles his meager possessions into a suitcase and takes a few personal effects, a computer, and two dictionaries that go everywhere with him—she'll cope with the rest—before putting the suitcase in the trunk of the car.

When he drives away, his sorrow descends on him like a blade of light. He'd almost forgotten it.

The sky's blue again, the air springlike.

He stops for a moment on the place de la République, just long enough to gather his thoughts and adjust his earphones—he does still have Massenet, at least—then he heads slowly, cautiously toward the Grands Boulevards, watching his image disappearing in shadowy shop windows.

42

In between jobs, I might come and see you in Philadelphia," she says, taking his hand.

Murphy opens his mouth to speak, then, disconcerted, says nothing. She seems unrecognizable, or at least so different from a few months ago that he has to make a whole series of hasty adjustments and transpositions in order to pick up the thread of their story.

They're walking across Hyde Park, through lawns filled with daffodils and crocuses, while down the hill from them early risers are boating on the Serpentine. Nora's clearly not interested in any of that. For some time now she's been talking about her plans as an actor—she's just come to London for a few days—and about the personalities she hangs out with in the theater world, people she seems to be on a first-name basis with.

"Your patience is going to be rewarded at last," he congratulates her, forcing a friendly smile.

Robert Wilson, she now confides with a conspiratorial twinkle, called her from New York to say he desperately wanted her to play Anne-Marie Stretter in the fall.

"That's probably commendable, but I have absolutely no idea who Anne-Marie Stretter is, or Robert Wilson," Murphy apologizes.

After that, if everything goes according to plan, she carries on, not listening to him, she'll play the young Violaine at the Odéon Theatre in Paris.

"The young Violaine at the Odéon," he echoes, thinking he can feel the earth's heartless rotation beneath his feet.

Nora's voice, her excitement and the worrying speed with which she's talking, suddenly remind him of a particular phase in their lives when her sullen moods and low spirits were regularly followed by slightly frenetic bouts of cheerfulness that tormented him even then.

In retrospect, Murphy realizes he's always found her worrying.

Although, right now, because of his usual combination of uncertainty and delaying tactics, he can't decide whether he should tell her the truth lovingly, as Saint Paul would recommend, or leave her to her ramblings in the hopes that some vestige of common sense will bring her back to reality one day.

· · ·

"NORA, I'M A bit worried about you," he says eventually.

"Worried about me?" she asks, astonished. "Why do you say that?"

"I don't know, intuition," he says, deciding not to explain, as they carry on walking side-by-side over the lawns.

For the first time since he met her, Murphy no longer feels anything in her presence except pity and despondency. Despite her anorexic pallor, she still has a sort of poignant beauty that devastates him.

He wishes he could believe she's achieved what she wanted with her life and it's no longer his problem.

At the moment she's telling him a muddled story—and this is probably why she wanted to see him—about a payment she still hasn't received and some rent she absolutely has to pay or she'll lose her apartment.

"Is it a lot of money?" he interrupts, eager to cut the conversation short but also trying to make her understand that he's not exactly living the high life either.

"Two thousand five hundred," she says quietly.

"If you like, I can give you a bit more," he offers, taking out his checkbook.

For two seconds, two tiny consoling seconds, he glimpses the radiation of her smile.

Then it's over.

Their whole story's behind them.

After gratifying him with a token kiss, Nora has left, and, with a heavy heart, Murphy watches for a long time as she walks across the park, looking about her in every direction like a disoriented crow.

WITH HIS BACKPACK hanging from one shoulder, he walks along the park railings, feeling the moist wind swirling around his legs. Apart from a few early-morning walkers, Buttes-Chaumont Park is empty, the swings covered up, the gardeners busy with their planting.

It is just after nine o'clock. Tannenbaum's waiting for him on the landing, leaning over the banister in his dressing gown.

"Blériot, my sweetheart, I was worried about you. Why didn't you come yesterday evening? You know I have to leave."

"I'll explain later."

Luggage is piled up in the corridor, the keys hanging behind the door where they can be seen, along with instruction manuals for appliances and telephone numbers in case of an emergency.

"I've told the caretaker, she'll bring you the mail. Make yourself at home now," Léonard says in a paternal voice, dropping into an armchair with a slight grimace of pain.

Blériot notices his swollen legs, his reedlike neck, his large transparent ears like those of a waxwork, but makes no comment and doesn't try to persuade him to put off his trip until he's better.

Because he knows he won't get better.

"I'd rather you told me about your disappointments in love," Léonard says, reading his thoughts. "Remember I'm your appointed spiritual adviser."

Except that this morning, in this state, straight out of bed, with his bag and his dictionaries under his arm, he honestly doesn't feel like going to confession.

"I'd like you to make me a coffee first, Leo."

"WELL?" ASKS HIS adviser. "You know I'm curious and I won't let you off that easily."

"It's an exhausting story," Blériot tells him, opting to go straight to the end: he's now a single man, dumped by his mistress and thrown out of his house by his wife—he's always known that the revenge of the one would precipitate the revenge of the other—and, for the first time in his life, he feels he's reached rock bottom.

"Which is a difficult but instructive experience," he admits.

"You see, my lovely, I'm afraid I don't really understand your heterosexual misery," says Léonard. "I really must be from a different species, with different pleasures and different kinds of suffering."

"On top of all that," Blériot continues, not believing a word of what Léonard has said, "I now find myself the proud owner of the sum total of two shirts, one pair of shoes, and fifty-seven euros in my bank account."

"I left you some bills in the dresser drawer, but if it's not enough, you can ask me for whatever you want," Léonard tells him, apparently convinced that this is a case of monomania.

"Would five hundred be too much?" asks Blériot at the precise moment that, in a London park, Nora's tapping into Murphy's pocket—they could be a couple of professional cadgers in action.

Blériot, just like his accomplice, doesn't bat an eyelid as he pockets the five hundred euros, already mentally subtracting half of it to deal with the most urgent issues; then he listens while Léonard gets dressed and tells him the details of his new idyll—he really does fall in love at the drop of a hat—with Omar and Samir.

Apparently, they're two fashionable cousins from Brittany, officially students, vaguely soccer players, and they've invited him to stay in their house in Casablanca.

"Apart from the time I devote to these boys, my life feels meaningless," admits Léonard, seeing Blériot's skepticism.

"It's up to you, but, given the state you're in, I'd still recommend you be careful."

"I've thought of that, can you believe it. I'm going to have to leave you, my dear, flawed friend," says Léonard, coming over all seventeenth-century again, "and the perils in which we both find ourselves make this separation all the more vexing."

"I'm sure everything'll be fine," Blériot reassures him, carrying his things onto the landing while Léonard, who feels constrained to travel dressed up like puss-in-boots, puts on his cloak and wide-brimmed hat.

"You know, my handsome," he says, kissing Blériot, "I'd have liked to end my days with you."

"Don't say that."

"I wanted to tell you. Anyway, it won't kill me, as far as I know."

"No," says Blériot.

A few minutes later he's all alone, sitting on a chair in the living room, gazing vacantly into the aquatic morning light.

43

He sleeps constantly. Some days, he sleeps twelve to fifteen hours at a time, huddled on his bed, his hair stuck down with sweat, overcome by a chilling lethargy. It's as if, so long as he refuses to get up, his core temperature is dropping one degree at a time, and his extremities are going cold. These are probably some of the psycho-physiological effects his pain is having on his body—but he feels too tired to think about it.

For days now the curtains have been drawn, the door locked, the intercom unplugged. The room where he's sleeping in the depths of the apartment is as hermetic and silent as a sensory deprivation tank. A digital alarm clock projects the time onto the ceiling (02:13 . . . 11:03 . . . 17:12 . . . 04:21) as if he were orbiting around the earth like Laika the dog.

Every now and then, when the telephone manages to wake him—it's never for him—Blériot gets to his feet shivering, takes a few steps across the apartment, and stays for a while stationed by the window like an astronaut shirking behind his porthole. It won't stop raining outside.

After drinking a cup of tea he goes straight back to bed, nestled in his crumpled sheets, closing his eyes and pushing with his feet to bury himself once more in the amniotic warmth of sleep, until he feels himself gradually tipping into the coils of a dark sinkhole.

And he sets off into orbit again.

SOMETIMES HE WAKES all by himself right in the middle of the day, tormented by a headache that gives him the sudden sensation that he's thinking with only one hemisphere of his brain. He decides to take two or three aspirins and have a scalding hot shower.

When, much later, the suffering has passed, he can get so far as brushing his teeth—his incisors have gone yellow like an animal's—and then shaving, by the open window, in the soft hubbub of the afternoon, as slowly and calmly as an opium addict. While he's there, he takes the opportunity to explore Léonard's medicine cabinet, and to relieve him of some Valium.

As he waits to get back to sleep, Blériot lies down on the bed with his hands crossed behind his neck, periodically in the grip of sexual desires with no specific object, like when he was thirteen or fourteen years old. At the rate that he's regressing, it's actually quite possible he'll soon end up bed-ridden, abandoned by the world, his body and soul ossified, and his mind preoccupied with libidinous longings.

And, when all's said and done, he'll know he had it coming to him.

THEN ONE DAY he stops sleeping. He's exhausted his sleep account.

He stays there on top of the sheets, detached, slightly doleful, his gaze turned toward the gaps in the blinds, which let through slender oblongs of gray light. Occasionally he hears a little girl laughing on the third or fourth floor, he listens to her laughter pealing like a little bell ringing in the wind, and the clarity of his senses reassures him about his mental state.

Outside it's raining so lightly, so imperceptibly, that when he opens the window to feel the fresh air on his face, he has to put his arm out to convince himself it is actually raining. It's as if, now that he no longer has anything to hope for or anyone to wait for, the world has finally been restored to him in its objectivity, with its empty streets, its wet dogs, its unknown couples, and its blossoming trees, and his field of consciousness is suddenly the wider for it.

If he didn't spend his days wondering what on earth he was going to do to fill the time, he'd be almost happy.

From time to time he does a bit of shopping in the local mini-market, at the end of the rue de Meaux, preferably late in the morning, because that's when the lazy, the idle, and the antisocial are there, and, all in all, he feels he sort of belongs to the same family. Besides, like them, he's very partial to those endless American series that he watches on a loop on television, telling himself that so long as he doesn't know the last word—and that won't happen anytime soon—nothing serious can happen to him.

On the few days when it doesn't rain, he catches himself midafternoon walking toward Les Lilas, taking the exact same route he used to, stopping in the same places, as if suffering from some barely suppressed ritualism. He parks himself by the gate to the house with his forehead against the metalwork—the lawn's crawling with weeds and wild grasses—as he remembers those evenings when Nora used to appear in the doorway, with her oversize shirt or her headscarf, like a young Russian peasant in a film by Eisenstein.

All around him the neighborhood hasn't moved, and he sometimes contemplates the fact that he doesn't actually have a single photo, a single piece of evidence that it wasn't a dream; perhaps if he rang the buzzer at a neighboring house they would tell him the place had been uninhabited for years.

WITH EACH PASSING day, thanks to his strange ability to bounce back, Blériot eventually emerges from this post-separation crisis fairly downtrodden but intact, still in possession of all his faculties.

He's been feeling a little more vigorous, or at least closer to his normal state, for a while, so he's even turned on his computer. He's working at a rate of three or four hours a day, translating an American paper on various degenerations of the neuro-vegetative system—you'd have thought it was written for him—full of esoteric terms such as "neuro-chemico-tactile processes" and "colloidal microtubules" that he troops out calmly without stopping to think.

To put his heart into his work a bit and to stimulate his own motor apparatus, he smokes and drinks pretty much nonstop while listening to Duke Ellington and his big band in the background.

When he looks up briefly from his work, he sees the evening light, muted and elegiac, coming to him along the walkways of Butte-Chaumont, and these few moments of beauty stolen from his work time are enough to afford him some contentment. Somewhere in this dull life, purged of passion and regimented by deadlines, he even finds himself thinking that he was born to live alone and translate pages of English, just as surely as the swifts perching in the trees in the park were born to swallow insects mid-flight.

In the evenings, he stands at the window smoking peacefully in sync with people sitting on café terraces or on benches along the rue Manin; it's quite a little community, each dragging on his or her cigarette as if communicating to the others through the dusky shadows with luminous signals.

Up until the evening in June when the thought that he absolutely has to go to London to find Nora—an idea that must have been buried inside the dark lobes of his brain for weeks—streaks through his head like a shooting star as he closes the window.

44

The next day—in the beginning was the deed—he's booked a seat to London with a low-budget airline, written a thank-you note to Léonard, watered the plants and cleaned the apartment from top to bottom, opening all the windows wide. Once the rooms are aired and exorcized, Blériot gathers his bits and pieces and slips away to the garage on the rue de Belleville (his wife's meant to be in Germany) to drop off some belongings and pick up his suitcase from the trunk of the car.

Committed to his mood of regeneration, he even grants himself a substantial breakfast in a brasserie and then hurries to catch the Métro to Charles de Gaulle Airport.

Leaving France suddenly feels like an acquittal, a release, or, at the very least, an alleviation of his pain. The proof of this is that, beneath his outward appearance of semi-depression, Blériot feels almost carefree again once he's inside the airport.

On the plane, the whole time he's flying over the sea, his head nods against the window as if his hypersomnia has taken over once more, while memories of Nora buried deep inside him like a microchip broadcast mental images of happier days, days when she was still impish and fun.

Coming back to reality is then all the more abrupt. The cold in the telescoping walkway, the rain-laden sky, the people waiting in lines, the bickering border police, and the rows of anonymous faces in the arrivals area: things that instantly restore his sense of his own fragility and abandonment. A sense that will materialize later in the baggage claim—after a wait of an hour and a half—when his small black suitcase is last to appear, trundling around on the conveyor belt on its own.

That evening, depressed by a thunderstorm and the deluging rain flooding the streets of London, Blériot stays shut away in his hotel room in the Barbican, lying in front of the television screen—one day he'll actually vote on *Big Brother*—while he empties the miniatures from the minibar one by one and waits patiently for the sandman.

IN THE MORNING, walking alone, he remembers Nora mentioning a café in Islington several times, somewhere she went regularly, the Bertino or Bernini—in the end it turns out to be Bernardino's; someone points it out to him at the far end of Upper Street, heading toward the old Highbury stadium.

He sits down inside for a while, not recognizing anyone but huddled in a corner, listening half heartedly to some students behind him—sound particles and flying dust motes—as he takes small sips of his first martini of the day.

The waitress is new and doesn't know any Noras. But she promises to have a word with the boss.

Blériot orders a second martini (alcohol apparently sharpens metaphysical awareness) and goes outside with his glass in his hand to make the most of a pool of sunshine on the terrace. Lost in the pleasure of his daydreams, he has no desire to talk to anyone at the moment. He watches people come and go in the street with a sort of wavering attention, his head slightly tilted, his eyes blinking as if trying to photograph the randomness of things.

The boss, a short, glum man with a striped tie, introduces himself and announces that he has a very clear recollection of Nora even though he hasn't seen her for a long time.

"She was a nice young woman, but a bit odd and eccentric," he remembers, using an obituary-like past tense that can't fail to disturb his listener until one small detail—the twin boys she sometimes used to take for walks in the area—eventually clears up the misunderstanding: they don't seem to be talking about the same Nora.

• • •

BLÉRIOT DOESN'T GIVE in to despair but hops in a taxi and goes to Camden, where she took an acting course, then to Earl's Court, where her best friend (whose name he's forgotten) lives, before crossing over the Thames, still in a taxi, and heading toward Greenwich, where her sister's supposed to have a house or an apartment.

With a tenacity he would never have thought he had in him given his generally irresolute personality, Blériot questions anyone who could possibly have known her or just had a glimpse of her around—starting with bar staff—but no one remembers her at all. You'd almost think she was transparent.

Still, he continues looking for her the following day and the day after that, walking along the streets of London against the wind, with a constant ache of missing their addiction to each other, and occasionally he ends up in driving rain in such improbable places as Lillie Road, Maida Vale, or Egypt Lane—where, instead of pyramids, he finds only a row of Indian grocery shops—without ever giving up or stopping his street-by-street pursuit of her like a pursuit for the ultimate sensation.

Until, aided and abetted by exhaustion and wishful thinking, Nora clones suddenly start appearing pretty much everywhere: a florist, a secretary in stiletto heels, a brown-eyed businesswoman, a student in a trench coat, and even an amazing schoolgirl who seems to walk without touching the ground—the latter pursued by Blériot all the way across Holland Park, until his nostalgia wears him out.

WHEN HE COMES back to Bernardino's, Blériot is still just as compulsive and can't wait to order a drink and sit down in the same spot on the terrace so that he can make the most of the fluid clarity of the morning light while he waits until the boss is good enough to devote a few minutes of his time to him.

Absorbed in his contemplation, he hasn't noticed that directly behind him there's a man sitting at a table, talking to the waitress and not taking his eyes off Blériot. After a while, this man gathers his things and he too comes out onto the terrace.

"Do you mind if I sit here?" he asks, appearing like a shadow across Blériot's field of vision.

In the time it takes Blériot to make a sketchy gesture of concession, he sees that he's facing a sort of blond giant in a three-piece suit with a pockmarked face and eyes hidden behind blue glasses.

"I'm Murphy Blomdale," he says; "you might know my name from Nora. They said you were looking for her."

His slightly nasal bass voice resonates oddly, as if emerging from the opening in a helmet.

Blériot has gone very pale; he seems to know this is the fatal moment, the moment he's been dreading so long. For a few fractions of a second he looks at Murphy with gaping eyes, before realizing he has no other resources available than to offer a handshake.

"Louis," he says, "Louis Blériot-Ringuet."

Given his state of shock, it wouldn't take much for him to try to touch the other man's arm and shoulder too, to make sure he isn't an apparition.

"TWO DOUBLE SCOTCHES," Murphy orders from the waitress, as if to celebrate the event.

Blériot now notices a timid-looking black dog lying at his feet, its nose on its paws and its rugged old coat buffeted by the wind.

"Is he yours?" he asks, patting the animal just to have something to do.

"Not at all," replies his counterpart; "dogs come running after me as soon as I set foot outside. I like them and I think they know it. Dogs have this ability to be happy, and I find that touching," he explains, removing his glasses and looking intently at Blériot with eyes as pale as a newborn baby's.

Blériot, who doesn't know what to say (he loathes dogs), also detects in his expression an area of unease that Murphy can't quite contain because a glimmer of pain keeps appearing and fading away again.

"I'm glad you came," Murphy says spontaneously, hiding behind his glasses again.

"Actually, I don't really know what I'm doing in London," Blériot admits. "I feel like I've come for an appointment and no one's expecting me."

"Nora's changed a lot since she got back from Paris," Murphy says in his strangely calm way. "She's living like a recluse at her sister Dorothy's place and I'd venture to say a visit from you would do her good, because she's very low at the moment."

"I thought she might be," says Blériot, who still remembers their last encounter at Les Lilas.

Both men then sit in silence, looking prostrate, like two widowers sitting on a park bench, each aware that he's the protagonist in a story that ended badly and it was partly his own fault.

"I suppose we have to try to put right what can still be put right," Blériot says. "Do you think her sister would agree to my coming?"

"I have no idea; she let me see her once and only once. I'd say the best thing would be to go to Greenwich—her address is here on this card—without warning," Murphy eventually advises him, getting to his feet as if he's already said enough for today.

"I hope I'll have the pleasure of seeing you again too," he adds, his voice deadened by alcohol.

45

When the time comes, his courage fails him and he feels like turning on his heel. His taxi's disappeared, so he stands outside the building for many a long minute, smoking one cigarette after another, not knowing what decision to make. Once he's on the stairs, his fears paralyze his muscles.

According to the nameplate, they live on the third floor.

"Could I possibly see Nora?" he hears himself ask a short, dark-haired woman with a rather sullen face, who he imagines is Dorothy. "My name's Louis."

"I'm not sure that's a very good idea!" a man's voice cries from behind them. "No one's even told your sister."

Then there's an awkward silence, and Blériot uses this to his advantage to slip through the half-open door.

"Come in for a minute," she eventually says reluctantly, while her husband stays at the far end of the hallway with his arms crossed, perhaps to demonstrate his disapproval when Blériot personally was all for postponing the meeting indefinitely.

Because of his modest height, his ruff of beard, and his cigar, the man has something of Sigmund Freud about him, though obviously a less profound version.

In the living room a tall, red-headed woman—who doesn't seem to have an opinion on the subject—is sorting through pills with the professional efficiency of a nurse.

"Maybe you've heard that Nora's not well," begins her sister, inviting him to sit down. "The doctor, who won't actually give us any prognosis, is talking about psychological exhaustion as a result of an impossible situation," she tells him, looking him right in the eye. "So we can try to treat the symptoms, but not the cause. Do you see what I mean? Not the cause."

Blériot, who's feeling more and more like someone brought before a criminal court, listens with his neck and shoulders rigid from the effort of concentrating, but he occasionally squirms on his chair in apprehension of what she might tell him next.

"Anyway, my friend, you can be proud of yourself, you've done the job well," Dorothy's husband concludes before slamming the door to his study to make it clear he's washing his hands of the matter.

After his initial surprise, Blériot does feel he should protest to Dorothy and challenge all these allegations concerning the abuses to which he is supposed to have submitted her sister.

"I loved her more than I've ever loved anyone," he admits very quietly, because of the nurse.

"I'll go and see if she's sleeping, but it'll probably be the last time you come to see her," she warns as she walks down the hallway ahead of him.

WHEN HE IN turn goes through the doorway into the bedroom, which is shrouded in shadow—it's a completely bare, cell-like room—Blériot feels as if he's been given a jolt from a defibrillator that knocks him back a good six feet.

Before him, he can make out a human form crouching at the end of the bed. A form that's breathing noisily. Because she's hidden beneath her sheet like someone camping in a tent, he can identify only the outline of her head and one of her legs through the fabric.

"I don't want to see you," she announces.

He's so dismayed that, for a moment, he stays rooted to a spot in the middle of the room (which smells of stale air and disinfectant), before it occurs to him to close the door for fear that the others might witness the scene.

"Did you hear me?" she asks.

Driven by a need to help her, to cure her, to reawaken her desire to live and get out of this dungeon, he goes over to the bed very softly.

"Nora, listen to me, I came to find you, I want to take you back to Paris," he whispers, risking a glance beneath the sheet and seeing an ashen arm and a hand so weak, so listless that he can't utter another word; just then the hand itself lashes out at him.

"Go away, Louis, your wife's waiting for you," she orders him in her peculiar, monotonous, slightly buzzing voice, as she recoils under her shelter again.

Blériot, now devastated, steps away from the bed and goes to sit in a chair by the window, resigned to letting her give full expression to her jealousy. But she says nothing. Apparently reassured, she's started panting quietly again under her sheet while, lost in his thoughts, Blériot looks out at the gray Thames across the street, absorbed by the sight of boats and seabirds.

"It's the room in *The Seagull*," he points out. But she doesn't reply.

What can he do for her?

She was always so hyper, so unstable, that he's known for a long time all this was bound to happen.

Right now she's like someone who's tried so hard to do the splits between normality and abnormality that she's literally split in two down the middle.

WHEN HE LOOKS away from the window, Nora is sitting half turned toward him, without her sheet, her thighs pressed to her chest.

She's watching him weirdly, turning her head toward the wall one minute and the window the next, with lifeless eyes, eyes with almost no light in them, as if they were no longer fed by an alternating current.

"Were you looking for me for long?" she asks.

"I've looked everywhere for you for days and days. I feel like it's all I've ever done."

"You looked for me and you found me," she concludes in a strange voice. "You must be having trouble recognizing me," she says, still swiveling her head. "I'm not young anymore, my springtime's over."

He doesn't know how to respond, and she starts crying silently there on her bed, wrapped in an old sweater, her hair half shorn off, her large, thin feet pressed tightly together.

"Come next to me," she orders him suddenly. "You can't stay in that chair all day."

He comes over and sits down like a robot.

"You're being all calm and patient with me because you're frightened you're going to explode. I can tell you're frightened of your feelings, Louis."

"You're right, Neville, but come on, stop crying."

As he strokes her ravaged hair and kisses her as mercifully as he can—because it is still *her*—Blériot briefly feels he's leaving his body for hers, like in some out-of-body experiment, and he too can feel himself shivering and suffocating on this bed.

They both stay there, huddled together, hand in hand, in the blinding white clarity of absurdity.

"Now listen to me," she says very quietly. And he listens. "Louis, I beg you, don't come back again and don't call me again, except to tell me you want a baby."

She puts her mouth to his ear and whispers, "You hurt me too much," just as her sister opens the door.

46

It's beginning to get dark outside. Blériot gulps back his tears as he walks hurriedly along the embankment, thunderstruck, helpless, stealthily drawn by the dark waters of the river. The Thames is as wide as an inlet of the sea here, and on the opposite bank large, glass-built structures seem to ebb and flow with the tide. The shops along the docks are deserted, the café terraces battered by onshore winds.

He stops every now and then to look at the current, and then pictures himself living by the water with Nora, listening to her rambling quietly and wasting her life on empty dreams, while he watches over her with the tender concern of a perpetually dismissed suitor. Until they're both too old or too deaf to keep their conversation going.

It would be a gentle and rather muted life. More enviable, in spite of everything, than this catatonic existence hidden under bedsheets.

Tired of the docks and overcome by heartache, he goes down to the underground on Jamaica Road, letting two or three trains go by, not sure where he's heading, before emerging at Waterloo and wandering at random through perfectly deserted esplanades.

Once he has crossed the bridge, the air feels warmer; cafés and restaurants are still open and people are sitting at tables in the dusk.

I need something to drink, he's thinking when he suddenly feels his cell phone vibrate.

"Louis, your mother's been pacing since six o'clock this morning. She's driving me mad. She's knocking everything over."

"Can't you stop her?"

"She's locked herself in."

"Turn the light off and go to bed," Blériot says. "She'll go to sleep eventually."

Submerged in his personal entropy, Blériot now orders two martinis, plus a vodka for the road. Only to notice on his way out that he's been stung for at least twenty percent more than the advertised price, as if there were some new tax on a customer's distress.

HE SETS OFF on foot toward the city center with an urge to dissolve into the crowds, and gets lost on the periphery of a station, where there are no crowds left at all—nothing but walkways and deserted streets—with a sudden, almost exciting feeling that he's walking through an imaginary city whose name is on the tip of his tongue.

On his travels, he ends up in a bar peopled by insomniacs, their eyes reddened by lack of sleep, and he buys himself a banana daiquiri at the bar, his ears straining to hear Otis Redding's voice—which doesn't make him feel any younger—while the woman on his right tries in vain to start a conversation with him.

"I can't hear you," he apologizes, pressing his hands to his ears.

On the street outside three boys standing with their legs apart are peeing in unison onto the wall of a warehouse. Their three heads leaning under the summer moon.

At closing time everyone breaks into small groups, some people supporting their friends, and Blériot sets off again, walking on and on, his legs stiff and his feet tortured like his mother's, continuing indefatigably through the night— he recognizes the area around Bayswater—as if he too has been implanted with a minute particle of the earth's energy.

IT IS JUST before ten o'clock and, hiding behind his blue glasses, Murphy is sitting on Bernardino's terrace with two balding dogs asleep under the table.

"Do you really think he'll come?" asks Vicky Laumett, stretching her legs in the sun. "What's his name again?"

"Louis Blériot something or other. I keep forgetting his name."

"Maybe he's the aviator's ghost."

"He's meant to be here by now," he goes on, unruffled. "Unfortunately, I don't have his number."

"What did he seem like to you?"

"Obviously, it was a pretty unusual situation, but I thought he was okay," he concedes after a moment's thought. "I even regretted not inviting him to come and stay with me in Islington. I'd have liked to talk to him a bit more and gone to see Nora together once."

"I don't know if I've already told you this but, ever since Coventry, Nora's always aroused dreams of a *Jules and Jim* type of solidarity around her, in girls just as much as boys. Which *is* a bit weird," she points out, looking sideways at him with a soft, slightly distraught expression on her face that he finds very surprising.

She too must have paid the price with Nora, he thinks.

"I'm probably going to get divorced, you know," she says out of the blue. "Life with David doesn't mean anything anymore. I even think it's months since I've been happy just for one day. You're not saying anything . . ."

No, he says with a shake of his head.

"The worst of it is, he looks so crushed in his own little corner, so childlike, that I can't bring myself to separate from him."

Murphy still doesn't say anything.

As if emerging from some distant era as long dead as

Nineveh, an image of Nora comes back to him, walking along a station platform into a strong wind and waving her sleeves about exuberantly.

"Oh, human attachment," she declaims, imitating Helen Mirren, "dreaded human attachment, incredible what it costs us!"

Why's she saying that now? And about what?

It's a station in Basque country, near San Sebastian—they were traveling together for the first time—with whitewashed walls, a small deserted town square, and troughs of white oleander. They were waiting for a connecting train, shivering in the sunshine, huddled in their coats. They looked happy. Their was a whiff of early spring to their shadows.

So why's he staying there hunched on his bench, not uttering a word, as if prey to a premonition?

Because of human attachment?

"Did you give him Nora's address in Greenwich?"

"Yes, he said he'd go over that afternoon," he replies after a slight delay, as if switching back to Vicky on another line.

"Dorothy says it takes her two hours to get from one part of the apartment to another. I don't want to see her in that state," she admits.

"Vicky, if you want something to drink," he interrupts, "I think we'd do better trying to be served inside."

"Do you think he might still come, this aviator of yours?" she asks, looking at her watch.

"No, right now I'm convinced he won't come," he replies, with no obvious emotion.

47

For days now he's been traveling toward Non-madness. Nora's beside him sleeping peacefully, with her legs on the seat and her head resting on the carriage window. She's wearing makeup and a blond wig, probably to hide the effects of her illness. Because she's aged ten years overnight, the way people age in fairy tales.

One morning they wake on the edge of a meadow beside the railway line, feeling they must have fallen from the train. The landscape of brightly colored fields and hedges is enclosed by hills in the distance. Banks of mist are starting to rise from the slopes exposed to the sun. The grass is long and they have to lift their feet high off the ground to walk, freezing in their summer clothes—he doesn't know why but he's put on a black tie—while, all along the path, poplar trees rustle in the wind as if endowed with feelings.

"But does Non-madness really exist?" He's been worrying about this for a while.

"Don't worry, be happy," she replies, singing in a strange, slightly unsynchronized voice.

Although he doesn't say anything, Blériot's amazed that she's so docile and carefree as they walk. She never gets stressed, doesn't take anything the wrong way, and completely defers to him as soon as they need to make a decision.

Actually, he's having trouble recognizing her.

Every now and then she still descends into long silences and her eyes instantly go blank, but, because she herself claims this is just a way of saving her energies, he adopts an understanding expression every time.

"Don't be so anxious," she reassures him, "I'm right beside you."

After crossing a bridge, they come to the edge of a wood and can see a large garden dried out by the summer heat, where a young woman with a rake is busy burning roots and dead leaves. Her embroidered clothes and the blue scarf tied under her chin make them think she must be Serbian or Bulgarian, and they aren't bold enough to talk to her.

"What are we doing at their house?" he whispers. "I don't understand what you're up to."

"They've agreed to rent the cottage behind their house to us, for when we have a child."

"When we have a child?"

"Louis, do you want a child or don't you?" she says impatiently, confronted with his incredulity.

"I don't know, maybe I do," he says to avoid upsetting her.

While they stand there keeping an eye on the fire—the young woman has disappeared—Nora says softly, "You see how simple life can be, Louis, and how happy we could be together."

"It's true, we could be happy," he says, noticing he's shaking from head to foot.

WHEN HE STEPS off the train, Blériot stays on the windswept station concourse for a moment with his jacket over his shoulder and his bag in his hand, almost astonished not to have Nora by his side.

He's here to do something specific, but what? Because of his dream he can't quite remember.

The manageress of the rental company patiently explains that his black Opel is on the right at the far side of the parking lot, opposite the Hotel Continental.

"And don't forget to fill up the tank on the way back," she advises as she hands him the papers for the car.

When he's sitting at the wheel, he undoes his collar because of the sweltering heat, then drops down the sun visor and looks at himself briefly in the mirror, struck once again by his resemblance to his father.

On the way out of town, just before the industrial area, he turns as shown on the map, taking an anonymous road edged with low-slung buildings and dated-looking houses.

The clinic should be at the end, over the roundabout.

For a while he sits waiting on a bench in the entrance lobby, painfully afflicted by the sight of the gray linoleum and the fingerprints on the windows.

"It's room twenty-eight, on the second floor," the girl at reception tells him at last.

As he goes into the room, where the window shades have been partly lowered, he sees his mother first, in a light-colored blouse and a black skirt, with her back to him as if she hasn't heard him. She's standing in the middle of the room with one hand on the bed, the other raised, apparently pressing a handkerchief to her face.

"I came as quickly as I could," he apologizes, kissing her.

Then his feet carry him over to the bed.

BECAUSE OF THE huge strip of gauze around his head, his father looks like a war-wounded soldier lying there under the covers. His cheeks are sunken, his nose pinched, his eyes slightly charcoal-like. He looks both very young and very far away, as if he's deliberately chosen to break off all communication with them.

"Did he leave a letter?" asks Blériot, hearing his voice echo in the room.

"Nothing, not even a note," replies his mother, who suddenly starts swaying on her feet like a pendulum. He catches her just in time and persuades her to sit.

"They took out the catheter and switched off the machine just before noon," she goes on, slumped in her chair, while he stares at his father with all his might, as if to wake him.

Perhaps, just as he was climbing over the parapet and getting over the security fence, a great gust of fear put out the tiny flame of his consciousness.

Perhaps he laughed. Perhaps he was already no one anymore.

"Could you leave us for a minute?" a couple of nurse's aides ask, coming into the room with their trolley and lifting the corpse to put him on a different bed.

For a few brief seconds, in the time it takes him to walk to the door and turn away, Blériot glimpses (without wanting to, of course—he doesn't want anything anymore) his father's great swollen scrotum dangling between his legs.

Then, too late, he closes his eyes.

After a short-lived fit of hysterics in the restroom, he splashes his face with water and stands for a long time scrutinizing it in the mirror, sucking his cheeks in. He re-emerges calmer, or at least sufficiently in command of himself to drive his mother home, as if he has already forgotten his pain.

And there's nothing shocking about that—the sun is now quite horizontal—given that his pain won't forget him.

"Please, Louis, don't leave me on my own."

"I'm here, you know that," he tells her as a great wall of very pure orange light comes toward him and he suddenly accelerates.

48

To people who are used to meeting him on the streets of Nice, Blériot must seem a rather gloomy, inexpressive, and to all intents and purposes oddly solitary man.

He's often seen having lunch near the place Masséna, eating salad and grilled meat with a carafe of wine. He talks to no one and seems to eat with manic care, his head right down by his plate, like someone counting calories. Then he walks in the sunshine along the promenade, his stride relatively elastic, wearing a sort of blouson jacket with a hood that reveals only his nose and the cigarette in the corner of his mouth.

His cell phone sometimes starts ringing in the inside pocket of his jacket, but more often than not he doesn't show any sign of reaching for it, as if he's taken a vow of silence. He carries on along the seafront, withdrawn, walking past people he's never seen before and whom he has no desire to know, while the festive mood of high summer throngs all around him.

For a year now he's been living in a small apartment on a backstreet, not far from the Jules Chéret Museum, a beautiful but pointless and deserted museum—just the way he likes them—in whose gardens he spends part of the afternoon reading the newspaper.

Below him, through the waft and weft of shadows, he can see the girls at a private school playing volleyball in white shorts and yellow shirts with numbers on the chest, like Pop Art images.

When the heat has dropped he heads home and goes back to the work that pays his rent, translating a few pages on adrenergic hormones before granting himself a small, premature martini and then doing his weight training while he waits for Helena to arrive.

AFTER A SERIES of misunderstandings, Helena left her bags at his place barely two or three months ago and unilaterally decided that they were made to live together. He didn't dare protest, as if, when all was said and done, she was a better judge than him.

Helena, a musicology student at the University of Bucharest, doesn't know Massenet—that's probably what upsets him most—but is teeming with ideas about everything, particularly the limitless development of the mind and diverse forms of transpersonal achievements. Other than that, she's so reserved about her feelings, so undemonstrative, that Blériot has given up trying to work out whether or not she really loves him. The only time he tried to broach the subject with her, she immediately clamped her hand over her mouth and he didn't press the point.

In fact, he's relinquished all curiosity in that area, as in many others.

His dispassionate interest in creatures and things could be seen as a sort of embittered wisdom or a weariness of life, and could be worth further investigation, but he doesn't feel like thinking about it and even less discussing it with Helena.

When she's finished showering and has slipped on her robe, her hair secured on top of her head with a large clip, he'd much rather treat her to a glass of champagne out on their little balcony. They both take up positions, resting their elbows on the railings as if to drink a toast to the setting sun, and stay there like that, chatting quietly, their skin glowing red and their senses raw.

When they get out of bed, they sometimes go out again to stroll through the streets of Nice with the excuse of looking for a restaurant or an appealing terrace café. Because of the accumulated heat in the stone walls along the streets, their legs are instantly dripping wet and they feel as if they're walking extraordinarily slowly, trying to find a breath of air.

"Louis, I haven't the strength to walk to the town center," she usually complains. "We should just sit down here. Anyway, there won't be any trams now."

"Whatever you like," he agrees, lighting a cigarette.

When they get home, their Italian neighbors have packed in every last one of their friends around their swimming pool and turned the music loud. To avoid looking like killjoys, Blériot and his partner generally agree to have a glass or two with them, before being sensible and going to bed—Helena has class at eight in the morning, he tells them—and falling asleep head to foot like children on New Year's Eve.

"IT'S YOUR CELL phone," she calls from the bedroom.

"Hello, is that the aviator?"

"It's you," says Blériot.

"I'm with friends in the depths of Brooklyn," Murphy tells him. "It's six o'clock in the evening and it's eighty-six degrees out in the yard."

Blériot recognizes his very American, quick-fire, nasal bass voice. He pictures him sitting on the garden veranda, with his massive legs and tinted glasses, surrounded by a troop of stray dogs.

"I thought you were still in London," Blériot apologizes. "I was going to call you sometime to get some news of Nora."

"The last time I saw her before I left for Philadelphia," Murphy replies, "she'd been to stay with her sister in Cornwall. I thought she seemed better, more stable at least, not so jumpy. But how about you, how are you?"

"I feel like I'm nowhere," admits Blériot. "I'm in Nice, but I could just as easily be in Tunis or Dakar. I'm sure," he adds with a surge of friendliness, "that you must miss her too. Do you resent her sometimes for never getting in touch?"

"Louis, one day our souls will recognize each other and all will be at peace," Murphy says, laughing, while a plane can be heard thundering overhead in Brooklyn.

"Do you believe that?"

"Of course I believe it," he says, still laughing. "She had grounds to resent me too and I'm sure she's already forgotten them."

"Maybe you're right," Blériot concedes eventually, aware that Murphy has a maturity he'll never attain.

NOW HE'S ON the balcony in complete darkness with his laptop on his knee—Helena must have gone to sleep. He makes himself work for a couple of hours in the hopes of reestablishing a bare minimum of existential stability and, as a secondary concern, finishing his medical article.

Noradrenaline, he translates—she does exist, then; he didn't invent her—*is an organic compound secreted by the suprarenal glands that acts as a neurotransmitter for effector organs.*

Noradrenaline, he carries on typing, *is noted for the powerful effect it has on alpha receptors and has a determining influence on the development of dreams and emotions.*

Which he's been saying for years.

THE SEASON HAS switched overnight. In the morning, almost before they're out of bed, they quickly do their shopping between two downpours. While Helena runs from shop to shop, umbrella in hand, Blériot sits closeted in the car, listening to the radio and watching the storm build a head of steam over the sea.

Endless oppressive rain just keeps falling over the region, flooding roads and raising river levels so that people and animals drown in them. The buses aren't running and the freeway's closed, adding to the general feeling of disorganization. For two weeks now they've been spending their days walled up in the apartment, like fugitives or stowaways cut off from their past, pacing around and around, not knowing what to do as they watch the rain streaming over the balcony.

There's so little going on that they're condemned to saying pretty much the same things to each other from morning till night, each stuck with his or her own mental output and sense of isolation.

"I can't wait for lectures to start again," she keeps saying on a loop.

"That's cheerful."

Quite often they don't even say anything and spend whole afternoons sitting facing each other, playing cards, and yawning like a couple of depressive cats.

In the evening, when Helena's lying on the bed in front of the television, Blériot sometimes parks himself next to her, with an imperious and puerile urge to hound her into a corner until she undresses of her own accord to get him to leave her in peace.

Afterward they fall asleep, turning away from each other.

Yet there are still times when he looks up and sees her—she's twirling around the apartment at the moment—and is touched by how fragile and beautiful she is, and wishes with all his heart that things could work out between them.

When he really should know that nothing ever works out and he'll probably always be a man without a woman or a descendant.

ON MONDAY, OCTOBER 8—the first fine day—he goes to the airport with her, pulling her big suitcase on wheels through the deserted streets. She has to spend ten days in Paris before going back to her family near Bucharest.

"We'll probably see each other in a few months or a few years," she tells him, laughing as he gets his feet caught up with her case.

Personally, he'd prefer it to be a few months, he admits, amazed that he still has his smile and a pair of legs to keep walking. Because he doesn't have many illusions now.

While she describes the various people she has to see in Paris—there is mention, among others, of one Emil, whom she's already referred to several times—Blériot notices the sea right at the end of the runway, dense and glittering in the sunlight, and he stops dead, no longer hearing a word, as if his ability to arrest time has been mysteriously restored.

When he comes back to his senses it's already over.

He's in a bus, she's screaming something unintelligible at him, he makes a random hand gesture and she moves in the opposite direction, her face slightly in profile, growing progressively smaller in the depths of that late afternoon.

49

A year later—but it feels like the same late afternoon—Blériot's sitting on his balcony, his head protected by a straw hat and his laptop on his knee. He's talking to his mother on the phone (she's staying with her sister in Clermont-Ferrand), and then hangs up, promising to call again.

After that, despite his best efforts, he keeps nodding asleep over his page of translation, as if afflicted with narcolepsy. At the end of the garden, he hears intermittent cries of excitement from the volleyball players. Every time he closes his eyes and lets his head drop, he pictures his wife singing in the living room of their apartment in Belleville—he's hiding on the stairs—*Bang bang, he shot me down, Bang bang, I hit the ground*. And her voice now resonates peculiarly on the stage set of his memory, as if amplified by distance.

A few months ago, when he was checking his bank account, Blériot noticed she had made a payment of five thousand dollars. He naturally sent her a little thank-you note, and, without going to very much trouble, she told him that she had to leave Paris briefly for reasons connected with her work. The following week she sent him two consecutive articles she'd written on Michelangelo Pistoletto, and then stopped broadcasting altogether, not answering any of his messages, like a satellite lost in the atmosphere.

All he can hope now is that one day, thanks to the invention of a new molecule, science will reconstitute minute by minute the memories of happy times they spent together—because there must have been some—with their thousands of tiny perceptions that would otherwise disappear forever, lost in the dark background of his life.

BLÉRIOT ACTUALLY REALIZED some time ago now that he likes the past. Not his own past: the past itself.

The distant glow of the past.

When evening falls, palm fronds stirred by the onshore wind start scratching at the shutters. The neighbors opposite have turned on the spotlights in the pool and some music.

For a few brief seconds, Blériot feels he's living suspended, shut away from the world, his heart free, his mind active—as he would always like to be. But then the telephone rings.

It's his mother again.

"Louis, there's something I didn't dare ask you earlier: Are you still living alone?"

"Yep. But don't worry about it, I'm not unhappy at all," he reassures her, feeling the shooting pains of his hemicrania spreading over the left-hand side of his head, starting above the ear, making him break off their conversation to take a couple of Antalvic pills with some Valium.

When the pain has eased he puts on an old Sam Wood film, curls up in a robe, and falls half asleep with his feet crossed on the table, while he waits for a very young Ingrid Bergman with curls like a lamb to be kind enough to make a bit of room for him beside her.

IN THE MORNING Blériot feels he's emerging from oblivion and wonders for a moment whether it's 2009 or 2019 before jumping out of bed and collapsing on the floor like someone falling from the fifth floor. He stays sprawled across the carpet for a few seconds, clasping his hands around his head and tasting blood in his mouth.

A brief examination in the bathroom mirror confirms that his lower lip is split, two incisors are broken, and he has several bruises on his forehead, which he is obviously quick to clean up and bandage.

But when it comes to raising his arms in order to get dressed, he has to acknowledge—in the midst of his mind-numbing exhaustion he's retained a sort of paradoxical lucidity—a disturbing stiffness in his movements as well as a lack of coordination. But he's not sure whether he should attribute this state to his dependence on alcohol and to the Valium or to some obscure degenerative illness.

If this is the case, Blériot remembers that after a collapse, injections of noradrenaline—he'll keep coming back to it—are used to raise the blood pressure instantly, thereby avoiding fatal decompensation.

But then he would have to have some noradrenaline in his medicine cabinet.

WHEN HE GOES out the air feels heavy, almost moist, like before a thunderstorm, as he walks cautiously along the seafront, making a conscious effort to breathe, and regularly sitting down on benches for fear of having another dizzy spell in the middle of the crowd and the deafening traffic.

His attention is now drawn to the folds of a huge, luminous cloud that has come from the hills inland and is hanging over the town. Its human forms are so explicit, so shocking—you can make out the man and woman clearly—that Blériot can't even understand why parents aren't making their children look away.

Instead there are hundreds of them milling on the beach in their swimming things and sunglasses, all eyes turned in the same direction.

Later, while he's still on his bench, not daring to move because his headache's getting worse and worse, Blériot is suddenly gripped with foreboding as he notices a second luminous cloud hanging over them like a flying saucer.

The people on the beach have fallen silent, huddled together, one hand over their glasses, shielding their eyes, as if to protect them from the light of the future.

And that is when, sitting there in his little black tie and with his Converse on his feet, his body lolling back, he starts slowly slipping off the bench.

50

It may well be recognized and generally accepted that we exist in only one form and only one state—with only one biological life—but things are very different in terms of quantum probability. Because the universe is endlessly subdividing into simultaneous worlds. In that case, there is inevitably one world where, as with Schrödinger's cat, Blériot died after having a stroke, and another where he's alive.

Here he is, in fact, sitting on the bed in his room a stone's throw from Buttes-Chaumont. Because his metabolism has slowed, he hardly ever leaves the apartment that Léonard bequeathed to him, a place filled with pizza packaging and Chinese takeaway containers. He spends the best part of his days in a semi-lethargic state, doing nothing but occasionally reacting to the buzz of the intercom: a sign that some of his nerve endings live on.

"Does Louis Blériot still live at this address?" someone asks into the intercom.

"That's me," he says with a jolt, unwittingly opening the door to a parallel universe.

He then finds himself on the landing face-to-face with Nora Neville, who is wearing a skimpy summer dress and a cloche hat, which slightly hides her expression.

"Do you recognize me?" she says, removing her hat.

His instant impression is that she's ageless, her beauty set firm, almost disturbing, reminiscent of the beauty of a prototype or a three-dimensional image.

Because it's so hot outside, they've gone in to drink cold white wine in the kitchen, Blériot leaning against the window and Nora sitting on a stool like in the Les Lilas days.

We can obviously assume that they each have their own ideas about what's happening here but have opted to keep them to themselves. In any event, they're hardly talking at all and seem happy to drain their glasses and smile beatifically at each other like a couple of simpletons.

At the exact same moment, as if it were happening in another part of the apartment, Murphy Blomdale is waiting for the same Nora to finish getting ready—she's come back to live in Islington—and to put the phone down at last.

"Do you remember Tyron?" she says, leading Murphy into the living room. "My sister's friend who asked us to the country that first time—it was him on the phone. Do you at least remember him," she asks again, "the pretty deer spying on us over the hedges when we went to the pond? And pounds and pounds of cherries that Max Barney brought on his motorbike?"

"I remember very well," he replies, meekly following her from room to room as if revisiting the ruins of their emotions in his thoughts.

"Are you planning to continue working in the States for long?"

"I don't know," he says, "it depends on lots of things. But you can stay here anyway, if you like."

Early in the evening they take a taxi to Rotherhithe and go for a walk together along the banks of the Thames, Nora still gently trotting out her memories and Murphy hiding behind his blue glasses and whistling Phil Collins tunes while summer lightning shoots over the surroundings, on roofs, cars, bridges and passersby on the bridges. Everything is illuminated.

IN THIS VERTIGINOUS, constantly expanding universe, there's also a world superimposed over the others in which Nora has always been alone. A world in which she acted in two or three films no one ever saw and eventually set up house with her psychiatrist, a very fat, questionably crooked man who's recently gone back to brokering wine.

They live near Toulouse in a sort of large manor house with stained-glass windows, where she spends her days as a lady of leisure, playing with the cats and reading whodunits.

She's never heard of Leibniz.

She's in her early fifties with a slightly puffy face, and wears black glasses and very short skirts, her inner age arrested somewhere around seventeen or eighteen.

In a universe parallel to that one, she looks so very young beside Blériot that she could be his daughter as they drive toward the sunset between fields of ripe corn, caught in a state of such distress, in such silence—they'll be splitting up soon—that they could be mistaken for dead astronauts orbiting a red planet.

Finally, it's also likely that there's an infinite number of universes in which neither one of them ever existed.